"IT IS TIME!"

The
Orb of Truth

BRAE WYCKOFF

www.theorboftruth.com

The Orb of Truth

The first book in the Four Horn series.
©2012. **Brae Wyckoff**
Published by LR Publishing

All scripture quotations, unless otherwise indicated, are quoted or paraphrased from the Holy Bible, New International Version®, NIV®. Copyright ©1973, 1978, 1984, 2011 by Biblica, Inc.™ Used by permission of Zondervan. All rights reserved worldwide. www.zondervan.com

The "NIV" and "New International Version" are trademarks registered in the United States Patent and Trademark Office by Biblica, Inc.™

ISBN: 1479313262
ISBN-13: 9781479313266
Library of Congress Control Number: 2012921173
CreateSpace Independent Publishing Platform
North Charleston, South Carolina

Request for permission to make copies of any part of this work should be directed to the website, www.theorboftruth.com
or the facebook page, *The Orb of Truth*
Author Photo by Lucid Impressions
Cover art by Brian Rollason
AKA "The Pixel Chemist"

CONTENTS

ACKNOWLEDGMENTS

I would like to dedicate this book to my wife, Jill, and my amazing children who encouraged me each step of the way. Jill, you are amazing and I'm so thankful to have you as my wife and best friend in life. I raise my glass of wine to you babe! Cheers…

A special thank you to my daughter, Michelle, for falling in love with my characters and nudging me to finish the book all those years. She is also the creator of the map of Ruauck-El!

Encouragement was around every corner with my friends…thank you Mr. Haney, Super Dan, and my rules "lawyer" Eric… "You people!"

Mom and Dad, you da best! Thank you for your love and support!

My mother-in-law, Peggy Koehler, paved the way by being the first published author in the family with her book, Our Legacy of Love. She is such an inspiration to me. Thank you Mom!

I would like to give a big shout out to the Rancho Bernardo Writer's Group for their amazing critique of my book. I can't say enough about you all…Peter Berkos (Academy Award Winner and Author), Karl Bell (RIP my friend)(Author), MJ Roe (Author), Lillian Belinfante Herzberg (Author), Rosalie Kramer (Author), Gerry Factor (Author), Debra Friend (Author), Mark Carlson (Author), and Terry Ambrose (Author)…thank you! I will keep making up words and you will continue to challenge me! As Peter Berkos would say, "Just need to tighten it up a bit."

And this book wouldn't be as good as it is without my wonderful editor, Krisann Gentry! Her valued insight and her passion for getting the content right was impeccable. I remember her telling me that she would apply pressure on my piece of coal and turn it into a diamond. At the time all I heard was her calling my work a "piece of coal". It is now a diamond…thank you Krisann!

Thank you "Bridazak" for coming into my life over 25 years ago…I look forward to the many adventures waiting for us all!

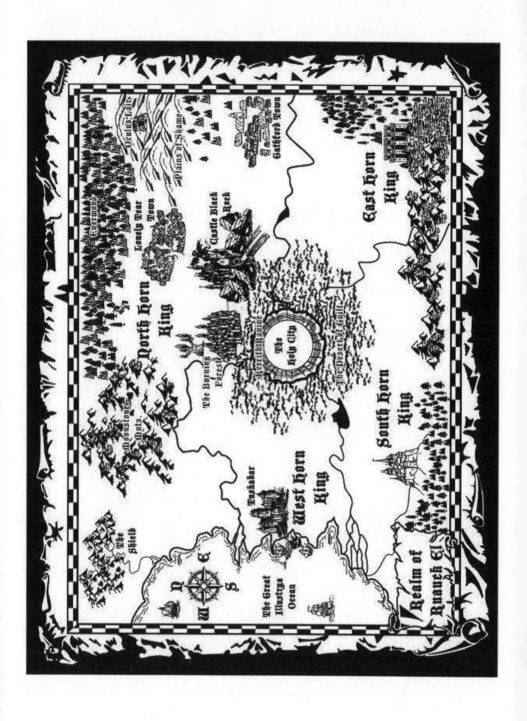

PROLOGUE

The Tree

Its leaves were like clear glass, and when the sun broke the horizon to announce the new day, a kaleidoscope of colors danced, dazzling the people who had gathered. It stood twenty feet tall, a glorious beacon of light, attracting all in the vicinity. Silver and purple woven wood harmonized to form the base, stretching up and then gracefully out. Hundreds of branches waved gently in the breeze, causing the crystal petals to chime, creating a beautiful chorus, like angels singing, harkening those with ears to hear.

On this day, the Tree was found on a grassy hill overlooking a small village. Residents of Brook Haven slowly emerged from their dwellings and began to assemble. The crowd of men, women, and children swelled until the entire community formed a half circle around the base of the knoll. None would approach the Tree any closer.

A man—carrying his sick child, pale as snow—broke through, streaks of tears running down his cheeks. "Please help me," he whispered as he laid his boy on the grassy slope.

One of the thousands of crystal petals snapped free from the strong branch and descended like a feather. As it fell, it slowly disintegrated, leaving a trail of shimmering dust which lingered, suspended in the air until the prismatic pattern faded. Each brief flash of reflected light was like a strum on a lyre. Everyone was entranced by the hypnotic action, including the father. They refocused on the debilitated child when they heard the boy speak, "Papa?"

"My boy!" he said as he lunged for him in a tight embrace, kneeling on the ground beside him. He peered up to the Tree, "Thank you, for my son."

Witnessing the boldness of the desperate man gave another the courage to step forward. "Pardon, um, Great Tree, I, well, I could use some advice." He lowered his head and grew altogether quiet for a moment, not noticing another petal falling. Then his posture and demeanor slowly changed. He turned and faced the hushed crowd of onlookers, but looked lighter and freer. Whatever burden had been bothering him had clearly lifted as he trotted off back to their town; another petal descended.

More people brought requests before it, and throughout the day a leaf would fall for each granted miracle. Finally, the brilliant, golden light of the setting sun illuminated the relic with a blinding halo. The people shielded their eyes from the intensity, and within seconds the aura dissipated, and the Tree, along with it, had vanished.

Sheets of blustery snow swirled around the shallow cave entrance and the howling wind echoed within. A mound of white fur huddled in the back recesses for warmth. Hot breath escaped in uneven heaves from the several gathered creatures. The cold air whipped at their backs. Their faces were hidden from the elements.

An intense light blared to life outside, followed by soothing warmth. The snow flurry settled and the wind calmed. A head popped up from the tangled fur, surprised by the phenomena. The large, rounded white pupils of the Yeshi reflected the sparkling petals of the Tree of legend.

One of the beings approached, crunching snow underfoot, tenderly holding one mangled, fur-patched arm. A not uncommon injury, the result of a recent battle within the inhospitable mountain range they resided in. He extended his bloody appendage, and watched a single petal fall as the damaged limb was restored to health. The creature turned and called out to the apprehensive clan in its language of Yeshi, "We host the Tree of Lore! Come while you can! Bring your requests and offer them without fear! Hurry before it departs!"

The lumbering, beast-like creature turned and fell to his knees before the amazing spectacle, bowing repeatedly. After years of suffering turmoil in these harsh mountains, never daring to hope the Tree would come so far to aid them, it had arrived. From this day forward, his clan would never be the same.

1

This Time it's Different

A cool breeze weaved through the dirt street, bringing with it a mixture of smells from manure, spices, cooked meats, and dust to the many patrons of the Gathford market. Sparse clouds and the midday sun warmed the small trading town. Nestled at the edge of a pine forest, three dirt roads connected the community where weary travelers could find rest and supplies to continue on their journey. Gathford was predominantly a Human community, now. This woodland location used to be Elven-occupied, where people of all walks would travel through for trading. In recent decades the tyranny of King Manasseh and his regime had pushed the other races away; the Dwarves and Elves had taken the worst over the centuries. Wars had decimated their numbers and now what remained of them were hidden in the mountains or forests. Then there were others who, driven by adventure, continued to taunt danger by mingling within the Human establishments.

A four-foot-tall, blonde Ordakian stood between one of the many vendor carts. He wore blue robes with a metallic sheen and a green scaled belt—simple but regal attire. His attention was focused on a nearby vendor who was selling rare feathers from creatures across the realm. The merchant made eye contact with the Ordakian from underneath his hooded brown cloak and gave a slight nod.

Emerging from the meandering crowd was a group of bodyguards surrounding a fat Noblewoman. Her blush silk dress caught every jiggle and shift of her excessive weight. A light blue, wispy shawl covered her shoulders and draped over her blubbery breasts. Diamonds adorned her from top to bottom—dazzling earrings, a sparkling necklace, and multiple rings on each finger. One ring in particular cradled the largest gemstone, and tilted to the side of where it rested on her enlarged knuckle. She stopped in front of the feather vendor.

"My people have informed me that you have a rare collection from Everwood," she said in a deep, husky voice.

"Why, yes I do, my lady," came a cheerful reply from the vendor. "What kind of feather are you lookin' to buy? I have the scary Nine-Tails going for ten gold pieces, or perhaps the intriguing Serapliss from Griffs Peak is more your liking? I have more, but some of them are quite expensive."

"Cost will not be an issue. I'm in search of a Varouche."

"Oh, that one. I'm sorry my lady, but I sold it just a bit ago."

Her pudgy brows wrinkled as she glared at the vendor, "Who could have possibly been looking for a Varouche and bought it before me?"

"He paid for it, my lady, but hasn't picked it up yet. He should be back for it soon. Oh, wait, here he comes now," the vendor pointed.

"Good day to you, Sally," greeted the Ordakian.

"It's Seelly," the vendor snapped back from under his hood. His voice was awkwardly raspy.

"Right, whatever. I've come for my purchased item." The Ordakian's voice was heightened.

"I have it right here for you." Seelly reached under his cart and pulled out a bright yellow feather covered with beige spots.

The woman was startled and stood motionless; her eyes widened as the plume was displayed out in the open for all to see. She took a step forward as the Ordakian held it up, carefully studying the rare coloring.

"Do you know what you are holding in your tiny hand?" she asked.

"A feather from some woodland area in the North, I believe," he responded.

"I am Lady Birmham of the House of Urmthong. I will give you what you paid and you can buy a replacement."

He paused at the offer. He almost felt sorry for her, until the sparkle from the large diamond ring on her hand caught his attention. Before he could respond she continued her plea, "The feather you hold, my dear little-one, is not just from the deep forest of Everwood, but symbolizes the greatness of such a mysterious and wonderful world that we cannot possibly imagine. The history of this creature is almost as legendary as the Unicorn. The Varouche is said to have great powers within the woods—to animate the inanimate or release a birdsong so fascinating that it would slow the heart to sleep forever. You see, I have been in search of such a plume for almost ten years now, and I don't intend on letting this one escape from my sight. I am sure we can come to some arrangement to complete this quest of mine."

She ended her petition and stared intently into the Ordakian's beautiful teal eyes. The rolls of fat around her neck bunched together as she peered down at him.

"Well, that's a great story and all, but I'm not sure you can afford what I paid for this, my lady."

"Preposterous! I have very deep coffers. Might I inquire what you intend to do with it?"

"Well, it is a personal matter. I use exotic feathers to help me fall asleep."

"How does a feather help you do that? Is it magical?"

"Oh, no, no. Nothing like that at all." The Ordakian leaned in a little closer and whispered, "I use them to lightly touch my feet," he reached down with the feather, wiggling his wide, hairy toes for embellishment.

The woman reeled back, appalled, "Stop! You'll ruin it! My dear child, that is disgusting!" She regained her composure. "I will purchase for you any two other feathers to help you with your sleeping disorder."

He paused, "It's common to mistake an Ordakian for a child, Lady Birmham, but I am almost three-hundred years of age. My apologies for being so blunt, but I really don't think your coffers go that deep, after having insulted me." The Ordakian started to turn away.

"No! Please wait. I wish to make it up to you. There has been a grievous misunderstanding," she pleaded.

He turned, "I still *could* possibly be persuaded."

"I will pay you double what you paid, in addition to what I already promised."

The hooded vendor slightly gasped at the proposal, but quickly turned the surprise into a cough, keeping his head down.

"That is indeed an offer I cannot refuse. It would please me to accept. I paid three hundred gold pieces for the Varouche, and will take two feathers of the Lamshan in its place."

A smile of joy overwhelmed her face. She quickly snapped her sausage fingers and waved her servants over to take care of the transaction. Seelly handed the Ordakian the Lamshans and the aids relinquished two small bags of coinage equaling double the amount he paid. He handed her the feather slowly. Her eyes were transfixed, and she held her breath until her hand was finally grasping the reward she had sought for so many years. A sigh of relief purged through her body as she realized what the little-one had done for her sake. She focused again on him and then bent over, planting her fat, moist lips on his forehead, as if he really were a child.

"Thank you so much. Oh, how I have dreamed of retrieving this, the rarest of my catalogued specimens," she said as she stood upright, holding the feather up higher to admire it more.

This was the perfect time to make his move. The Lady and her bodyguards, who had been scrutinizing the transaction, were now watching her new prize, and not him. They all looked upon this thing as though it had some spiritual significance—as if it were holy.

"You are very welcome, my lady," he said quietly as he gently grabbed her large hand and laid his dry lips on the back.

As he retracted his face, his small, dexterous paws slid away from hers, along with the loose-fitting diamond ring. The job was a success so far. He kept his eyes on the lady and took a step backward. She was still fondling her treasure and paid him no attention.

"Well, I must be off now. Thank you and well met, my lady."

"Yes, yes. Thank you again." She barely took her sight off of the Varouche as she waddled away with her entourage.

The Ordakian thief turned and instantly bumped into a leather-clad guard patrol.

"Didn't I tell you men that we would find something interesting in the market?"

The patrol erupted into laughter. "What's the password, Halfling?"

He gulped, "Hail King Manasseh?"

"Good try. Where are your other misfit friends?"

"C'mon Thule. We're not worth the time."

"You got that right, Bridazak. Do you know what this insignia means?" He pointed at the patch on his chest of a black dragon.

Bridazak glanced at the feather vendor, who kept his head down.

"I'll tell you what it means. It says that I can tell you to leave my town or I'll have you arrested. Why don't you run and hide in the mountains and forests, like the rest of your kind?"

"Yeah fine, we will leave first thing tomorrow."

"You've said that before, but I will have the power to do something about it. Tomorrow I get sworn in by the official magistrate of the King, and then you and your other outcasts will be all mine. I will do my part and make sure there are three less of your kind in the world. C'mon, boys." Thule spit on the ground. His phlegm splashed in the dirt and sprayed Bridazak's hairy pads.

The squad followed their leader. Several of them bumped into the Ordakian on purpose as they passed, knocking his shoulder to the side. He sighed, glanced back at the hooded vendor with a slight nod, and then disappeared into the crowd.

Bridazak entered the small cottage and leaned his back up against the door as he closed it. He let out a deep sigh and shut his eyes. A strong smell of pipe tobacco hovered in the bare room. Only a single bed, a dining table with a couple of chairs, a charred fireplace, and a few knick-knacks adorned the chamber. Two sets of blankets from travelling bedrolls were on the floor in one corner.

"What's got you all rattled?" A deep voice asked from the opposite side of the room.

Bridazak opened his eyes and looked at the red-bearded Dwarf leaning in a chair against the wall, smoking his pipe.

"Thule and his goons," he sat at the dining table.

"They deserve a good Dwarven beating. Did you sell that damn feather you and Spilf concocted?"

"Yes, the noblewoman came through. We will have enough to live on for a while."

"Good. I need a good drink tonight, so cough up some coin."

Bridazak tossed a leather pouch filled with gold pieces onto the table and the coins jingled loudly. The Dwarf tilted forward in surprise of the amount, showing more of his face in the dimming light. He had a large scar on his left cheek that was partially buried by his thick, foot-long beard.

"Whoa, you made how much for that feather?"

"Three-hundred," he fibbed; Bridazak was distracted with other thoughts and responded mechanically.

"I'm impressed, you came out ahead this time, what with all of your costume regalia purchases. Where is your sidekick?" Dulgin moved to the dining table and inspected the coinage by feeling the weight in his ruddy hand.

Just then, the door burst open and another Ordakian, several inches shorter than Bridazak, came through. He held a large cloak rolled up in his arms. His short brown hair matched the color of his eyes.

"Do you know how hard it was to balance myself on those wooden crates? That was incredible Bridazak," the excited Ordakian said. "I wish you could have seen it, Dulgin."

"Ah, it's not my way, and you know that."

"You should have seen Bridazak in action. He played his part like a pro, except when he called me Sally. I told you it was Seelly."

Spilf was smirking toward his long-time friend, but he could see that his mind was elsewhere. "What's wrong, Bridazak?"

"What? Oh, nothing. You did well today, Spilfer Teehle." Bridazak gave a half-hearted smile.

"It's Thule, isn't it? He got to you this time," Spilf pressured him.

"It was something he said that really bothered me."

"What?"

"He said he would make sure there are three less of our kind in the world."

"I'd like to see him try," Dulgin interjected.

"I don't know. It's just…"

"Just what?" Spilf asked.

"He needs a drink is what he needs."

"Good idea, Dulgin. C'mon Bridazak, let's get our table at The Knot."

"Not this time. I'm going to sit this one out and get some rest. You guys go on without me."

"Suit yourself. C'mon Stubby," Dulgin said as he grabbed the loot off the table.

"You know I hate it when you call me that."

"You'd think you would be used to it, after two decades of travelling with me." Dulgin headed for the door.

Spilf followed, "I don't mind a nickname but pick something with some pizazz, like Amazing or Magnificent."

"Sounds good. Let's go Amazing Stubby," the Dwarf laughed.

The door shut behind them and their voices trailed off as they made their way down the path toward the tavern. Bridazak was now alone with his thoughts. His long-time friends were right; they had heard all the ridicule among the Humans before, so why was it bothering him this time? Thule brought up his kin in hiding. Why was he not with them? Why had he not succumbed to the pressure, like the Elves and Dwarves?

"Thule did have one thing right; we are misfits," he thought aloud as he hopped down off the chair and made his way to the bed. As he lay there, his mind began to race. Snippets of feelings came to the forefront of his memory and sparked to life. He closed his eyes and allowed them to continue. Ruauck-El had changed over these many decades, especially as the Horn Kings continued to dominate the good folk of the realm. A century ago seemed like yesterday—when he first met Dulgin on the road through Ogre's Pass, and their years of adventures across Ruauck-El since. The Dwarf had been his only family until they found Spilf, another orphaned Ordakian, stealing food from a vendor on the streets of Baron's Hall. Bridazak connected with Spilfer. He was alone, abandoned, and looking for something more to life than hiding their existence from the world—a true thirst for adventure. Spilf had been a younger brother to him these last twenty-seven years. Bridazak drifted deeper and soon fell asleep.

His eyes opened, but he knew that he was still sleeping. Above him was a soothing, brilliant white light. He turned his head and peered down the side of his bed. Below him was darkness—a pitch-black that had no end. A cold fear forced him to look away. His bed hovered between the nebulous dream realms. The silence was broken by whispering above. He squinted his eyes, as he saw amorphous beings approaching. Bridazak felt waves of peace emanating from the aura above. The two ethereal figures were outlined by the light flooding from behind them. Their muffled voices became clearer the closer they came.

Suddenly, his bed began to shake as their mysterious words finally resonated clearly, "It is time." Their voices were hollow and their bodies ghostlike. The frame beneath him shattered and he could feel the hay-filled mattress give way. He didn't fall with it; he was pulled on from both directions. The spirits stretched their hands, holding something, and he instinctively reached for it. As soon as he touched the object, a jolt of electricity shot through his arms.

Bridazak lurched violently from his dream and awoke back in his bed inside the dark cottage. He could feel sweat trickling down his forehead and the cold chill of damp clothes. The intensity of the dream still seemed real. He told himself to breathe; he was safe at home. He swung his legs over the side of the bed and something fell from his lap and crashed onto the wooden floor. It startled him.

He fumbled for the candle at the nightstand next to him, but before he could get it lit, the room suddenly glowed in a blue aura. The source was a small rectangular item on the floor. The words from his dream came back to him, *"It is time."*

2

Bridazak's Destiny

Bridazak sat at the wooden table, staring at the candle's fickle flame. His hairy, fur-topped feet were propped on the table's edge. He heard his comrades' muffled conversation as they returned from the tavern. The click of the lock and the slight squeak of the door swinging open alerted him, as it would have any skilled thief, of his friends' arrival home.

"Why do you always have to end a perfectly good evening in a fight, Dulgin?" Spilf sarcastically questioned.

The weathered, red-bearded Dwarf lumbered in behind him. "Wasn't much of a fight but, he had it comin'. I could see it in his eyes," he responded in his gruff voice.

"In his eyes? Are you kidding me? What, did they say, 'punch me in the face'?"

"Yeah, something like that. Best be leavin' it alone."

"Are you going to hit me too, or, hey - Bridazak, you're still awake? Are you feeling better?" Spilf continued as he closed the door behind Dulgin.

"Hey guys," he said in a low voice.

"What's wrong?"

"Another nightmare," Bridazak responded.

"Same one?"

"Yeah, except—" he paused.

"Except what, ya blundering fool? It's just a dream. I don't know what the big deal is. Every time it is the same. You are in bed, it's dark, there's a light, you wake up," the Dwarf said.

Dulgin ignited a match for his tobacco pipe. His eyes squinted as he tugged on it with short breaths to get the hot embers going. Smoke billowed out from his mouth and nostrils, escaping through his red hair on his face.

Spilf joined Bridazak, taking the place opposite him at the table, "Leave him alone, Dulgin. Dwarves wouldn't understand nightmares. All you know is drinking and picking fights," Spilf retorted.

The Dwarf's eyes flared wide and he gave a mocking snarl. "Come over here little-one, and I'll show you a Dwarven nightmare you will never forget."

"You are all talk, and you have too much drink in you."

"I'd say not enough, after coming home to this Troll-shit dream talk, again!"

"Enough, you two! This time it is different," Bridazak interrupted their bickering.

"Ah, what do you want us to do about it?" Dulgin grunted. He tilted back in his chair, balancing on two legs against the wall.

"I have to agree with the Dwarf for once, Bridazak. What can we do? It appears to be a childhood nightmare, and we have no skills in the area of dream walking."

Bridazak, with a concerned look, gazed at each of them. "This time is different because of this—" he pulled open his tunic, which had been concealing the mysterious item, and then placed it on the table next to the candle. The wooden container was three inches high and five inches wide, with ornate writing encompassing it. Spilf edged closer so he could get a better look. Dulgin's chair clopped to the floor from his tilted position. As he approached, a steady stream of pipe smoke trailed behind him.

"What is it?"

"I'm not sure. Been trying to figure that out all night."

Dulgin's brow furrowed in thought as he inhaled.

"Look at the writing," Spilf stated in amazement, and continued, "I don't understand what it is saying, but it looks like an ancient dialect. How does it open?" He did not touch the box, but leaned in close to inspect every square inch.

"What do you mean you can't read the writing? It's written in Ordakian, clear as day," Bridazak stated.

"No, it's not; at least not to me. It's a language I have never encountered. What does it say, then?"

"It says, *"I have given you eyes to see. Knock and the door will be opened."*"

"If you see it in our language and I can't, then it's definitely magical, but I have never seen anything like it. Very clever, and look at this craftsmanship! I don't recognize its workings to be from around here, or even from this region," Spilf continued examining the box, still reluctant to touch it.

The mysterious item had no seams, no lock, no apparent way to open it. Embossed gold writing in the strange script wrapped around the edges of the ebony wood, imbuing it with a sense of importance.

"What does this have to do with your dream?" Dulgin asked.

"You wouldn't believe me if I told you."

"Try me. It can't be any worse than the tall tales Amazing Stubby tells me all the time." Spilf gave Dulgin another glare and slightly shook his head.

"It came from my dream," Bridazak blurted.

There was silence as his friends digested his statement. Dulgin placed the pipe tip back into his mouth; bright red embers came to life as he breathed in the tobacco. He walked toward the window. It was late at night. The fragrance of his pipe filled their small cottage.

"You're right, I don't believe you," Dulgin finally responded.

"Spilf's never seen anything like it. Can you tell me where it came from then?" He paused, then continued, "I want to find out what this thing is, but I need your help."

"So let me get this straight, you want us to help you uncover the mystery of this box that supernaturally appeared out of your dream?" asked Dulgin.

Bridazak looked up at him, nodding in agreement.

Spilf reached his hand out to touch the container, but it strangely pushed away from him the closer he came to it. He retracted his hand in fear and the other two looked on in amazement. His legs suddenly became wobbly. Bridazak lurched and grabbed hold of his friend to stabilize him.

"Are you alright?"

"Yeah, did you see that?" Spilf slowly asked. "Dulgin, try touching it. There was a strange sensation that I felt when I reached for it. I can't explain it."

Dulgin scoffed, "This is ridiculous!"

"Bridazak, have you tried knocking on the box? You seem to be the only one who can touch it," Spilf spoke, still watching the oddity, but now with a sense of fear.

"Yes, I've knocked. I've tried everything."

"Someone is playing a practical joke on you, Bridazak. They snuck in here and placed this, whatever it is, in your hands and then left. They are probably laughing at us right now," Dulgin placed his pipe back into his mouth for another tug.

"No one sneaks up on Bridazak," Spilf defended his friend. Then Spilf caught his Ordakian brother's glint in his eye, "Bridazak, you have that look on your face that I have not seen for quite some time." Dulgin ignored them and walked back to his chair. He leaned again, and rested his head against the wall.

"What look?"

"The look you have when you're making a plan."

Bridazak paused, "Matter of fact..."

"I knew it!"

"Hold on Spilf, it's not a plan, just an idea."

"Yes, and?" A smile of anticipation froze on his face.

"I think we have been cooped up too long in Gathford. Thule and his goons are getting on our nerves. Plus, we will have Lady Birmham on our tail. It is time for us to move on to bigger and better things; to get out of here, onto the open road, and start adventuring again. Roam the land and be our own kings." Bridazak knew wanderlust called out each of their names.

"Finally! I'm ready to break into some serious coin for once, and stay out of these treasureless, small towns," Spilf said, already on board.

The Ordakians peered over to the quiet, stubborn Dwarf.

"You don't know what you are talkin' about."

Bridazak slid, bare-footed, on the smooth wooden floor. He leaned in and whispered, "Did I forget to mention gold?"

Dulgin didn't flinch, but his right-eye shot wide open and glared into Bridazak's teal eyes. "How much and where?"

"That box on the table is highly magical and probably rare. Worth more than you can possibly carry, I'm sure of that."

"I'm in, as long as it doesn't involve any of those damn Horn Kings. These humans are leaving a bad taste in my mouth that I would love to be rid of."

Spilf then asked, "How much do you think we can sell it for?" he pointed at the mysterious item.

"Yes, about that," Bridazak hesitated. "We are going to need to find someone who would know about such things. Someone who," he paused, "someone who knows magic beyond magic itself."

Spilf cocked his head slightly, his eyes narrowing as he processed what Bridazak was after. He feared to say it out loud. Bridazak nodded as he understood his friend knew what he was alluding too.

"You have gone mad, Bridazak. We have done a lot of crazy things together, but this one takes the prize," Spilf walked to the window, contemplating Bridazak's hidden agenda.

"What are you Daks talking about now?" Dulgin asked while still resting his head, eyes barely open.

"He is talking about things that shouldn't be talked about! Leave it alone, Dulgin."

"Okay Daky, don't be telling me what to do," Dulgin glared at Spilf a moment, then questioned Bridazak again. "What are you getting at? Stop with all your cryptic dances with Stubby over there and spit it out."

In pure frustration, Spilf yelled out, "He is talking about the Oculus!"

Dulgin stood up out of the chair and walked to the table where the mysterious item lay. He slowly moved to touch it but it pushed away the closer he came. He retracted his hand, and looked at his friends who held their breath, waiting to see if he felt what Spilf had experienced earlier. The Dwarf visibly resisted something. His eyes then focused on Bridazak.

"No way in Dwarven hell am I going down into those smelly, rotting, rat-infested sewer tunnels! Are you crazy? Is this thing worth risking your very soul?"

"I know it sounds crazy, but it is the only way that I can see to figure this out."

"I said yes to gold, but Oculus? That thing is an abomination! Why, Bridazak? Give me something else besides treasure, cause going there just doesn't make any sense."

"We have been through a lot my friend, and this is yet another adventure. You are the one that always told me the greater the threat, the greater the reward. Time to find out if that is true."

"Whatever is inside that box has to be worth a lot. It doesn't make sense, but I'm in," Spilf said.

"Both of you don't make a bit of damn sense!" Dulgin shouted.

"Your four-hundred and fifty years as a fighter brought you here, a year spent in this cowpeck town of Gathford," Bridazak quickly resounded. "When exactly is the last time your axe has been truly put to use?"

Dulgin looked long and hard before responding, "Alright, alright. It's not in me to back away from a challenge. Let's go and see what the Great Oculus is staring at these days."

"Spilf, we will need supplies," he said while placing a reassuring hand on Dulgin's broad shoulder.

"I will get what we need. It will most likely take us a good three to four days to reach the lair; could be a hard journey."

"No harder than it was for us cutting through King Cerberus's garden."

"Yeah, good point. This will be a snap," Spilf smirked, and then he was off.

Dulgin gathered his belongings. He paused as he looked at his dented metal armor on the floor, waiting to be donned. Entranced in a flood of memories, he recalled how every nick and scratch came about, and it warmed his heart. As stubborn as he was, he had missed the thrill of adventure.

Bridazak wandered over to the window and watched Spilf move through the shadow of night until he could not be seen any longer. He stared down the small street to Gathford. The shadows were heavy as the night waned. He caught a sudden but slight shift in the blackness. Yes, there was something hiding within, but it was far down the street, three structures beyond, just past the old candle shop. Bridazak's eyes narrowed to focus in.

"What are you looking at?" Dulgin asked as he walked behind Bridazak and looked out the window.

Bridazak saw the shadowy figure move back deeper into the black of night, and then it was gone. "Nothing, my friend. Just lost in my thoughts is all."

"Yeah, well, you should gather up your stuff cause first light will be here soon," he said as he picked up his satchel and resumed packing.

The Ordakian continued to search, and saw the mysterious figure once again. Bridazak nodded his head ever so slightly.

"I see you. Whatever you are," he said under his breath, edging closer to the window.

It vanished back into the night. Bridazak peered at the table to see the wooden box, where it waited patiently. He scooped it up with his small, dexterous hands. "What do you hide inside, I wonder?"

3

A Disturbance

The darkness was his masterpiece. His cold heart mirrored the black of night, and whispers of his impending world domination echoed in the halls of his domain. It was only a matter of time before the four kingdoms were completely under his reign, and the people left without hope. He had separated the created ones from their creator five hundred years ago, and forever silenced the god of light.

This entity sat upon a black glass throne, revelling in the thought of his conquests throughout the known realm. Pride welled up inside and there was a slight smirk on his face. His eyes were red and his skin black. Cold blood coursed through his body—a being so full of hate that his appearance was hideous to the forsaken world.

His followers, cast down from The Holy City alongside of him, bubbled up out of the murk: demons and the undead. Slowly, his army had infiltrated the land, encouraged wars, brought more greed, and created more gods to be worshipped. Ultimately, he had established four strategic puppets, known as the Four Horns. There was nothing to stop him as he continued to squeeze the life out of the people and the land, and swallow it up into his realm of shadows. The scraping of claws reached his ears and caused him to conclude his thoughts of the past and his future.

"Yes, Sigil. I could smell your foulness approaching. What news do you bring?" the creature whispered from the throne.

"My Lord, a situation has been reported from the land of Manasseh that needs your attention," the beast gurgled with confidence. Sigil, the Dark Lord's commander, was foul indeed. Spikes protruded from his muscled body, and his skin glowed a darkened red, as if he showered in blood. He stood nine feet tall with four arms, and had claws as razor sharp as any magically enhanced weapon ever created. His teeth were black and pointed. Pupil-less eyes revealed no life.

"What has our puppet done now that I need to be bothered with, Sigil?"

"It is not him, but a strange disturbance from a small town on the edge of his land, my King," Sigil replied.

"What do you mean, disturbance?"

"A strange aura manifested, and one of our agents within the town was spotted by a created one."

The dark being on the throne turned into smoke and simultaneously transported twenty feet away, softly growling his discontent in Sigil's face. "Show me what the agent saw," he whispered into his commander's deformed ear while circling him. The Dark Lord bested Sigil's height.

Sigil opened one of his clawed hands to reveal a sapphire of extreme value. The gem activated and produced a ghost-like image of the recorded scenario. The dark pair watched the soundless chronicle as faded images told the story of the encounter. The creature of the night was on top of a structure, overlooking a small town of a hundred buildings of various sizes, scattered about in clusters. Trees swayed in the night breeze and the moon was partly showing behind the clouds. A sudden flash of light ignited in the community, brilliant and blinding. On the far side of the hamlet a glow pulsated, like the rhythmic beating of a heart. The spy glided to the ground and then made his way through the shadows until it finally reached the lambent source, emanating from an open window.

Before the agent could move closer to the domicile, an Ordakian came into view. He had a bright glow all around him. The Dak stared out into the night, and spotted the agent. A red-bearded Dwarf stepped behind the child-like race to peer out, but soon walked away. The spy tried to move further back into the darkness, but the light intensified from the room and flooded the area. The Ordakian nodded his head to show that he could still see the shadow creature. Vulnerable to the mysterious beacon and the increased power it radiated, the agent teleported back to Kerrith Ravine. The vision ended and the dazzling gem returned to normal.

"What creature can see my shadow agents in the natural when they do not want to be seen, Sigil?" the Dark Lord rhetorically asked.

"There is none," the red behemoth replied.

"I would say you are correct, until now. Very intriguing. I have not seen this before," he paused, "perhaps one of the fallen ones created a magical item that allows one to see our realm of shadows."

"Shall I send more to investigate?" Sigil responded.

"No, I will discuss this matter with Manasseh and have him deal with this. It is time that I reveal myself to this manufactured king of ours."

It had been a long day for Manasseh, the ruler of the North Horn. A grueling schedule of overseeing expansion efforts, training his growing army, deployment of spies and assassins, and strategizing in council with his mystics. The night had come and it was his time to quiet himself in the solitude of his private wing. He walked to his chamber, the thumps of his gold encrusted boots resounding throughout his halls. His black cloak of the finest linen of the realm swept in behind the gliding movement of his six-foot frame. Jet black hair fell to his shoulders, straight and flawless. Steel blue eyes, angled face, and a muscular body exuded power in the sight of his subjects. He brought a strong presence wherever he went, and his reputation for brutality permeated the land. A click sounded as he unclasped his cape, letting it fall to the cold, slate-tiled floor. Before him was his bed, the grandest in the region. The walnut frame was a lacquered black finish with ornate carvings of dragons in flight. Descending from the ceiling and cascading over the edges were silks of rich colors, draped in thick layers to prevent anyone from seeing inside. Candelabras on either side cast shifting shadows about the room.

Relaxed in the stillness, he sat in his replicated throne—the soft red velvet chair captured his tired body as he pulled off his heavy boots and silk shirt, tossing them to the side. He fell back into the high, cathedral shaped seat and closed his weary eyes.

He opened his eyes when he thought he heard someone shuffling on his bed. It wasn't unlike his head mystic, Vevrin, to send him someone to keep him company, but he was always informed. Vevrin knew not to surprise his King.

"You can leave. I'm not in the mood." His voice echoed through the stark room. There was no response, but again he could hear someone shifting in the confines.

"I said, leave," his tone was deeper. Again, no response. He stood and glared toward his sleeping haven. A silhouette of a hand brushed along the silk. Angry with the intrusion and the defiance, he strode to the bedside and pulled the draping away, "I will have you flogged—" He stopped short when he found it empty.

A strange garbled whisper echoed behind him, and he swung around with a summoned dagger now in his hand. The King could sense a presence of someone in the room. A chill encompassed his exposed chest and arms.

"Guards!" he called.

Instantly, two men in black armor with red painted shoulders burst through the double doors. They wielded polearms; the halberd consisted of an axe blade topped with a spike, mounted on a long wooden shaft. Helmets adorned with two horns shielded their faces. They scanned the room with their weaponry lowered.

Another whisper reached his ears, "I'm behind you." He sharply turned to see nothing but the fixated shadows of the room.

"Fan out," he ordered his men.

He turned at the sound of a clash behind him to find his guards on their knees. Their weapons clattered to the ground and blood sprayed out of their open necks. Headless, they collapsed to the floor. There was no sign of the intruder, or the guards' heads. The doors slammed shut.

"Show yourself!"

"How is it that a human can live for four centuries?" a booming voice questioned. King Manasseh did not respond as his eyes darted around the room. "Where does your power come from? Who gave you your strength?" it mocked.

"Who are you?" Manasseh countered.

"I've watched you. I've groomed you."

"I demand you show yourself!"

20

A seductive female voice spoke behind him, "I'm right here."

He spun around to face her. The naked brunette stunned him as he stared at her chilling beauty. Her stance was awkwardly stiff as her head was bowed and her palms faced up, at her sides.

"How did you get in here, woman?"

Another voice startled him from behind, "I have my ways."

He turned quickly and the same woman stood before him. "Let me rephrase that. How did you get in here, witch?" There was venom in his voice on the last word.

Her bowed head lifted and her closed eyes sprang open in a flash. They were pearl black. She broke a smile to reveal black, jagged teeth, and took a step towards him. The half-naked King backed away and then fell into his throne. She mechanically moved closer—each step was rigid. He was fear stricken, but attempted to slide over the arm of the chair. Her slow posture suddenly shifted as her hand hastily swatted at Manasseh. He caught her arm in mid-swing and then plunged his dagger deep inside her chest. She instantly disappeared, but he still felt the evil presence. Jumping out of the chair, he scanned the room defensively.

"I'm not afraid of you, demon," his resolve returned.

"You should be. You will be," the Dark Lord responded. His voice echoed through the room so that Manasseh could not pinpoint his location. He was enjoying this first meeting, playing with his puppet.

"What are you and why have you come?" Manasseh yelled.

"I am your Master and you will bow to me," said the self-titled King of Kings. Manasseh's blade suddenly turned white hot in his hands. He released the weapon and tried to stop the pain of the burn with his other hand.

"Sit!" Manasseh was launched forcefully into the red chair and his hands were pinned down on the arm rests. Out of thin air, a wisp of smoke manifested as the evil visage unravelled: standing ten feet tall, the red eyed, black skinned behemoth smiled. He soaked in the fear emanating from the pathetic human before him.

"I am your Father. I have groomed you from birth and brought you into greatness. It is finally time for us to meet and for you to ascend to the next level of power. I am the ruler of death itself. I am the creator of all the chaos and corruption you see in the lands. I am your destiny, and I am the god of all gods; you will worship me as they do."

King Manasseh was shocked by the words this creature spoke. Could it be true? His source of power and strength rested below his castle. He could sense the connection under his feet from the depths as it flowed into him. *"Yes, can you feel it?"* Centuries had passed without a word from this deity and yet his voice seemed familiar. *"Yes, it was me."* How? Why? Yet here he stood. His thoughts battled his soul as he tried to reconcile the truth. This dark one had power he could only dream of, and he wanted it. He could see the advantage of having such an entity by his side, and pictured overtaking all the Horn Kings and ruling the entire world.

"My Lord and my God," he bowed his head. His hands were released by the unseen force and he moved off of the chair to kneel.

"I accept your worship. Now rise and receive my instructions." The human lifted his head and stood. "I want something to prove your worth to me."

"Anything," Manasseh said.

"Good. You will capture an Ordakian for my pleasure. This creature was last seen in Gathford. He travels with another of his race, and a Dwarf. I only need the blonde one. When you have retrieved him, call upon me and I will hear you. Do you understand?"

"Yes, my Lord. I understand and it will be done."

A smooth stone, cradled in gold and attached to a leather strap, appeared magically around Manasseh's neck. Smoke swirled inside it, and he marvelled at the depths of the darkness. When he looked up, his master had vanished. He knew his marching orders. This Ordakian would be his before the next full moon. His mystics would locate his prize and teleport with twenty of his best fighters. What a simple task this would be, and then, he would have his deity's favor to crush his enemies.

Manasseh began to laugh softly and then it built into a hearty roar. It was a night that would rival all his nights; he soaked in the glory of what transpired.

"I'm coming for you, Halfling!"

4

Oculus

"Welcome to the Plains of Shame," Dulgin announced. The shimmering golden fields went beyond their vision. A dry smell of wheat mixed with a tinge of berry briar patches washed over them as a slight breeze rustled across the open land.

"Oculus's Lair resides deep inside. C'mon." Dulgin, now wearing his rusty plate mail, clattered ahead of the Ordakians. His weapon matched his attire; a huge Dwarven battle axe rested on his shoulder.

Spilf nudged Bridazak, "You know what this means right? Dulgin's History Hour." Spilf wore his leather armor under his dark green shirt and pants. A grey cloak draped down his back and his ornate dagger, with a snake-head hilt, was sheathed at his side.

Bridazak gave a slight smile. "It gives him something to do while we travel, and I never mind his stories." He also wore leather protection underneath his brown pants and beige shirt. Strapped around his back was a quiver of arrows. His short bow he carried in his hand. A sheathed dagger on his hip completed his ensemble.

"A great battle in the Bronze Age of Ruauck-El was fought at this very location. Why, you ask? I will tell you why."

"Can't wait," Spilf whispered sarcastically.

"It was said that the Orcasians and Humans arranged for this land to be a neutral trading ground, until the Orc scum betrayed the union."

"How so?" Bridazak asked, now curious.

"The Orcs invested in dark magic and their leader was transformed into the likeness of the Human King, Darius, because he knew the royal family was scheduled to make a tour of the new establishment. The doppelganger timed his visit with their arrival, and slept with the Queen. She eventually birthed a son from that ill-fated night, and the hideous half-orc child revealed the truth of what had transpired. A war ensued and many thousands of Orcs were slaughtered. An easy victory for the Humans as their cavalry swept across these golden plains, which were renamed The Plains of Shame."

Spilf chimed aloud, "Speaking of cavalry, are you guys ever going to tell me why we don't use ponies to get around? It would be so much faster and less wear and tear on our feet."

"I will defer that to the Dwarf. Dulgin, why don't you tell Spilf about the ponies," Bridazak said sarcastically. He knew that Dulgin would not ever talk about that event. Their bearded friend had vowed to never ride a pony or horse again.

Dulgin growled at the two Daks. "It's not my fault that your kind doesn't wear boots," he spouted.

"That still doesn't answer why we can't ride."

Dulgin turned sharply and cut the Ordakian off, "Listen here, Daky, we ain't ever going to ride those damn things and that is final. Got it?"

"Yeah, sure, whatever, *Dulgy*." Spilf jabbed back in retaliation.

Bridazak smiled at the confrontation. It was quite entertaining. Dulgin did not respond and continued walking ahead of them.

Not alerting their burly friend, Bridazak lowered his voice, "Hey, by chance did you mention anything about the full amount of our score with Dulgin the other night?"

"He was too busy drinking."

"Good, I'm afraid he'd have spent our nest egg on all the Dwarven Ale in sight. It's getting more and more difficult to find as the years pass."

"How much do you think that diamond ring is worth?"

"I would say double what we received in coin."

There was a lull in the conversation. Bridazak then asked, "Did you see anything on the streets in Gathford when you went out to get supplies?"

"No, why?"

"I saw someone hiding in the shadows, but couldn't make out who it was."

"Do you think it was Thule?"

"No, this individual was extremely gifted in stealth. I think I was lucky spotting him myself."

"Actually, come to think of it, I had a creepy sensation at one point, like someone was watching me. There was a cold shiver that went up my spine, but it went away and I didn't think anything of it."

"Let's be mindful of the possibility that someone might be following us."

"Now that we are out of the town, it's our laws that reign. Dulgin would love to put his axe to use again, and when's the last time you used that bow of yours?"

"Not since the Gathford archery contest several months ago."

"Oh yeah, that's the reason Thule and his goons started bothering us. You gave them an education in archery, that's for sure." They laughed at the memory as they continued to slosh through the waist-high, golden stalks.

"I've almost got it." Beads of sweat trickled down Spilf's brow.

Bridazak watched his friend methodically maneuver his tools of the trade to bypass the trapped entrance. "What is it with you and those rusty picks you like to use? I just don't know how you do it using those things."

Spilf peered up with a cocky smirk, "Someday I will have to let you know my secret." He went back to work and a moment later, announced, "There, got it." The magical glyph of fire fizzled away in a puff of smoke around the sealed, debris-covered entrance. Dulgin continued to scan the area. It was a desolate land—dry, rocky, and depressing. They had arrived at the lair of Oculus—an ancient, abandoned keep, crumbled and scattered. There was a foreboding about the place, a sense of depression intruded into their minds.

"Are you sure about this entry point, Dulgin?" Spilf asked.

"No, it was over three-hundred and fifty years ago when my brother told me. He was known to be wrong before, so we enter at our own risk."

The Ordakians looked at each other, shocked at the mention of a sibling he'd never told them about. "You have a brother?" Bridazak questioned. "Where is he?"

"*Had* a brother. He went off on a damned crusade to Kerrith Ravine with a thousand other good clerics from across the land. They were never seen again. My brother, El'Korr of the Hammergold Clan, will be forever remembered for trying to restore the Lost Kingdom." Dulgin's voice trailed off as he thought of his brother. He had been a great Dwarven warrior who deserved a burial worthy of his caliber. The last time he saw El'Korr was at their father's passing, just before the elder brother left on his crusade. The deaths of these two Dwarves had altered his attitude, he recognized; he'd grown more cynical, and more stubborn than ever. He glanced at the only thing he retained from his past—his father's axe; an heirloom meant to be passed down in the lineage of his family, but now only a symbol of what was. His home was long destroyed and any remaining Dwarves had scattered across the land as they escaped the wrath of the Reegs, the shadow demons that came out of Kerrith Ravine.

Spilf released the lock, snapping Dulgin out of his thoughts of the past, and the dull grey, metal portal hissed open. A gust of putrid smelling air escaped to meet the three intruders, air so strong that it pushed them to the ground. On their rear ends, hands covering their faces, they looked at each other in bewilderment. They slowly edged their way over to peer down the dark tunnel. After a moment, the faint sounds of scuffling and whispers below reached their ears.

"Maybe it's rats," suggested Bridazak with a shrug.

Dulgin stared at him with irritation, "I don't think so, my friend. Rats don't whisper."

Spilf unslung his pack and pulled out a torch, a flint, and a piece of steel. Within seconds a large spark ignited the oil-dipped piece of wood and he tossed it into the black hole. Landing twenty feet below, it revealed the disgusting sight of piled and decaying bodies. Dulgin glared at Bridazak.

"Alright, alright, I'm going," he surrendered.

"Remember, this was your idea in the first place," the Dwarf countered.

"That smell is rank. Are we sure we want to go down there?" Spilf pleaded.

"It's called the smell of adventure. Now get your Daky-ass down there!"

One by one, the three friends climbed down the cold, metal rungs. Their movement echoed throughout; the creaking of leather, the tap of boots on metal, and then soft padding of bare feet on stone as they reached the bottom. Picking up the torch to get a better look around, Bridazak snapped his head in one direction where he heard more scuffling sounds in the distance. Dulgin followed his change in stance and quipped sarcastically, "Maybe it's those rats you were talking about."

"Too big to be rats," Spilf responded.

"Maybe it's *really* big rats, coming to ask you for some fresh meat. Looks like they could use it," Dulgin continued his joking.

They surveyed the carcasses that were strewn about. Humans, Orcs, and Goblins. Thirty decayed bodies that bore signs of battle: slash marks and punctured armor.

"The sounds are coming from the north passageway," whispered Bridazak. The echo of his childlike voice glided smoothly down the dark corridors.

There were four tunnels leading away from this main junction. Bridazak moved toward the source of the sound, and the light from the Ordakian's torch faded as they went deeper into danger. The aroma of rotting flesh dwindled and the corridor slowly transformed into a cleaner, dryer habitat. Bridazak and Spilf were walking a little ahead of the gruff Dwarf. The stocky redhead intermittently walked backward, watching for any surprises. He had done this several times without any problems, but finally bumped into Bridazak who had stopped walking for some unknown reason.

"What is wrong now?" Dulgin harshly whispered.

"Look at the torch."

They gazed at the twisting fire and watched it flutter and move to the left. An air source was coming out of the right wall. Simultaneously, they spoke softly, "Secret door."

Within minutes, they had discovered and opened the elusive portal by pushing it in on one side. It was a swivel set-up that was well crafted. The torchlight did not penetrate the magical darkness beyond.

"It smells even worse in there!" Spilf stepped back, covering his mouth and nose with his sleeve.

From the darkness a voice echoed back, "I would be saying the same to you, little-one." The hidden voice sounded scratchy. They backed away, waiting; they could not see through the magical barrier, so no one moved. The voice crackled again, "Why are you here? You are not welcome, so your answer had better be to my liking."

Bridazak looked at his friends and Spilf nudged him to respond. "We are here to see Oculus."

"I am her loyal servant."

Bridazak was suddenly able to see outlines of creatures inside the darkness. At least four pairs of eyes glowed red, looking down on them. He was uncertain how he was able to see through the magic. He wished he could sense their intentions and an impression came just as quickly as he thought the question. *"They plan to kill you."*

"We are sorry to have bothered you. We meant no disrespect," Bridazak stated promptly and started to tug at his friends to move back away with him. They were surprised at the statement and the action, but trusted his leading.

"I have not permitted you to leave," the creature responded in a threatening, raspy tone.

"We don't need permission, whoever you are," Dulgin retorted.

The conversation was meant to keep their defenses down, but now Bridazak moved quickly to pull forth his short bow and notch an arrow, as he knew that Dulgin's chime was not diplomatic enough to hold them back any longer.

They rushed the group from the darkness. Claws sprang out of paws attached to shaggy, light brown fur. A hateful expression of rage was on their distorted rodent faces. These *were* giant rats.

Bridazak's shot unerringly hit his first opponent between its eyes. Without hesitation he quickly pulled out another arrow and struck the second rat in the chest with deadly accuracy. It slammed it into the cold stone floor. Dulgin pulled out a throwing axe and hurled it toward his mark. The vile thing fell dead with the hatchet buried in its head. Five other sewer scented creatures engaged the combatants.

Spilf was knocked to the floor by one of the beasts as it launched itself at him. He was able to pull out his snake head dagger and slice its back foot as it jumped upon him. It snarled at Spilf in disgust and then lunged again. The Dak rolled to avoid the grapple and then quickly swung his blade back to hit the thing squarely in its gut. It screeched and tried in vain to stop the blood that poured out. The magic of Spilf's dagger had unleashed its venom. A gurgled last breath was heard as the poison took over.

With lightning speed, Bridazak released a volley of arrows. One dropped, then another. Dulgin had just delivered a punishing blow with his huge battle axe to drop one more. He wielded his weapon masterfully, as if it were an extension of his hands. It slammed into the last one, breaking and severing the backbone of the creature. A blood-curdled yelp resounded, and then there was silence.

"I got four and all you could do was take out three?" Bridazak scoffed over at Dulgin.

"Ah shut your mouth, ya blundering fool!" Dulgin was pulling his throwing axe out of the dead carcass.

"I got one," chimed Spilf, after picking himself up off the floor. "Or, at least my magical dagger got one."

"I told you that them rats wanted to talk with ya, didn't I?" Dulgin teased Spilf.

All three chuckled at the comment.

"How did you know, Bridazak? How did you know they were going to attack us?" Spilf asked.

"I was able to see an outline of them somehow. I can't explain it"

The magical darkness had disappeared, and down the new corridor was an iron door twice the average human size. Ancient and mysterious, the shadowed entryway loomed before them. Cautiously, the three adventurers approached. Bridazak nodded toward Spilf, "Check it out."

"You got it, boss." He brought out his rusty picks once again and inspected the locking mechanism. "It's all clear." Spilf then pulled open the great iron door with surprising ease. Almost too easy, they all thought, as it glided with little effort.

Beyond, a short corridor ultimately brought them to a large room on the left. It was an enormous chamber, with the only shadowy illumination coming from their torchlight. They could hear the sound of water splashing deeper within, and as they cautiously entered, the source was revealed. In the center of the room, a stone statue portrayed a hideous, frightening creature, the likes of which were otherwise found only in nightmares. A round boulder shaped beast, ten feet in diameter, with a gaping maw and an eye the size of a large wagon wheel, magically hovered above the pool.

Several tentacle eye-stalks protruded from the top. A strange red liquid poured out of its mouth into a basin below. It floated above the reddish pool, casting a menacing stare in their direction.

"What is that?" questioned the Dwarven fighter.

"That is the legendary Great Eye of the Deep. A statue of whom we seek—Oculus. It's a good thing that this is not real, otherwise we would probably be dead by now," Spilf explained, grasping at his dagger again.

They crept into the chamber to search the area in hopes of finding another secret door, keeping a wary eye on the stone figure.

"Tell me Bridazak, what do you think that red liquid is in that fountain?" the Dwarf hesitantly asked.

"Probably just your ordinary everyday blood sucked from the lives of innocent people."

"Great, just what I needed to hear."

As the three searched the confines of the room, a loud thundering voice crackled to life around them. Bridazak instinctively drew forth his bow, as did Dulgin with his battle axe. They scanned the area to try and pinpoint the threat.

"Who dares to enter my domain?" The deep voice bellowed.

Bridazak hesitated before speaking up, "I'm Bridazak and these are my friends. We seek an audience with The Great Oculus."

The voice thundered once more, "Two Ordakians and a Dwarf, in a place they should not be. Many seek my voice, but find only fated death. What has brought you to the door of oblivion?"

"A mystery, one that came from my dream. We seek your help, oh Great One," said the Ordakian.

"Show me what has turned from a dream into reality."

Bridazak produced the ornate box in his small hands, and began to speak, "We don't know what the writing—"

"Silence!" The ground shook under their feet. "I know what you seek, but you must answer my riddle. If you are correct, then I will reveal to you the meaning of this gift. If you fail, then you will be sent to the grave. There will be no rest inside the gates of the netherworld, your soul will thirst for death again for all eternity and generations forthcoming will never know you existed."

"What about my friends?"

30

"You came here together as one accord and you will live or die in the same manner. Your riddle is this, little-one:

Rigid but born to perfection
I wonder who brought me my blissful conception
I am gazed upon by many lonely eyes
Standing there to be portrayed with lies
There are questions that surround me
Thinking, feeling, hearing, I can see
No movement comes from within
I am forsaken because I lack earthly skin
So true is my heart without a beat
Now I drink the rainwater, tasting bittersweet
Crafted by art in life's forgiving hand
Brought from afar to this known fatherland
Trying to find the meaning of my existence
A voice comes here and there showing the eminence
The task performed in drought of the grandmaster
Born in stillness could have been my disaster
Braving the depth of a complex web
Weaved and woven in the delight of the ebb
Now and forever in eternal agony's darkness
Never to move to touch, only to feel a sweet caress.

Of what do I speak?"

Dulgin contemplated the intricate riddle and then asked, "Can you repeat the saying once more?"

"You have until the end of the torch light you hold," the creature responded. Silence overtook the room once again, interrupted only by the sound of the fountain splashing into the pool.

"Do something Bridazak, the torch has only a few minutes remaining."

"I'm trying to think. Born. Emotions, no movement. I can't recall everything it said. I wish I could see it." The sounds in the room around him began to fade as the Ordakian strained to grasp something in his mind.

He saw the round rock sculpture illuminated with a soft light. His body felt raptured inside a somnolent vision. The outlined effigy slowly came alive, and the once-still representation of Oculus moved to face him. Then it suddenly ended, snapping him back into reality. The sounds of the room returned, Dulgin and Spilf were yelling at him to find out what was wrong. He could see the torch on its last chokes of breath.

"Bridazak, there is no time!" Spilf's words echoed.

"The light—it was showing me the answer. That's it. I've got it. Great One of the Deep, the answer to this riddle lies before me. It is a statue," Bridazak's words faded at the same time as the fire in his hand.

They waited in anticipation, not breathing, motionless. Uncertainty surrounded them. The pitch-black room seemed like a tomb.

"No one has ever answered this riddle, for it was created by the gods themselves." A soft glow permeated the area as a beautiful human apparition appeared. She glided from inside the immense statue. Translucent, grey-colored, ghostlike clothing fluttered about. Her eyes emanated a hypnotic, dazzling blue light as she hovered gracefully before the group.

"You don't have much time, as you are being tracked by mystics," she said without her lips moving. Her voice was powerful and soothing, and spoke within their minds.

"Why are we being tracked?" Bridazak asked, a puzzled look on his face.

"Listen to what I have to say. I am Kiratta, once the helper of mankind, but now forever condemned inside the creature you see before you. You must find the Lost Prophet inside the endless forest of Everwood, in order to set in motion all that must come."

"What are you talking about? We don't know about anyone in Everwood," he responded, confused.

"Bridazak, you have been called. Now it is up to you to heed that call. Do not worry, little-one, it will unfold in due time."

"But what is inside this thing?" He lifted the box toward her.

"To open this gift you will need to bare your heart to the One that has given it to you. Protect this gift at all costs, Bridazak." She paused and then continued, *"You will know you have found The Prophet when he says, 'I will reveal my strength through weakness'."*

"What does that mean?" Bridazak questioned.

"It is part of the prophecy, but there is no time left to explain. Assassins have entered, and there is a mystic among them. He teleported inside my domain."

32

"There is only one entrance, how do we get out of here?" Spilf questioned.

"There are many doors throughout Ruauck-El hidden from natural sight. Go to the town of Lonely Tear and follow the river against the current into Everwood." She twisted her arms in movements that mesmerized the group. Elegantly, she weaved her spell to completion. Behind the adventurers, natural sunlight poured out from a magical portal. They turned and shielded their eyes from the sudden brightness.

As she finished, twenty men wielding assorted weapons and wearing black studded armor entered, and skidded to a halt when they saw the monstrous statue. Their eyes refocused and spotted the heroes on the other side of the room. Then out from behind the soldiers came the feared mystic, adorned in blood-red robes with a wooden staff as twisted as himself, bearing a human skull with sapphire gems embedded in the eye sockets on top.

"And where do you think you're going?" The thin, pale-faced human mage spoke confidently.

A large roar of rage echoed throughout the room and caused the magic wielder to redirect his attention toward the statue. The strange red liquid ceased to pour from the mouth, and the loud cracking of stone pierced everyone's ears. The workmanship of rock fell away and smashed onto the floor, revealing a fleshy chitinous hide underneath. It was moving—coming to life—screaming in anger throughout the transformation. Kiratta was forcefully pulled back into the statue. Her brief time of freedom had come to an end. "Go!" she yelled. "Oculus awakens!"

"What dark magic is this?" the Dwarf asked.

A crossbow bolt whistled by their heads and ushered them back to the immediate threat. Several of the troops fired at the hideous creature, their ammunition bouncing off its natural armor harmlessly. A few others hugged the wall and started to make their way toward their exit. One of the assassins was instantly burned to ashes as an eyestalk of Oculus delivered a black ray that hit the warrior directly. Flashes of red, orange, and blue colors flared in the room as the ancient beholder of the deep unleashed her fury.

"Come on! We need to get out of here!" Spilf yelled over the screams and sounds of battle, pushing Bridazak and Dulgin to move forward. The Dwarf watched the mystic point his staff in their direction as his little friend moved them closer to the portal. A magical, dark bolt of force shot forth and the Dwarf's instinct kicked in—time seemed to slow down as he moved to push Spilf and Bridazak out of the way of danger. The energy bolt struck him in the left side of his back as he shielded his friends. The smell of burning flesh was undeniable, and Dulgin fell forward to the ground. Bridazak and Spilf helped him to his feet, and they rushed the portal which had now started to fade away.

They jumped through together as a group. The brilliance engulfed them and a moment later they landed in the middle of a dirt road. It was daylight, and the surroundings showed no life except for some birds chirping in the distance. Sparse trees dotted rolling meadows in every direction. A cool breeze brought the smell of dried vegetation.

"Are you alright, Dulgin?" they asked.

"Yeah, of course. Just a scratch. Let's move on," he tried to lift himself up but quickly fell to the ground in pain.

Bridazak and Spilf inspected his wound by turning him over on his side. Small wisps of smoke wafted up from the hole that penetrated the armor, revealing a black sludge pouring out from the opening in his flesh. Spilf riffled through his pack and produced a vial with blue liquid inside.

"Our only one." He uncorked it and then poured it directly on the wound. Dulgin lurched at first but settled in as the magic of the fluid produced its healing affects. His wound slowly closed and the black sludge dissipated. The Dwarf slowly turned over to lie flat on his back. Then he winked at them and smiled.

"Gold or not, you sure know how to show a Dwarf a good time."

They all stood up on their feet and surveyed the land. Dulgin began to cough uncontrollably. Blood was on his hands after the fit was over.

"I think that mystic gave you a little more than an open gash in your side, my friend," Bridazak stated with concern.

"Who were those people, and why are they after us?" Spilf asked.

"I don't know, but they looked angry about something," Bridazak responded.

"They were military, and that could only mean King Manasseh." Dulgin coughed again.

"Good news is, I think they improved the look of your armor, my friend."

They laughed and then began to walk down the road—a road that they had never been on before.

5

Lonely Tear

The sun beamed its last rays across the landscape, giving a golden hue to the terrain. There were no distinguishable landmarks, and the name of the town of Lonely Tear had never fallen on their ears before. Dulgin was still experiencing the hidden effects of the magic that the mystic unleashed into his body. He lumbered along with gritted teeth and concentrated on each step he took. The Ordakians watched him and gave periodic glances of concern to one another. Time was against them.

"Bridazak, how did you know the answer to that riddle?" the Dwarf winced as he tried to distract himself from the pain.

"It was strange. A light outlined the statue and then I felt an impression in my mind that I cannot explain."

"Did Kiratta give you the answer?"

"No, it was more powerful, like a spirit directing me from wthin. Time stopped, and—I'm not sure how to explain it."

"You were possessed by something?"

"No, not like that. It was an impression that welled up inside me."

"It was the box, Bridazak."

He looked at Spilf, surprised, but deep down he knew he was right. *What could he possibly be carrying?* Bridazak withdrew the impenetrable container, and a soothing warmth flowed through him as he grasped it once again.

Dulgin suddenly doubled over and grunted, jarring him from his thoughts.

"Are you alright?"

"I need to sit and rest. I will be fine." He could feel a cold sensation running through his veins. In his stubbornness, he resisted to inform his comrades as they lowered him down onto a slightly inclined grassy slope along the dirt road.

"Bridazak, he needs a healer."

"I know. I wish a caravan or someone would come along to let us know where we are."

Bridazak and Spilf heard faint neighing from a horse behind them. They made eye contact, making sure they both heard what they thought they heard, and simultaneously turned around slowly. A caravan in the distance approached. Spilf looked at his friend and lifted an eyebrow, indicating the box his friend still held. Bridazak quickly tucked it away again, and they waited along the worn roadside for the oncoming group of merchants.

"Well met!" Bridazak yelled towards the first horse drawn wagon.

"Bugger off," responded the man. "We don't pick up stragglers!"

A thick cloud of dust enveloped them from the movement of the more than thirty wagons being pulled by horses in a single-file line. They covered their faces, coughing.

Within seconds a woman's voice could barely be heard over the rumbling noise of the moving caravan. Her words fought through the tumbling of wheels and the thuds of hooves.

"Come, I'm over here!" her voice carried mysteriously.

Bridazak hustled to one of the slow-moving vehicles. He pushed aside the thick velvet draping to reveal the silhouette of a robed woman, confirming his instincts—he had found the right wagon. Inside, it was cozy and warm, but dark.

"Thank you and well met," said Bridazak, helping his two comrades finish the climb inside.

"Where are ya headed?" Dulgin asked with grimaced face.

"The next town, I suppose," replied the veiled woman.

"Why did you help us?" asked Spilf.

"I have my reasons," she elusively responded as she lit a dangling oil lamp.

She threw off her hood and revealed her breathtaking face. Her complexion was impeccable and her red hair seemed almost on fire. Her eyes sparkled an orange hue, and an enchanting glow surrounded her face, soft and alluring.

He stuttered, "I'm Bridazak. This is Dulgin and Spilf."

Dulgin was also captivated by her stunning appearance, but went into a coughing frenzy. He clutched at his heart; his legs spasmed and he fell hard against the wood framed wagon in excruciating pain.

"Oh my, you are hurt Dulgin," she quickly pulled her leather gloves off and knelt at Dulgin's side. Before the Ordakians could say or do anything, she closed her eyes and began to recite an unknown incantation, "Shel-ouck-noh-kah-thoom-kay-labra."

Her hands weaved and jostled in the movement of the arcane. Her gestures were fluent, and the sounds emanating from her vocals were charismatic and capturing. Her chanting ended; she opened her eyes and smiled at the gruff looking Dwarf. She placed her delicate hands onto his armored chest, and a glow permeated. Dulgin forced his eyes shut while his friends watched hypnotically and helplessly. Energy flowed through her hands and then the radiance dwindled. She backed away and gave a genuine smile toward them all.

"You are a healer," Bridazak chimed in amazement.

"Yes, at times I can be," she responded pleasantly.

"Thank you my lady," Dulgin initiated a bow of his head. "I am in your debt," he added, checking himself over. He noticed his coughing had stopped. His muscles relaxed and he felt strong once again. "What is your name?"

"People call me Ember."

"That's your real name?" asked Spilf. His life of surviving as a thief had taught him when people were not being entirely truthful.

She paused for a moment," No," she admitted, "but I like to go by that name when I meet new people, such as you."

She focused again on Bridazak, "Would you like for me to reveal your future? If I concentrate hard enough, I might find the answer that you seek."

"What do you mean? How do you know that I have a question?" he asked curiously.

"You have an aura of confusion about you that I can sense."

"Actually, I do have a question on my mind. Maybe what you say might shed some light on the answer." Thoughts of wonder burned inside, and every step they had taken brought a need to know what he carried even more. He tried to breathe calmly, but his heart pounded furiously. Moving closer, he sat upright and attentive in hope.

Dulgin quietly gazed at the angelic, red-haired woman. He was suspicious of her, even though she had just miraculously healed him from the poison that was wreaking havoc inside his body. He glanced over at his companions. Spilf's mouth was open, still held captive by her allure. Bridazak sat waiting for the mysterious woman's prediction like a puppy waiting for its food. Dulgin had a feeling this female wasn't all she played up to be, but he waited quietly as she began to tell his friend's future. Her eyes were closed and her head cocked back, her hands resting on her knees. She was deep in meditation. The light of the lamp seemed to pulse, but not enough to alarm them. Her blue robe in the dim light appeared black at times. There were no symbols or family crest to identify any lineage or regime she may have belonged to. Everything was plain and simple, but at the same time, her beauty nullified the most magnificent thing you could think of. No blemish was on her face, no wrinkle, nothing out of sorts. She was as perfect as he imagined one could be.

"There is someone coming," she started. "Someone of great importance, and someone you will meet. Evil follows you wherever you may go, but destiny has awakened once again. In time, the truth will be revealed and this truth shall set you free." Her eyes opened and she locked into Bridazak's, "That is all that I am permitted to tell you."

"Who are you?" Bridazak questioned, knowing she was more than what she appeared to be.

"I am someone full of regret, and though there is no hope for me, I have chosen my path." She shifted her focus, "Dulgin, keep your suspicions high, for they might save you and your friends. Spilfer Teehle, you might spend your time in the shadows, but the brightness of your heart shines strong." The woman suddenly faded away like a dream, disappearing right in front of them. The wagon stopped abruptly. Dulgin swung the heavy curtain aside, and discovered more time had passed than they realized; the deep of night was upon them, and the saturated air clung to their skin. The rest of the caravan was gone. Vanished.

With the light from the oil lamp inside, Dulgin spotted a weathered wood sign that read *Lonely Tear—One Millari*, and an arrow that pointed the way. Hanging from the wooden post was a medallion on a chain. Bridazak hopped down and grabbed it from the aged marker to inspect it. A symbol of flames adorned the jewelry piece. A circle of gold encompassed the image. Bridazak placed it around his neck and then looked back at his friends, who still sat in the back of the cart, feeling foggy and stunned.

"Let's get moving," Dulgin shook off the numb feeling. He made his way to the front of the coach, helped Spilf right behind him and then grabbed the reigns.

"Thought you said you wouldn't ride any horses," Spilf stated.

"I didn't say anything about a wagon, just none of them four legged meat-walkers."

Bridazak smiled, "Let's see what awaits us in Lonely Tear!" He climbed on with a renewed spirit.

The Dwarf whipped the horses and they all jolted backwards. Within minutes they had reached the outer walls of the small town. Two guards, roused by the sound in the early morning darkness, stepped out and halted their approach.

"State your business," declared one human guard, suspicious of the three little-folk.

"We're merchants delivering silk goods," replied Bridazak.

"Silk goods, huh? Why are you travelling at odd hours of the night?"

"The late hours are more favorable in getting the goods delivered faster, as there is less traffic," he said with a cheesy smile, which Dulgin and Spilf did not share as the other guard approached the back of the wagon to inspect the merchandise. Knowing full well there was no silk onboard, Bridazak glanced over to Dulgin and gave him a look that begged for forgiveness.

"Ya blundering fool," whispered the Dwarf harshly, nudging him with his elbow.

"I didn't know they were going to check. I'm sorry."

They dropped their heads and waited to be chastised by the guards for lying, and then probably detained and questioned. At least they would have a place to stay the night, once arrested.

"Everything checks out, Tulk. There are about ten silk bolts back here."

Spilf quickly peeked through the canvas, and saw the guard inspecting the imagined rolled thread in the barren hold of their wagon. He shrugged his shoulders, informing his friends the human seemed to have gone mad.

"Okay, you're clear to go through. Welcome to Lonely Tear," the guard Tulk waved them to enter.

"This is just unbelievable," whispered the Dwarf as they rode past the alert pair of troops.

Spilf nudged Bridazak to get his attention, whispering, "It's the box again. It's helping us."

Bridazak wanted to respond, but whether it was fatigue or not, he had no words to challenge his friend's insight. "Let's just find a place to rest," he sighed.

The town was quiet, except for the wagon wheels on the hardened dirt and the clopping of the horses' shoed hooves. Lonely Tear was a hamlet of five hundred humans that had survived on its fishing industry. They could see a bay of water clearly now as the moonlight shimmered off the glassy surface. The town was situated on a hill with a considerable slant heading towards the bay. An occasional human staggered from one of the taverns down the street and the wind created a slight whistle between the structures as it raced up from the water.

"Lady Luck Inn. That's a great place to stay," Bridazak pointed to direct the attention of his friends.

"How do you know that, ya blundering fool? You've never been here before."

"Because it has 'Luck' in its title. That's how I know," he defended himself.

Upset and tired of the day's happenings, the Dwarf's rough voice quaked to life, "Oh, come on. Let's get some rest and just forget about today. I'm tired of all these games and ghost tricks."

Dulgin went off to settle things with the stable caretaker and then they walked into the Lady Luck Inn. The stone building was a two-story structure with a thatched roof and double paned windows. It was very plain outside; a simple sign dangled above the entryway. Inside was much the same; nothing adorned the walls, and a few small tables were set around a fireplace where sparkling embers faded. There stood a small registry station to the left of them, but no one was present. All was quiet, like the town. A dim light from behind the counter in a back room mingled with the darkness of the main lobby. They tried to peek over the human-sized wooden counter to see where the innkeeper might be. They had hoped their entrance had alerted someone, but not a soul stirred from the back room.

"There is no one here, late night travelers," said a creaky, unknown voice from behind them near the fireplace. "Come, sit by the fire while you wait for the innkeeper," the midget voice spoke again.

The fire suddenly erupted, illuminating the lodge enough to see more clearly. In the light, they recognized that the small creature was a Deep Gnome, an underground race with wood-brown skin, pure white hair, gray-blue eyes, and a plump nose, pitted and almost three inches in length. Smaller than the Ordakians, he was only three feet tall. He wore earth-toned clothing, leather boots adorned with strange writings, shiny gold bracers around his arms, and a small, thin, dark brown cape that was slung over his left shoulder. The Deep Gnome glared at them with a cocky confidence.

"Who are you?" Bridazak asked suspiciously.

"My name is Mudd, but you can call me Aloysius Davadander Ashenkoombi, for short."

The Dwarf and Daks looked at each other, bewildered and confused.

"I don't like him," whispered Dulgin.

"And I don't care," the mysterious Gnome grinned, apparently hearing the Dwarf's comment from across the room.

"What do you want?" asked Bridazak.

"I wanted to see with my own eyes the ones that are causing so much grief."

"Grief with whom?" Dulgin questioned as he took a step forward.

"Yes, an interesting question indeed," he sighed, "You have no idea what is happening, do you?"

"No, we don't. But we would appreciate some answers," chimed Bridazak as he moved into the sitting room and sat on the end of one of the benches. His friends followed, but did not sit.

"Things are changing rapidly—things that no one can stop. You, Bridazak, have awakened the destiny of this realm. The prophecy has been unleashed. I have seen much over my thousand years, and have found that men of all races are springs without water and mists driven by a storm. The blackest darkness is reserved for most, but for what they were not told, they will see, and what they have not heard, they will understand." Mudd narrowed his eye slits while staring intently toward Bridazak.

"Since you know who I am, are you the one Ember spoke of?" asked the Ordakian.

"Not even close, but interesting that you should mention her name. She told you of him, didn't she? Now I see that she has granted you protection, for what it is worth," Mudd pointed at the medallion around Bridazak's neck.

"What is it worth?" Spilf's interest piqued at the thought of getting a few more coins in their purses.

"Worthless to those it was not given to, and no help in preventing me from locating you. What matters now is the time of the prophecy. It has called out for centuries, but none have heard, until now. I will give you a word of advice before I depart. Keep moving, because as I found you, so can others. You can stay in my room, if you dare, and the key I leave behind opens more than one door." The mysterious gnome became blurry and slowly transformed into a ghostly image. He produced a soft aura as he rose from the chair and hovered.

"The creatures of this world never cease to amaze me. We will see if you are one of them." Mudd flew up higher and then soared down toward the group. They ducked and watched the apparition as he plummeted into the roaring fire. A burst of flame erupted, and then reduced to its original dying embers. Spilf noticed a glint of gold, and upon inspection, discovered a golden key on the chair where Mudd sat.

Bridazak sighed as he put his hands over his face. *What have I gotten us into?* He reached for the box again, but thought better of exposing it, remembering Mudd's warning. It didn't matter though, as he found that just the thought of it calmed him and returned a warm feeling to his otherwise nervous soul.

Spilf retrieved the key with a room number etched into it. He looked back at his friends, waiting for someone to say what to do next.

"Come on little-ones. Let's rest for a few hours before we leave," Dulgin spoke solemnly. Silent in their walk, they trudged up the stairs to room number four. The sound of the Dwarf's boots echoed on the hardened wood floor, and mingled with the slight stomping sound of the Daks' hairy feet.

They entered a large suite that overlooked the bay and all of its beauty, but it was the three beds in the room that had snared their desires. Their eyes were heavy and their adrenaline had run its course. Perhaps more answers would be revealed tomorrow, but at this point nothing seemed to matter.

Hours passed and the night turned to day. Bridazak was startled awake by the neigh of a horse outside their window on the street below. He sat straight up in his bed to find Dulgin and Spilf already awake and staring out of the opening from the side.

"What is it?" He asked groggily.

"A few humans in dark clothing. They appear to be looking for something, or should I say, someone," Dulgin indicated his friend with a quick look.

"What could they want with us? I don't understand," Bridazak said while throwing his hairy feet to dangle off the bed.

"I've been thinking the same, and have come to the conclusion that it has something to do with that small wooden coffer inside your backpack. You haven't opened it yet," the Dwarf pointed over at his friends' belongings.

Without a word, Bridazak hopped down and slid the tiny chest out of the leather sack.

"To open this gift you will need to bare your heart to the one that has given it to you. Remember, that is what Kiratta said," Spilf echoed her words. "Oh, and I found out what this key opens in the room."

Dulgin and Bridazak looked confused by Spilf's last statement. "Remember, that gnome Mudd, last night? He said this was his room key and it would open more than the room. Ah forget it; I will just show you." Spilf scurried across twenty feet from where he was standing by the window. He placed the key to the wall and magically, an outline of a small door appeared. Spilf looked back at his friends with a smile, "See? We could use it as an escape route if the men in black find us."

"But where does it go?" asked Bridazak.

Spilf pondered the question, "I imagine to the other side."

"Yeah, brilliant. You came up with that all by yourself? When there is magic involved, who knows where that will lead? Maybe another portal," Dulgin spat out.

"I didn't think about that."

"You did good Spilf. Don't mind Dulgin. Hopefully, we won't have to use it," he expressed protectively, and then returned his attention to the mystery of the box in his hands. He realized he felt just as protective of the box as he did Spilf.

Dulgin glanced out the window once again, but this time found the cloaked figures gone. He rushed the opening to get a better view of down below. His head darted back and forth, not locating any of the mysterious tall folk.

"Look alive. We might have company."

The Ordakian grabbed his knapsack and shoved the box back within its domain. He shuffled to his feet and readied himself. Dulgin's axe was out and ready for battle. Then it was quiet as they waited. They stared at the door to their room with the keen sense of danger that approached them. A knock at the door didn't rattle the Dwarf, but the Daks nearly jumped out of their skin. Dulgin calmed his friends with his gruff hand waving downward slowly.

"What do you want?" Dulgin responded to the knock.

"Town guard wants a word with you," sounded the voice beyond.

"Yeah, what about?" Dulgin continued the charade.

"It has to do with the silk goods you brought into town. Open the door."

"Don't know what you're talking about. Now go away, before I introduce you to my axe."

There was no response to Dulgin's threat. The Dwarf looked at Bridazak and motioned him with his eyes to check outside. He moved quietly, and immediately saw one of the assassins, already climbing up the slippery thatched roof toward their window. Another strong impression suddenly entered his mind, *"There are too many. Use the key."* He waved for Spilf to open the secret door. Spilf already had the key in hand, and reignited the outline, prying it open. The knocking to their room became pounding.

"Open this door immediately, by the order of King Manasseh!"

As he approached, Bridazak could hear the sound of a traveling horse and smelled the pungent odor of hay just beyond what he was now sure was indeed another portal.

"You guys go through first. I will close the door behind us," said Spilf.

"I'm gettin tired of all this portal-hopping, not-knowing, riddle-answering, goldless adventure of yours!"

A crash behind startled them as the assassin shattered the window with his crossbow. Spilf quickly started to push his friends toward the dimension door, but he gasped for air as a crossbow bolt slammed into his back and gave him enough momentum to topple the burly Dwarf. Off balance, Dulgin fell through the opening. He was engulfed by the magical effect of the portal and disappeared. His yell faded from the room, and he was gone. Bridazak saw Spilf sprawled out in front of him with a large black bolt buried in his back.

"Spilf!" He cried.

"Bridazak," he coughed. "Quickly, take the key—and take this, my friend." Spilf handed him the golden key, so the intruders could not follow behind them, and a small leather pouch that he had tucked within his sleeve.

"No Spilf. I won't leave you."

The assassin was loading another crossbow bolt at the window ledge when the door to the room exploded open with a fury that sent the locking mechanism and fragments of wooden door frame, scattering in pieces.

"You have no choice Bridazak. I will miss you, my brother. Now go!" He pushed his friend one final time, but Bridazak still held his ground, until a force from behind grabbed and yanked him into the portal. Spilf slid over to close the door; a door that no man would be able to open again.

"Take care of my secret, Bridazak," he said as darkness overtook him and he slumped to the ground, lifeless.

6

A New Ally

Dulgin emerged from the open gateway to find he was engulfed by vibrant yellow, fresh-smelling hay. He was inside a large, hollowed mound on a horse drawn cart. He could hear the clopping hooves and feel the wagon wheels rolling over the uneven terrain. Only a small amount of light trickled into the confined space. He turned around and saw the opening he had fallen through. Faded edges outlined the portal and he saw his friends struggling, and the door busted open to unleash more men. What caught his attention most was the mystic coming into view—the same one that almost killed him had somehow survived Oculus. Dulgin could feel his temper rising, and wanted to finish what Oculus did not. Bridazak didn't notice the robed mage, as his attention was focused on the fallen Spilf. Dulgin was unable to hear any sound from his side, but he understood well enough. He stretched his arms into the opening and felt the portal's resistance. Pushing with all of his Dwarven strength, he broke the barrier and grabbed hold of Bridazak's shoulders, yanking him through. Bridazak was consumed by the magic gateway and landed inside the hollow haven with the Dwarf. They watched Spilf close the gateway and the magical exit blinked away. The faint sound of crackling energy dissipated.

"Let me go back!" Bridazak shrieked. Dulgin planted his gruff hand over his friend's mouth, hoping the driver would not stop to inspect. The Dwarf put up his other hand, motioning him to be quiet; they couldn't be sure if they were out of danger just yet.

He released his cupped hand and then pulled apart the hay pile to make a peep hole. Dulgin dug through enough to see the driver—a young human lad of about fourteen. He wore peasant clothing, soiled by farm work. It was too loud for the boy to hear anything; he determined they could talk openly as long as the cart continued to move. Bridazak made another opening directly opposite, revealing the town of Lonely Tear in the distance as they made their way along a dirt road next to a river. Realizing Spilf was not all that far off, and yet farther than he could now reach, was too much pain for Bridazak. He fell back into the hay mound in shock.

"We are safe to talk now, my friend—but keep your voice low. It appears that we are on a hay cart, bound for a farm I suspect. A young boy is the only driver," Dulgin said.

"Safe? Spilf is gone!"

"I know he is."

"Why? Why, Dulgin?"

The ruddy Dwarf shook his head slowly, not able to answer the question, and fighting his own emotions. He recalled his brother's faith, and the blessing he spoke in honor of those fallen. "Kawnesh di lengo mi diember faustuuk," he whispered.

Shyly, Bridazak peered up, "What does it mean?"

"It is a Dwarven prayer: 'May his light shine brighter in the realm beyond'."

Bridazak broke down; his entire body shook as he wept in a silent despair. The event rolled through his mind over and over again, counting the ways he could have done more to save Spilf. Dulgin sat down beside his friend and put his arm around his shoulder to comfort him. The Dwarf's eyes began to well up, but he quickly replaced his sadness with anger. He envisioned the triumph of standing over the body of the red-robed mystic, his own axe buried in the evil bastard's chest.

An hour passed, and Bridazak had fallen asleep from the exhaustion of his grief. Dulgin stayed alert and waited for an opportunity for them to move out from their hay-covered haven. That opportunity arrived when the boy pulled up the reigns and they came to a complete stop. The burly Dwarf nudged Bridazak awake and held up a finger to his mouth to quiet him before he could ask any questions. They listened as the farm boy hopped down, patted the horses, and then moved away into a thatch-roofed barn. Dulgin watched until he was out of sight and then gave the go ahead to climb out of the burrowed hiding place. Hay tumbled aside everywhere and straw clung to each of them; yellow strands littered their hair and clothing. There was no time to brush it off as they quietly scurried away down to the river's edge. Cowpecks and shepps grazed on the farmland, and fresh air mingled with the scent of animal droppings. The terrain was flat in these parts, except for an occasional rolling hill and some sparse trees where several of the farm creatures gathered to rest in the shade. There was a barn along the road, and a farmhouse not too far away with a smoke plume rising from the chimney. It was brisk in temperature and even colder next to the river. The smell of the fire and the manure dissipated as they hustled away to remain out of sight. Before them lay open country as far as their eyes could see as they ran toward their destination: the famous Everwood.

They finally stopped when Bridazak plopped onto a large boulder. Dulgin knelt down by the river's edge, cupped his hands, and splashed his face. He craned his neck and saw his friend staring into the rushing water, numb.

"So, what is the plan, Bridazak?"

"Plan? I don't have a plan, but apparently someone else does!" Bridazak snipped bitterly, as if he was talking to some invisible entity.

"I know that you are angry, my friend."

"Angry? They killed him. He is dead—and for what?" He pulled out the mysterious container, "For this?" He threw the box into the river with a scream, full of anger.

It splashed into the moving water and submerged like a rock. The deep sound of the impact reached their ears above the rushing flow. Dulgin stared at it and spotted a faint glow under the surface. "What is that?"

Bridazak's reddened face calmed and his focus shifted to follow Dulgin's. The aura intensified and the river began to swirl. The water showed more turbulence as it fought against the unnatural flow. A funnel opened in the center of the thirty-foot expanse and continued to enlarge. The current changed as a sudden wall of the green liquid exploded into the air. Another wall emerged. The fast paced river suddenly stopped, as if it was blocked by an invisible barrier. They looked upon a narrow opening which revealed the riverbed. Smooth rocks of various size laid scattered across the bottom. The box waited in the middle, with radiant beams of light sprouting in all directions. They were mesmerized, mouths agape. Bridazak sighed, and timidly approached. Cautiously, he stepped into the dry riverbed with a wall of water on each side of him. *"What are you doing Bridazak?"* he asked himself, but continued to traverse until there at his feet was the bright container. He slowly knelt down and picked it up. Holding it flat in his palms, he proceeded back to the shore where his friend remained motionless.

"By all the gods of Ruauck-El," Dulgin said in awe.

The water was suddenly released as the walls fell. It collided and crashed to connect once again. Waves splashed on the banks and the original flow returned.

Bridazak felt a strange peace come over him. The storm of emotions inside calmed.

"I'm tired, Dulgin. We need to find a place to rest and get ourselves back on track for whatever lies ahead of us."

"This, whatever it is, is beyond us now."

"I understand, my friend. It is okay if you want to leave."

"Leave? I'm not about to leave. They killed our friend and almost got me. I will see this through alongside of you. They have messed with the wrong Dwarf."

Bridazak nodded gratefully. "What is in this thing?"

"I don't know, but now it has caught my interest. C'mon, let's keep movin.'"

They walked in silence until they found a rocky area with a twenty-foot-high alcove nestled in the granite. It was a perfect location for shelter from the biting wind that swept through, and would give them a chance to get their bearings straight. The precipice of the naturally formed rock had a wide and flat dirt area that the weary travellers discerned others had used in the past. Remains of bones from an animal and a long forgotten fire pit were the markers, but no one had been here in quite some time. Dulgin began to scrape together loose wood in the area, mainly from the river's edge. They would need to have a fire on this chilly night.

The failing light produced a brilliant color spray of oranges and pinks on the sporadic clouds in the distance. Bridazak had watched many such sunsets with his lost friend throughout the years, and it stung deeply as he realized he was watching this painting unfold alone.

"Spilfer, why couldn't you be here to see this?" he whispered.

The red-bearded Dwarf started the fire quickly, and then moved to unravel their bedrolls which were attached to the packs they carried. He tossed some dried rations to Bridazak, who was warming his hairy pads by the fire. Bridazak nodded his thanks but continued to stare deep into the flames. The wind howled around them, but only lightly touched their protected campsite. Lost in the light of the fire, the world he now lived in seemed a lifetime away from all he had known just a few days ago. He counted the previous events, grasping to restore some understanding: his dream, the mysterious creature hiding in the dark, Kiratta, the prophecy, Ember and then Mudd, and now, the ache at the loss of the only person he had ever known as a brother.

"Hey! What about us?" A metallic voice sounded within Bridazak's ears. He quickly scanned around and noticed that Dulgin was at the perimeter of their camp, kneeling down to grab from the pile of wood he had gathered.

"Did you hear something, Dulgin?"

He gave Bridazak a puzzled, squinty-eyed stare. "You okay, my friend? I only hear the wind," he finally responded.

"Stop talking to that ugly Dwarf over there and let us get a good look at you," the same strange voice pronounced. Bridazak looked down and noticed the wrapping tucked in his belt—the one that Spilf had handed him before he was pulled through the magical gate. It suddenly wiggled and startled him. Dulgin noticed his friend's jerky movement, and dropped the wood he had in his hands to reach for his axe.

"What is it?" Dulgin asked.

Bridazak didn't respond, but instead slowly brought the bundle out to inspect. It laid flat in his palm and he slowly unwrapped the supple leather. His eyes widened in amazement as he unveiled the two thieves' tools Spilf had used to disarm traps and pick locks. They were no longer rusty as he had seen them before, but shined bronze. They were two inches long, skinny, and highly magical. The pair of tools each had eyes and a mouth, and were staring back at the Ordakian. Dulgin peered at what his friend had uncovered.

"Hi Bridazak! My name is Lester, and this is my brother Ross," the animated pick introduced himself. Bridazak looked up at Dulgin, smiling incredulously. Dulgin squinted with a blank stare, waiting for something he was supposed to notice, but heard only an uncomfortable silence.

"Can you see them? They are talking to me."

"What are ya talking about, ya blundering fool? Them are just some ugly-looking, rusted tools ya got there. I thought you were in danger or something. Don't be getting the mad fever on me," he muttered in frustration as he moved back to the wood he had dropped.

"Ah, don't worry about him, he is always grumpy," Lester chimed in response to the Dwarf. The other pick spoke, *"We are now at your service. There is no lock or trap that we can't get through,"* it boasted in a demeanor of pride.

The items had distinct voices. Lester spoke with a deeper, metallic tone, while Ross had more of a squeaky, tinny whine.

"So this was his secret. Where did Spilf find you? This is amazing," Bridazak sputtered.

Dulgin looked back over at the Ordakian and shook his head. Worrying his friend had lost his sanity, he went back to tending the fire.

"You can talk to us through your mind Bridazak, so as not to alert anyone around you. That is how we are talking to you right now, and that is why Mr. Grumpy can't hear us."

Bridazak tried it out, *"Can you hear me?"*

"Yes, we can hear you."

Bridazak slid his satchel over next to him and retrieved the strange wooden box. *"Can you find a way inside this?"* he asked in his mind.

"Why, sure we can. Lester's specialty is finding traps and mine is unlocking the best of locks. We can see anything invisible or illusioned. There is nothing in the entire realm that we can't bypass or find," Ross replied.

Bridazak moved the picks back and forth, side to side, under and over. They studied the container until Lester finally responded, *"Except for this. I apologize, but we are unable to locate any opening, lock, or trap. This is not from this realm Bridazak, which means our reputation is still intact."*

Ross added, *"Wow, that was a close call, brother. Good thing it is not from this realm. I can't imagine our reputation being blemished—like that Dwarf. I would lock myself in a room and throw away the key. Wait, that doesn't work. I could still get out. Well anyway, just look at that scar on his face. He scares me, Lester."*

Ross continued talking, but Bridazak tuned out his voice, remembering what Kiratta had told him, *"To open this gift you will need to bare your heart to the one that has given it to you."*

"Bare my heart," he whispered.

"*What did he say?*"

"*Never mind, Ross. Just let our new boss be. He is trying to figure something out, I can tell.*"

"*Oh, okay, yeah, I will let him be. Do you think he will be long, Lester?*"

"*Ross, this is not the time. Now be quiet so he can concentrate.*"

"*Oh, yeah, okay. Good call Lester. We will just be quiet now.*"

Their exchanges didn't phase the Ordakian as he continued to whisper, "bare my heart." He closed his eyes and focused on the words.

"*Hey Lester, why did he close his eyes? Is he going to sleep? What about us?*"

"*Ross! Be quiet! He is not sleeping.*"

"*Oh, okay, good, I just didn't want him to forget about us. Don't be so angry with me, Lester.*"

"*I'm not angry, but if you keep talking I will be.*"

"*Why? What did I do? Don't be mad, Lester. I cannot take another silent treatment from you. Those years stuck in this bag, alone, with you in silence, were torture. I can't handle it again.*"

"*Oh, just be quiet for once, Ross!*"

Bridazak's surroundings began to fade away as he searched deep within himself. His body stilled; there was no sound of a fire, or Lester and Ross, or the howling wind—just peace in this state of apparent solitude. There was a familiarity of his surroundings; it reminded him of the dream that haunted him for centuries. He saw a pinhole of light far off in the distance of his mind's eye. As he focused intently on the source, it began to expand and move toward him. He was soon inside a tunnel with waves of warm energy gently washing over him. He felt the presence of a being so powerful that he could no longer stand, and dropped to his knees. There in the center of the splendor was the silhouette of a person.

"Are you the one who gave me this?" Bridazak asked, and was suddenly holding the ornate wooden box.

"Yes," came the response; the voice, soft, pure, and comforting, yet somehow also terrifying and strong, penetrated his heart like nothing he had ever heard. He recognized this as the same sensation he'd felt while carrying the container, but it was no longer like looking through fog, or hearing underwater. He realized the door separating them was now open.

"I don't understand what I need to do, or why I have been chosen," the Ordakian replied.

Suddenly, Bridazak was standing before a mirror, endless in all directions. Inspecting himself quizzically, the voice returned, "For now you see only a reflection as in a mirror; soon you shall see me face to face. Now you know in part; soon you shall know fully, even as you are fully known. In time I will return and have already. Arise and return to me what was never lost; only waiting."

The mirror liquefied and wrapped itself around Bridazak. An intense heat wracked his body, and he felt like his heart might explode. His eyes opened and he gasped for air. The ground lightly trembled under his feet. He realized he was back at the campsite and looking straight at Dulgin, who stared, mouth open and eyes wide, beyond Bridazak's head. He slowly turned around to see what Dulgin was looking at—it was a two-inch in diameter perfect sphere of gold hovering before him.

"Do not be afraid, Bridazak," it spoke with a deep, authoritative voice. The same strange sensation still enveloped him, though the peaceful realm he had visited seemed to be a distant memory. Dulgin's knees slightly buckled from the Orb's presence, but he stabilized himself.

"Who are you, or what are you?"

"I am Truth," it answered.

"You are the reason for the trouble I am in, and the reason my friend died, aren't you?"

"I am the reason for the trials you are facing."

"Why are you so important to have? Why does everyone want you? I have so many questions."

"I know your burden, Bridazak. I have been hidden from the world for hundreds of years. An ancient prophecy speaks of my release—a part of the prophecy that you have fulfilled."

"I don't understand, so the prophecy is fulfilled? Can we go? What do I do now?"

"You must complete what you have started, and bring me to the temple in Everwood Forest. The road ahead of you will be difficult, but you will not be alone. I have summoned a foreigner from the East to accompany you, and I will protect you from scrying eyes; you will not be found by magic known to any being while in my vicinity. Before you is a great task, with great rewards."

"What is worth more than my friend? I thought this would be different. You came from nothing—out of my dream. I felt that I needed to know what kind of magic could come from dreams, because I needed to find meaning in my life, but my wish for some unknown good to come out of my fearful imagination has only brought loss. How am I supposed to do this without Spilf?" Bridazak backed into a large rock and slid down, burying his head between his legs in sorrow.

"Things are not always what they seem. Spilfer Teehle's destiny is fulfilled. You have a choice: to seek the truth, or continue in uncertainty. What must be, will be done, Bridazak. There is a finish line ahead of you, and you must endure the hardships to complete the race. Your heart has led you this far."

Bridazak sat still as the words from The Orb of Truth weighed heavily in his mind. He slowly peered up, to find that the golden sphere had drawn nearer to him.

"Are you taking me to the one that I am to meet? Is he at the temple?"

"No."

"Who is he?"

"He is the one that was, that is, and that will forever be."

"You are not answering anything, and yet you say you are Truth. Who are you talking about?"

"I will supply you with all you need when the time is right."

Bridazak resigned himself, "Well, will you at least tell me about this foreigner you have summoned? Who is he?"

"His name is Abawken Shellahk and he comes from the province of Zoar. He is a fighter who will aid you in your quest." The Orb moved toward the Dwarf, who stepped backward in surprise. "Dulgin of the Hammergold Clan, you were ordained to protect Bridazak and to continue your travels alongside him, no matter where they will take you. Do you accept this quest?"

The Dwarf regained his composure, "I respectfully decline. I recognize you are of importance, but," he turned toward Bridazak, and continued, "he is not a quest. It has been and will continue to be a privilege and honor to fight for my friends. I will go anywhere and do anything for him."

Bridazak smiled; he could feel Dulgin's words resounding inside his soul. Their long-standing bond had just grown stronger.

There was suddenly no wind and no sound of water rushing in the riverbed. They both heard the faint scuffling of movement on the rocks below their camp.

"I have allowed you to hear Abawken's approach so you can see the truth that I speak. Now wait and greet him. He does not know why he has been summoned; you can inform him when he arrives."

The Orb suddenly disappeared, but the Ordakian felt the weight of the object in his left pocket. Bridazak took a couple steps over to his friend and then whispered into his ear. When he finished, he slinked back into the recesses of the dark. Dulgin sat on a small rock next to the fire with his weapon of choice resting on his lap as he poked at the charred wood with a stick. It was only a minute later when the stranger approached the perimeter of the light given by the fire.

"Take one more step and it will be your last," Dulgin confronted the intruder.

There was no reply for five long seconds, "I am sorry to disturb you, Master Dwarf. I thought I might find some company and share your fire this cold night."

"You thought wrong. Dwarves don't share anything," he responded.

"I apologize once again, and will be on my way."

"What brings you out here all alone, traveller?" Dulgin quickly asked.

The mysterious person entered the campfire light. He stood six feet tall and was lean but well-built. He was wearing tan clothing that had seen better days. Leather armor was showing under his attire, and his boots were wrapped intricately with more cloth and strips of brown hide. A gold, tassled sash draped around his waist and dangled down on his left side. The human hid his face with a tan-colored scarf which revealed only his eyes.

"Nice weapon," Dulgin said.

He had noticed the stranger's scimitar dangling at his side the moment he laid eyes on him. The hilt was masterfully crafted in gold and platinum with jewels inlaid throughout. The blade bore intricate etchings from top to bottom. It was a magnificent piece that rivaled anything Dulgin had seen before.

"I'm alone, stranger. Why don't you sit for a few minutes to gather yourself before you take off?" Dulgin continued, since there was no response from the human.

The foreigner took a step toward the fire and then began to unwrap the linen from his head, revealing chiseled facial features which contrasted against a dark brown beard and untrimmed hair descending to his shoulders. His eyes were the color of the bluest ocean. The Dwarf motioned with his poker stick for the traveller to sit down by the fire.

"My thanks, Master Dwarf."

"So, what are ya doing out in these parts? You are definitely not from around here," Dulgin continued the dialogue.

"I am on a quest, Master Dwarf, that seems to have no end in sight. I have traversed the land beyond measurement and fought to survive on my own in a world that doesn't relent in danger. My apologies for the long reply," the human responded sullenly.

"How long have you been on this quest?"

"I am approaching the twelfth full moon."

"What would be worth heading out into the world all alone for so long?" Dulgin's interest was sincere.

"It is difficult to explain, kind Dwarf. It is something that I wrestle with myself, to be honest. With each day that passes, I question why I should continue. None the less, I will walk all my days if I must, in order to complete the calling that I have received."

"Calling? Who called you?"

"More like a vision."

"Oh, Dwarves get those all the time, after a good night of drinking."

"Well met, Master Dwarf. I thank you for the brief warmth of your fire."

Dulgin's eyebrows both shot up. "I see no harm with you staying the night, Abaw—" he tried to stop himself from saying the human's name, but it was too late.

Abawken instantly stood in alarm, hand on hilt, in a defensive posture. "I never revealed my name to you, Master Dwarf, and yet you know it. Who are you?"

Dulgin stood frazzled, not accustomed to the position he had been placed in; this was Bridazak and Spilf's territory. He fumbled for the words to keep things moving along, but gave up and sat back down to tend to the fire.

"We know who you are, and we mean no harm," Dulgin relinquished.

"I know there is another Dwarf in your camp that hasn't revealed himself yet, as I saw that there are two bedrolls," Abawken laid out the information he had gathered.

There was no movement for weapons, but everyone was cautious and slow to react.

"You have found what you were looking for," Dulgin slowly stated as he continued to poke and spark the embers.

"I am in search of a Halfling, not a Dwarf," he responded quickly and confidently.

"They are known as Ordakians, or 'Daks, in these lands."

Bridazak emerged from the shadows to reveal himself. Abawken's eyes focused on him for a moment, then he quickly dropped to his knees and bowed before the Ordakian. Bridazak looked at Dulgin, smiled, and shrugged his shoulders. The Dwarf went back to his grumpy mood, shaking his head in unbelief.

"Figures this would happen," said Dulgin smugly.

"This might sound strange to you, Master Bridazak, but I have received a vision and a calling to find you. Many times I doubted you even existed. Happily I stand before you now, and solemnly swear to protect and serve you. My life is bonded to yours, a bond that no man can break."

"Well, I don't know about this bonding you are talking about, but believe me, it's not strange at all to hear this, in light of all that's happened to us in the last couple of days. How did you know my name?"

"A voice told me, in my dreams," Abawken replied.

Bridazak pulled the metallic sphere from his lining and revealed it to Abawken. The Orb gently lifted from his hand and floated between the two.

"Abawken Shellahk from the province of Zoar," the voice began, Abawken falling face down in reverence, "you have done well—you heard my call and followed my leading. This was your first test. Rest this night and awaken to a new day, for your travels are far from over," the Orb finished and again disappeared back inside Bridazak's pocket.

"Welcome to the insanity. Let's get you caught up on our situation. You might change your mind and head back home after you hear what we have to say."

They rested next to the dying embers of the fire to keep warm as Bridazak and Dulgin explained what had transpired up to this point. Abawken also told his tales, of how he was lead to this distant and foreign land.

Dulgin asked, "So, what do we need to do with this Orb of Truth, exactly?"

"We need to give it to the Lost Prophet inside the temple within Everwood."

"That's it, then we are done?"

"I guess so. The Orb of Truth will let us know when the time is right."

The night waned and they finally settled in. Their eyes were shut, but their minds were wide open in thought, in question, and in hope.

7

Everwood

Abawken was frequently ahead of them by twenty yards, always scanning their surroundings. Three days of travel had been a bit of an adjustment for Bridazak and Dulgin in learning their new companion's ways. He seemed always busy around camp and never idle, but the journey was otherwise uneventful. They left the flat terrain and entered rolling hills. The fighter reached the top of a larger incline and stopped to survey the region.

"Master Bridazak, Dulgin! Come look!"

"We'll get there when we get there! Stop rushing me, Huey!" Dulgin fired back; a nickname he had given to all humans.

They soon reached the summit to view what their companion had hurried them to see: a breathtaking vista of the great Everwood Forest, about a mile distant. Bridazak's eyes followed the Kullithian River until it reached the enchanted foliage where it was swallowed by a regiment of trees. Birds of this majestic paradise soared over the tree tops and monstrous mountain peaks jutted out of the depth of Everwood. The sea of green stretched beyond his natural vision. The stronghold of the woods was intimidating, and the thought of entering the forest sent shivers through Bridazak's body.

"We're going in there?" asked the Dak.

"We'll set camp here and get a fresh start for the forest in the morning," said Abawken.

"Great! I'll start gathering some wood for a fire tonight."

Abawken gave the Ordakian a look of concern for a moment before responding, "Alright, but a small fire. We are in dangerous territory. There is no telling what kind of creatures we will attract if they spot smoke or smell the embers."

Abawken cleared out a section nestled between some rocks to hide the determined campfire. They tore at their dried rations as a requirement for sustenance to end the long day. Bridazak took the first shift to watch for trespassers while his comrades slept for a bit. It was an hour into the night, he withdrew the Orb, wanting to study it. The warmth returned to his body as he rolled it in his palm. Bridazak spoke softly, "Are you there? You said you would supply what I need when the time is right."

"Yes, Bridazak."

"We have faced so much, but this place we need to enter has only been talked about in rumors and legends. I am not sure I can do this. How will we know where to go?"

"Follow the river, and follow the signs."

"Can you tell me about the Everwood, and what lies within?"

The Orb of Truth pulsed and then rose several inches; it seemed to glow in a way that Bridazak had not yet seen. The power in its voice both calmed him and caused his heart to flutter, as it began to expand his knowledge of the mysterious woodlands.

"Deep, dark, ancient and unfathomable, the vast Everwood Forest dominates the Northern central marches. From its southern edge near Shree to its northern reaches near Everpass and Pike's Plume, it stretches nearly five hundred millari. It is like and yet unlike other woods in the North, remaining virtually untouched by woodsmen's axes.

The Everwood is the wildest of all woods in the North. Trees are bigger here, some approaching gigantic stature, and wildlife is more numerous, also usually of larger size. It is a fairy wood, home to bright creatures like Brownies, Pixies, Sprites and the legendary Unicorn. It also houses dark creatures like the Kechlings, Vesps, Stirges, Night Droppers, and Tree Walkers.

Many have entered the forest confines and few have left unscathed, as this place does not conform to civilized regions of law and order, but beats to its own heart."

The presence of the Orb relaxed him, bringing a sense of peace, more so than he had expected, especially while waiting at the doorstep of the scariest place he had ever heard of. Bridazak's eyes dwindled and he tried to fight exhaustion, but sleep captured his mind.

"I wonder if I'll get to see one of these creatures," he tried to speak, but the words faded like a dream and he wasn't sure if he was talking at all.

The night was calm and soon the sun broke the eastern horizon, shedding its magnificence across the realm.

Dulgin kicked Bridazak awake, "Did you get enough sleep, guard?" he mocked.

"What happened?"

"Good question. Abawken, did this Daky ever wake you for your shift?"

"I'm sorry Dulgin, I don't normally do that. When have I ever fallen asleep on watch? The last thing I remember was feeling nervous about going into Everwood, and asking the Orb to tell me about it. I'm sorry."

"Well, that explains everything. Maybe we should have the Orb keep watch for us next time!"

Abawken stepped in, "Come, we need to keep our wits about us. Nothing happened to us Master Dulgin, so now, let us focus on that," he pointed below their vantage point, to the edge of Everwood. They remained quiet while gathering their few belongings, and mentally preparing for the trek into the vast green sea of trees.

They entered Everwood with caution. The sounds that emanated from within grew increasingly louder the further in they went, resonating like an orchestra without a conductor. Exotic birds, animals, and insects were bountiful. They remained alert as they trudged forward, trying to keep near the river's edge, though it wasn't long before the foliage thickened and made it impossible to stay along the bank. The sound of the river was now their guide in this foreign place, and they treaded uneasily deeper and deeper. Bridazak found himself lost in the beauty of the ancient forest. He gazed up into the dense tree limbs to find a minuscule amount of light being allowed inside this old domain. He wondered if he was the first Ordakian to set foot in any part of the Everwood.

The sounds of the day faded and morphed into something that chilled them to their very bones. Whirring, creaking, rustling, and frightening squeals echoed throughout the area beyond. What little light penetrated the thick overhang slowly waned. A distant rumble of thunder announced a storm, and moments later droplets of water descended upon them. A musty smell encapsulated them as the rain awakened the decaying layers of foliage underfoot.

"What a wonderful place we have discovered. I could have been in a nice tavern enjoying a good Dwarven remedy to warm my body," Dulgin scoffed.

"And miss all the fun? Well, at least your armor is getting washed."

"Listen, Stubby—" Dulgin stopped in his tracks. Bridazak gave him an understanding look. The playful title that for so many years had belonged to their now lost friend, had slipped.

"It's okay, Dulgin."

"No it's not, dammit! I'm sorry, I didn't mean to say that."

"I consider it an honor, my friend." Their eyes locked, rain water cascaded down their faces as they silently remembered Spilf.

Abawken gingerly interrupted, "I found a place up ahead where we can rest, fill our water skins, and get cover from the rain." The two felt more settled, finally having taken a quiet moment to grieve together. "My apologies Master Bridazak, I didn't realize you were in a private moment with Master Dulgin."

"Lead on. We could use the rest."

The human brought them to a large, hollowed tree. It was a massive timber that had toppled over and now rested on the ground. Its days of reaching toward the sky had ended centuries ago; moss and thick vegetation now overtook it. They clamored inside and placed their weary bodies against the moist internal casing. The roaring river fought to be heard through the rain pelting their damp haven.

Dulgin settled in and took his pack off while Abawken climbed through another opening to the top of the fallen tree. Bridazak took the opportunity to refill his water skin. The biting cold of the rushing river caused him to slow as he made his way further in to gather the clean water. He stopped when he was shin-deep; the river bed dropped off to a much deeper level just a step away from where he stood. The water skin swelled to capacity. He capped it off and turned around.

"Hey Dulgin, you want to pass me yours so I can fill it up for you?"

The Dwarf produced his half full leather pouch and caught his friend's at the same time as he tossed his own to Bridazak, who turned to fill it up, hunching over once again, but something caught his eye under the water in the deeper area. He focused, lowering his head to get a better look. A claw suddenly stretched up towards his face and grabbed him. It had greenish skin and sharp, three-inch long fingernails. Another clawed hand reached out from the depths and took hold of his torso. He was yanked into the deep blue water with a splash.

"Abawken!" Dulgin yelled, scrambling up.

The human quickly looked behind him and saw the Ordakian was no longer there. Without thinking, he dove from above into the river. Dulgin readied his axe, but was unable to pursue the creature. He couldn't swim, but didn't have to, as a second leathery, green-skinned beast suddenly burst out of the water and towered over him. The water troll opened its mouth to let out a territorial roar, displaying sharp yellow teeth behind the long, pointed, wart-covered nose.

Dulgin responded, "C'mon ugly! It's gonna take more than bad breath to put me down."

Meanwhile, Bridazak was pulled deeper and deeper toward a cave entrance directly below the surface. His lungs were already beginning to burn, and his ears felt like they were about to explode from the pressure. The monster moved quickly, but just before it passed safely into its lair, Abawken penetrated the surface above them and moved even more swiftly through the water, as if it didn't exist at all. He was unimpeded by the fluid—his scimitar in hand led the charge.

Abawken soared toward Bridazak with lightning speed, thanks to the magical power of his weapon. He could breathe underwater and move through it with no effort. Ordakian blood began to flow from Bridazak's ears. The water troll noticed the human as he glided through the red, inky cloud, and let go of Bridazak to engage him. As soon as he was free, Bridazak reached out toward the surface and began to swim for his life. Abawken grabbed the Dak's tunic and pulled him hard, launching him toward the air above that he so desperately needed. The gangly creature attacked, but Abawken moved so easily that the monster was unable to grab him.

Meanwhile, Dulgin rolled away from a flurry of clawed weaponry. He had sliced the troll with his axe, giving it a deep wound in its left thigh, and puncturing several of the puss-filled cysts that covered his body. He had no time to think about what was happening below the surface, as this beast attacked relentlessly. It turned and began another assault on the Dwarf.

Dulgin instinctively parried with his axe and then countered toward its midsection. It lurched backward, avoiding the killing blow. Dulgin went with the momentum of his axe and turned quickly for another swing. The second one took a chunk from the troll's forearm. Green blood shot out and it yelped a horrible cry of pain.

Below, Abawken battle danced around the troll, and inflicted several wounds with his magical blade. The life essence of the creature quickly began to ooze, engulfing them both in a cloud. Again, it lunged for the human with reckless abandon. Its eyes glowed brighter in rage and it gave a high-pitched scream. Abawken darted aside to avoid its deadly claws, easily dragging his scimitar through the belly of the creature. Guts streamed out like tentacles waving in the water and the red glowing eyes faded. The monster floated away, swallowed up by the current.

The water troll above backhanded the Dwarf, and he sailed through the air like a rag doll into the berm. Dirt and debris crumbled and fell on top of him. The troll was standing over the defenseless Dwarf when Bridazak suddenly emerged behind it and made a loud sound of splashing water and gasped for air. It only took a second for the green beast to be distracted long enough for Dulgin to regain himself and swing his axe from where he was lying. Bone cracked and shattered as the mighty weapon severed its leg just below the knee. It fell to the ground clutching the stump, whimpering a horrible, gurgled sound. The Dwarf buried his father's axe blade into its head, killing it instantly.

"That'll teach ya." He turned from his attack posture just in time to notice his friend swept away by the current, as the Ordakian had no strength left to try to swim to shore.

Abawken shot up out of the water and then ran on top of the flowing river to retrieve Bridazak. He circumvented the granite rocks and then soon lifted the little-one up and into his arms. The human quickly assessed— Bridazak's chattering teeth told him he needed to get him next to a fire to return his color. He ran back, still on top of the fast moving river, to where Dulgin waited in anticipation and awe once he saw Abawken walking on water.

"What magic is this, Human?"

"No time to explain, Master Dwarf. Quickly, gather some wood so we can start a fire."

"Everything's wet, Huey! It won't ignite," Dulgin responded.

"Trust me. I will be able to start the fire."

Dulgin did as instructed. Bridazak was exhausted and barely awake. He had instinctively curled himself into a ball on the ground where he had been set down, trying to gather any warmth he could. Abawken was setting small river rocks around in a circle to contain the heat that would be generated from the fire. Once the Dwarf set the wood inside the stones, Abawken pulled out his scimitar once again and touched its tip to the wet wood, uttering a simple command word, "Esh". It ignited into a brilliant fire as the magic of the blade was unleashed. He moved Bridazak closer to the flames and the rocks; the chills soon retreated and the rosy coloring returned to his cheeks. Bridazak heard little beyond the crackling snaps of the blaze next to him as he tried to rest. His fragmented thoughts dominated, *"I almost died today. If I did, would I be with Spilf? The Orb sent Abawken, and if he wasn't here on this very day then I would surely be dead. I will have to thank the Orb. I will have to thank Abawken. I will have to thank Dulgin, or he will get upset for being left out of the thank-yous. Maybe I should apologize after the thank-yous for dragging them into all of this. I don't know. I'm just so tired."* He drifted off and fell asleep.

"Damn trolls," Dulgin said under his breath. He addressed the human, who was staring into the fire, "You mind explaining what happened out there?"

"The water trolls have a home below the surface, and they grabbed our leader to have a snack later."

"I'm not talking about that, ya blundering fool. How does someone walk on water and then start fires from thin air is what I'm after!"

"Oh, my apologies, Master Dwarf. This is called The Sword of the Elements." He drew his blade and held it out for inspection, "It has been imbued with magical properties that revolve around fire, water, earth, and air."

"And where does one find a blade such as that, might I ask?"

"Well, it was a gift."

"Mighty fine gift. What did you have to do to get it?"

"Another time perhaps, Master Dwarf. It is a grand story and one I would like to tell, but let us be vigilant while we watch for our fearless leader here to come back to reality."

"Ahhh, whatever Huey," Dulgin relinquished the conversation and then dug inside his pack for some food.

"Why do you call me this name, Master Dulgin? I don't understand," the human questioned.

"That's right, you wouldn't understand so I ain't bothering."

Abawken smiled and then returned his attention back to Bridazak. "His life is strong. It is still unbelievable that I found him. I had searched for so long, for what I'd thought was a ghost."

Dulgin poked a stick at the fire, "The Orb led you."

"This is true, but there was a faith inside of me that drove me on each day."

"I have faith in my axe."

"As do I now, Master Dulgin. You are indeed skilled, but faith is the confidence that what we hope for will actually happen; it gives us assurance about things we cannot see."

"Speaking riddles to a Dwarf is not wise, but I get where you're going with it."

Abawken smiled again, "Excuse me, Master Dulgin, I will gather more wood and fresh water for Master Bridazak."

The human lightly shook the Ordakian awake. He instantly sat up, startled and shouting. Bridazak's eyes darted about, until he realized he had been dreaming. He was inside the fallen tree and the fire was now embers. The rain had ended, and rays of light broke through the upper canopy high above. Smells of wet leaves mingled with the musty mildew and the camp-fire inside their hollowed home. "How long was I out?"

"Several hours. How are you feeling?"

"I'm fine. Let's get moving." He tried to get up on his own, but his legs wobbled. Abawken assisted him to his feet.

"Here, eat some of this, and make sure you get your fill of water."

"I'm fine. I can eat along the way. Where is Dulgin?"

"He's outside waiting, let's say, eager to get started—to put it nicely."

"You will get used to it. C'mon, the longer he waits the grumpier he gets." Bridazak grabbed his pack and climbed out the opening. Abawken followed.

"Finally! I was starting to grow leaves hanging around here. Let's find this temple and get out."

"Glad you asked, my friend, I'm feeling better."

Dulgin broadened his shoulders in true Dwarf fashion, and responded, "Good, cause I was going to leave your Daky-ass behind. Well, Abawken, you waiting for someone to hold your hand or are you going to lead?"

"My apologies, Master Dulgin." The human quickly took the reigns and scouted ahead as always. They followed in tow, continuing their trek along the river.

Hours passed as they navigated the brush and woodland debris. Dulgin complained most of the time as the humidity increased and pesky skets were swatted with occasional slaps on arms and necks.

Bridazak heard it first—a new sound—a strange guttural clucking in the distance. "Do you hear that?"

"What now, ya blundering fool? I don't hear nothin'."

"It is coming from that way," Abawken pointed a slight direction off from where they needed to go. "It sounds birdlike."

"Mmmm, bird. That sounds good right about now. I could use a hot meal," Dulgin rubbed his armored belly.

"Let's check it out, then," Bridazak said, feeling the hunger pangs also.

As they made their way through the thick green overgrowth, they heard the clucking turn into a clicking bravado which transformed slowly into a melodic whistle of soft tones. A wall of shrubs separated them from the mysterious prize that they tracked. Abawken pushed through slowly. The rustling of the branches caused the creature to cease its chime as the human broke free of the grasping leafy twigs. They emerged into an umbrella of the largest tree they had ever seen. It was impossible to see the top as the tree-sized trunks extended from the thirty-foot gargantuan base in all directions. They were completely shaded from any light, and fallen leaves were firmly matted down from something walking over them. The deep, earthy aroma of the environment mixed with the smell of a hen-house filled their nostrils. There was no sign of their prey as they entered its domain.

"Here birdy, birdy, birdy," Dulgin whispered.

"I will look for a nest. Perhaps we can gather some eggs," Abawken suggested.

"I don't eat anything that comes out of a creature's butt," the Dwarf scoffed. "I'll be getting the birdy while you forage for ass-droppings."

They spread out. Bridazak spotted something at the base of the immense tree. He cautiously approached the odd, twig-like piece nestled amongst the leaves. He reached down and unearthed it from the colorful leafed layers and quickly realized it was a feather—a bright yellow plume covered in beige spots. A worried expression of realization hit him, "It's a Varouche! We need to get out of here!"

"A what?" Dulgin questioned.

Suddenly, materializing behind the Dwarf was the legendary avian creature. Its chameleon power relinquished as it fanned out its glorious extended feathers behind its body.

"Dulgin, look out!"

The Dwarf turned to the see the eight-foot-tall beast. It's long neck was a metallic, blue and green hue. Smaller decorative purple strands of frizzy fur topped its crown. The eyes were a prismatic display of beauty and the bone-white beak snapped a couple times in preparation of its meal.

"Nice birdy," Dulgin backed away slowly.

The Varouche spun instantly and its colorful fan of feathers with whirling colors of the rainbow became a sharp blade-like weapon. Dulgin was slashed across his chest, straight through his armor. He winced from the pain of the deep gash, kneeling on the ground.

Bridazak pulled out an arrow and notched it quickly. He let it loose, but the Varouche brought up its plumed fan, blocking the arrow like a shield. The long-necked legend turned toward him and stomped with its clawed talons. It let out an ear-splitting cackle that caused Bridazak to drop his weapon and cover his ears.

Abawken curled around the base of the tree and slid to a stop, surveying the situation. He pointed his scimitar at the Varouche, uttering the simple command word, "Avir!" A funnel of air ten feet tall instantly shot forth and swallowed up the beast. Debris and leaves were gobbled up, spinning out of control inside the twister. A scream from the distressed bird bellowed from within. Abawken backed away to allow his magical entity to rip it to shreds. Electrical discharges sporadically sizzled around the whirling cyclone. The squawk of the Varouche finally dissipated, and the fighter waved his sword, dismissing the summoned elemental. The large bird fell to the ground and feathers shot out in all directions. Shredded patches of skin with strands of tuft was all that remained on its body. A silver colored tongue hung out of its beak.

Bridazak rushed to help Dulgin up. He was bleeding profusely and grimaced with clenched teeth as he stood.

"I worked up an appetite. I can smell it already," Dulgin sputtered. "Abawken, start a fire with that fancy sword of yours."

He gathered the wood while Bridazak helped his friend out of his armor to get a better look at his wound. A purplish, powdery substance stained the Dwarf's skin around the cut. The Dak used some of their water supply to clean the area and shredded an extra tunic, wrapping it around Dulgin's barrelled, red-furred chest. In the meantime, Abawken prepared their meal and soon the sweet smell of roasted Varouche captured their hearts.

"Too bad we don't have any Dwarven Ale to go along with this."

Bridazak picked at his food and stared at the pile of mixed feathers. He stood and walked over to grab one of them. "I'm keeping this, in honor of Spilf."

"Me too," Dulgin said. "Bring me one of them, would ya?"

"Make that two, Master Bridazak." Abawken surprised them. Bridazak smiled in recognition of their new companion's respect for their fallen friend he never met.

He held his feather up, as a toast, and his two comrades joined him, "We wish you were here with us Spilf, but we know you will always be here in spirit. We honor you my friend, my brother, and we will never forget you."

"Well said, Master Bridazak. I look forward to getting to know him through you both. A part of him resides in each of you; as you have shared life together, he helped shape who you have become."

"You are some talker, Huey, but I like it. Your words touched me." Dulgin grimaced in pain again, and looked at Bridazak, "I recognize poison. That critter gave me something to remember."

"We need to find a way to get him healed. Maybe the temple has someone there," the Ordakian suggested.

"Come, no time to waste. Let us get back on track."

Many hours of traveling had passed and the sun was quickly moving down to the west. The already dark environment was losing the little light that was allowed within its confines for the day. Abawken spotted a clearing up ahead, and hurried them to follow. They came to the opening along the river's edge; it was circular in design with a strange, grassy field nestled inside the immense forest—an oddity that they might never be able to explain. The green blades of grass came to Bridazak's chest as it swayed gently in the cool breeze that brushed over the top. There was a mysterious and strange glow to the meadow before them, but it didn't stop them from entering into the confines. As they began to wade deeper into the sedge, the magical effects of the field made itself known to them. Small bits of dust floated into the air with each step they took.

"I feel strange," Bridazak softly muttered.

"I feel good," Dulgin responded with a drowsy smirk.

"Something is wrong." Abawken's speech slowed. He fell to one knee and then collapsed face first, pushing the grass blades down from his weight.

"Look, Abawken is sleepy," Dulgin chimed slowly.

"Sleep is a good idea," Bridazak said as he, too, collapsed.

"You guys are lightweights. That is why I can out-drink any of you blundering fools," he slurred as he fell to the powerful enchantment.

It was as if time had slowed. Their muscles relaxed and their eyelids lowered. The deep of sleep consumed them and all was quiet except the thumping of their heartbeats. Bridazak had never really imagined the end of his life, but there was always the assumption that it would come with another quest in pursuit of some trinket or treasure. But in the end, it was instead just a beautiful, enticing sward within the great Everwood Forest. He relaxed, and realized he didn't care about dying this way, or dying at all. It was actually quite nice. He fell further into the depths of his end.

Bridazak felt a sharp sting in his side. The pain hit him again and his eyes opened wide. He felt instantly transported back to reality; back into the grassy blades where he thought he had died. His blurry vision refocused to see, looming above him, a magnificent, pure white steed with a large spiraled horn protruding from its forehead. The legendary Unicorn, flawless, not a speck of dirt on its gleaming body, made him wonder whether he wasn't still dreaming after all. Bridazak slowly stood, not taking his eyes off of the mythical creature, until something flew by his face and distracted him from his stare. The new visitor was not much bigger than the length of Bridazak's arm, and was difficult to see. Several of these beings fluttered about the area as they flew in a protective pattern around the Unicorn.

Abawken sat up yelling, "Fairy dust!," as he came to his senses. He peeked over the blades of grass that rustled from his movement. He grabbed his head to try to stop his mind from spinning and then he let out a groan of discomfort. Dulgin also stirred awake.

One of the small critters squeaked in the common language, "You will follow and not stray."

"Who are you?" Bridazak asked.

"We are your guides, and you will follow Chaadra."

The fascinating steed hurled its front hooves high into the air and then came down with a thud. It turned and began to walk toward the forest, then stopped and looked back at them with its beautiful almond eyes.

"Go. Chaadra will not wait," the small creature indicated with his hands to follow once again.

The others had stood up and regained their composure. Dulgin noticed his wound was completely gone, healed magically.

"Where is Chaadra taking us?" asked the Ordakian.

"You will find out soon enough." The fairy-like being mischievously giggled.

"I hate Pixies!" Dulgin blurted openly.

More laughter erupted around them and then they purposely zoomed pass the Dwarf's ears. Dulgin swatted the air in frustration.

Bridazak saw the other fairies fluttering about, but their bodies appeared clear as glass. The steed had also passed from sight and he quickly spotted the fabled legend across the grassy field at the base of the dense forest. It seemed to be waiting for them to follow and bobbed its head up and down.

"Maybe it will let us touch it. Come on, let's go!" Bridazak chimed with enthusiasm and headed off, not wasting any more time.

"I'm not interested in the creature, but in where it is taking us," said the human under his breath as he also complied, following behind the Ordakian, with Dulgin bringing up the rear.

"I can't take much more of this, ya blundering fools!"

8

The Door of the Divine

After several hours of traveling they came upon a crumbling structure. The unicorn, Chaadra, never let them get too close, but just enough to not lose them within the sylva. It stood at the foot of the rubble and lowered its head, bowing before something unseen. The breathtaking steed began to blur; the heroes squinted as they watched the distorted form blend into the surroundings.

In front of the adventurers laid a large pile of fragmented rock. The ancient dwelling was overtaken with vines that intertwined through the stone scattered about the area. Bushes had grown in pockets and several small creatures had taken residency over the many years since the edifice fell. They walked the perimeter and saw nothing of interest. Bridazak took it upon himself to climb and maneuver to reach the precipice.

"Get up here! You need to see this."

Soon they were all gazing upon the skeletal remains of a small humanoid, roughly four feet tall. It was clothed except for its bare, boney feet.

"It was probably an Ordakian," surmised Abawken.

"How do you know that?"

"Well, for one thing, it has no boots, just like you, and the other is that it's very small in height, just like you. My guess is it was some kind of Halfling."

"So I'm not the only one of my kind to set foot in the Everwood after all."

Abawken studied the scene, "I think we will need to head in the direction of where his boney finger is pointing."

Indeed, this fallen Dak was indicating a direction that led further into the forest; probably its final message before dying, but a message for whom to receive? Surely not them. Bridazak stood and prepared to make his way back down.

Abawken stopped him, "Where I come from, the living show their respect for their race by burying them where they lay. It is said that the dead will then bless you with favor. We call it 'mouton'."

Bridazak was pondering the foreigner's suggestion when Dulgin spoke, "I agree with you, Huey. Dwarves have similar burial procedures."

"I'm not sure of the Ordakian's ways of death, but any favor we can get is great with me. Help me cover him up." Bridazak grabbed a broken rock and stopped when the others did not move to assist him. "What's wrong?"

"Master Bridazak, it is your duty as his kin to cover him."

"But," Dulgin added, "we can hand you pieces to help you out."

Bridazak grinned as his friends helped him, handing him one fragment at a time. He felt something inside of him that he had never felt before—a sense of honor.

He carefully laid each piece of stone, slowly covering the remains. Some of the bones crumbled from age, and the tattered clothing fell away like fine powder. After the body was completely covered, Bridazak spotted a message etched into one of the pieces of rubble next to the forgotten kinsman. It was written in the Ordakian language, again confirming Abawken's suspicion.

He read it aloud, translating it to the common tongue, "Loyal Follower Billwick Softfoot," as he placed it near the head of the newly formed grave. He stopped and peered up at his companions, who seemed to be waiting for more, "That's all it says."

"A follower of whom, is the question."

"Maybe he worshipped whomever this temple was built for," Dulgin surmised.

"Good point," said Abawken.

They each made a final bow to the loyal follower, Billwick Softfoot, as they turned to move out, but Bridazak stopped as he spotted an ornately carved wood piece protruding from the rocks close to where the deceased Ordakian lay. He veered away after tugging at Abawken's shirt to let him know of his detour. After removing several stones, a short bow was birthed. Once again, there was Ordakian writing carved all over it.

"What does it say?"

"Let's see." Bridazak began to inspect it, "It says, 'When you notch, I will be ready. When you pull with desire, I will be the The Seeker.' This bow is incredible. Would any of you like my old short bow?" Bridazak asked innocently.

"My axe is good enough," Dulgin scoffed.

"You are truly favored, Master Bridazak. Now, let's get moving. It should be getting dark within a couple of hours."

Bridazak tossed his old bow away and then strung his new find, testing the pull strength on it. When he stretched the string back without an arrow notched, his eyes focused on something else in the distance. Abawken noticed the Ordakian's eyes change in focus.

"What is it now?" he whispered.

"Something sparkled off the sun's light over there, but now I can't see anything."

"What sun, ya blundering fool?"

The fighter admired Bridazak's keen senses, and a deeper appreciation of his Master's bestowed giftings began to shift his duty-bound motives. Normally, he would insist they press on, but he surprised himself and said, "Let us investigate, shall we?"

As they moved toward the general area, the shaft of a gold-painted flight arrow emerged into sight. Bridazak removed a rock piece that pinned it down, unveiling yet a bigger gift—an entire quiver of arrows. Eleven were nestled beneath the twelfth he had originally spotted. He slung the case over his shoulder after pulling it out of its confines.

"Okay, I'm ready. Let's go."

"Anything else, Master Bridazak?" Abawken asked, amused, gesturing to their view of the entire rocky area.

"Nope, that should do it."

"Just leave it to the Daks; they seem to sniff out treasure like a vampire does blood."

They headed off with no more detours or distractions and discovered another part of the temple complex that still stood intact. The same vine network that had established itself amongst the rubble also covered this structure. A wall of the woven green growth now stood between the heroes and the building. Two faded ivory pillars stood on either side of an immense stone door, rivalling the size of a mountain giant. They approached the ancient entryway and began to remove the vegetation.

Bridazak found something strange about the stone doorway. He noticed hundreds of miniscule holes, from top to bottom, which left a grey powdery residue covering his fingertips when he touched them to inspect more closely. He also spotted several inscriptions, and realized they were magical in nature, and most likely strong glyphs of protection.

"Look here, Abawken."

"What is it?" he asked.

"This is a magical trap, set for any who might open this door. I am not sure exactly what it will do, but I am guessing it has something to do with those tiny holes. Basically, if we open it, something bad will happen."

"Can you disarm it?"

"Maybe." Bridazak pulled out the magical thieves tools. In his mind he said to them, *"Okay, now it's your turn. We need to get inside, and this entrance appears to be trapped."*

"Let's take a look. I am so excited to help our new master. Ross, can you see if there is anything hidden?" Lester's metallic voice sounded.

"Sure thing, Lester. Now you are going to see some real skill. Master, can you show me the door and let me inspect it? Move us in closer."

Bridazak moved methodically with Lester and Ross in hand. The animated objects mumbled several words as they instructed their master to move them.

"Yes."

"Oh, wow."

"Interesting."

"Mmmm."

"Okay, we got it." Lester announced.

"You disarmed it?"

"No, we understand how to open the door," Lester responded.

"We sure do, Lester."

"So, how do we open it?"

"Um, we cannot open it."

"Yep, you are right about that, Lester."

"*What do you mean you can't open it? You said you can unlock any door and disarm any trap.*"

"*I am happy to tell you that this is not a trap and the door is not locked, and thus our reputation is still intact.*"

"*Good call, Lester. Yep, reputation is still there.*"

"*I don't care about your reputation right now. How do we open the door?*"

"*Lester, he doesn't care about our reputation!*" Ross whined.

"*Calm down Ross. I will explain it to him.*"

"*Yeah, okay, explain it.*"

"*What is it?*" Bridazak charged through his mind link.

"*This is a door of the divine. It has no lock and there are no traps.*"

"*And?*"

"*It will require a sacrifice to open it—the shedding of innocent blood. The magical writing embedded into the door itself gives the instructions. There are two sections, one on each side. You attach a rope or chain to the rings in each section and pull the door open from a distance. Whatever is standing in front of the door will be sacrificed. If it is worthy, the door will remain open for several minutes, before closing again.*"

Stunned, Bridazak placed Lester and Ross back inside his belt pouch. He could hear Ross complaining to Lester while he put them away. Abawken saw the change in his demeanor.

"What did you find, Master Bridazak?"

He didn't respond until Dulgin smacked his shoulder to knock him back to reality, "He asked you a question."

"It's a divine doorway, and it requires a sacrifice to gain entrance."

"What?" the Dwarf asked. Bridazak explained in detail what was revealed to him.

Abawken thought for a moment before responding, "I see. Then we have a dilemma here."

"What are we going to do, boys? I didn't go through all this just to be stopped by some door." Dulgin's gruff voice broke the lingering silence.

"I don't know, Master Dulgin. Perhaps there is another way inside that we haven't found yet."

"Well, let's get a searchin' then." He investigated a walled section covered in vines.

Bridazak hesitated, and then reached into his pocket and pulled out the Orb. The perfect golden sphere was warm to the touch and once again brought him the strange peace he had felt before. If ever there was a time they needed the promised provisions, it was now. "We need your help." It rose from his palm. "How do we get inside the Temple?"

"A door of the divine requires a sacrifice, the shedding of innocent blood."

Dulgin stopped ripping the strands and stood beside his comrades.

"But we have nothing to sacrifice. There must be another way," Bridazak continued, scanning the building for something they might have missed.

"The Temple is impervious to magic, and to any method known to man. There is no other way."

"Why would you take us to this place knowing we don't have anything to open this with? Why didn't you warn us?"

There was silence and then Abawken rested his hand on Bridazak's shoulder, "I was warned."

"What are you talking about?"

"The same voice in my dreams, which called me to you, told me of a time that would require a great sacrifice. This is that time."

"What? We have to find another way. This is not right."

"Are you saying you want us to sacrifice you to get inside this temple, ya blundering fool? I don't think I will ever understand you humans. This is ridiculous," Dulgin scoffed.

"I believe in this quest, and I believe in you, Bridazak. A great shift in this world—to restore what it was meant to be—is upon us. My sacrifice is for that change. It is my choice and my wish."

"It's not my choice, nor my wish," Bridazak protested. "Abawken, we need to find another way."

The human fighter withdrew a two-inch tall statue of what was known as a lizard man.

"What is that?"

"This is a magical figurine." Abawken spoke a word in his native tongue of Zoarian, tossing the figure to the ground. Within seconds it grew into a five-foot-tall lizard man, holding a long sword and shield. It was combat-ready, and very alive. It spoke with a slithering lisp, "Your wissssshhhh massssssterrr?" It waited for Abawken's response.

"Hello, friend. I ask that you protect me."

"Azzzz you wisssshhh massssterrr. Froommm whhooom?"

He looked at Bridazak, "Honor me in this realm, and know that I will be holding the doors of the afterlife to greet you when you arrive." He turned back to address the lizardman, "Protect me from the Dwarf and Ordakian."

"What!?" they both resounded in unison. The scaly opponent suddenly brought its shield up to bear, and its longsword rose in a posture of offense. Bridazak and Dulgin backed away. Abawken turned, exhaling a deep breath, and approached the door.

"No! Don't do it!"

Time elapsed rapidly and all breathing was held in check, as they could do no more than helplessly watch Abawken's choice play out before them. Knowing he could not get to the brazen human in time to stop him, Dulgin whispered a Dwarven blessing, "Diegg mu domosh."

The booming voice of the Orb spoke, "Do not open the door, Abawken. You have passed the test given to you."

The sound of an animal's gurgled baying behind them forced their attention away. There, caught in a thicket of vines, was a horned ramshod. It's spiraled keratin was worthy of a trophy. It squawked again.

Bridazak quickly turned toward Abawken, only to find the human already standing behind him, in awe of the provision. Each of them let out a sigh of relief. Dulgin extended his arm toward Abawken in congratulations, but retracted hastily when the lizardman swung its steel blade in his direction. The human quickly spoke, "Shirezz!" and it diminished back to its figurine form. He picked it up, whispering, "Thank you, my friend," and placed it back into his belt pouch. He then embraced Dulgin and Bridazak.

They followed the instructions, laced rope through the loop holes and then took positions behind the barriers. The Ramshod was wrapped in the vines and placed at the foot of the doorway. As they pulled, hundreds of the tiny openings glowed red, and then shot out an intensified blast of energy. The sacrificial creature was engulfed by the intense heat of the magic released. It disintegrated instantly. They quickly ducked, avoiding the sweltering wave as it passed over the stone wall in front of them. The energy finally settled and the adventurers approached with trepidation. Now open, a passage led deeper inside the strange temple. Abawken turned and knelt down on one knee. The Ordakian watched him as he gave a silent moment of thanks.

"Are you okay?"

"Yes. I am prepared for whatever lies ahead. Ready your weapons, Master Dak, for I sense combat approaches," he unsheathed his curved blade.

9

The Fallen Temple

Their senses were heightened in the breadth of the moment when all natural light was severed and countless years worth of dank, stale air met them as they entered the temple. Torches magically sprang to life along the walls to the left and right of them. The entry room was completely bare. On the other side, a wide corridor continued into more blackness, as did the vaulted ceiling, which stretched far above them. Faded murals decorated the walls, severely damaged by the years of neglect. A fine dust had settled on the floor and revealed no tracks; no one had set foot in here for countless years. Bridazak marveled at the workmanship and began to lightly touch the ancient paintings that time had forgotten. Abawken continued to scan the room for any threats.

"Stay alert," he said.

"Nothing gets by these Dwarven eyes, Huey. Me and my axe are ready."

Bridazak seemed lost in the cracked and faded pigments, trying to find something of importance. A shivering sensation caused him to snap out of it.

"It feels strangely cold in here all of a sudden," he announced, clenching his hands around his arms. He looked up to where Abawken's attention was focused and saw through the pitch-darkness two sets of yellow, glowing eyes; a stare that was familiar to him. He had seen eyes like these in Gathford, outside their cottage. There was a hiss of hatred as two shadow creatures descended upon them. A cold feeling of death emanated from the dark, wispy assailants.

"REEGS!" Dulgin shouted.

Abawken shoved the Ordakian out of the way of the first attack wave. They were attracted to life itself, trying desperately to consume it, to destroy it. The fighter made several swipes at one of the fiends, and hit it solidly. There was a shriek as the magic of his blade pulsed with the impact. The creature cringed backward, but immediately retaliated with greater speed. The Reeg penetrated Abawken's defense—the single touch of the cold-bearing effects lingered; his knees weakened as he felt his strength diminishing.

Humanoid in shape only, these beings were made from the lifeless void of darkness itself. They darted and flew through the air like spirits called to the opposite of their essence; a shadow whose only purpose was to devour the light of life.

Bridazak dodged the evil touch, but then took a miscalculated glance toward his friends and the creature of the dark struck him square in the chest. He felt no pain, though he should have. His body clenched in anticipation, but there was no ill effect. The dark shadow stood stationary for a moment, confused. Before he could try again, a bright flash came from within Bridazak himself. Like lightning, it blasted the creature. A huge thunderclap erupted within the temple room from the awesome magic released.

Abawken and Dulgin were propelled into the wall from the force of the blast. They witnessed the brief magnificent light eat away at the shadow, dissipating it before their eyes. The incorporeal shade's horrific screech faded away. Bridazak leaned against the wall in shock.

"Are you alright, Master?" Abawken asked.

"I—I think so. What happened?"

"I was hoping you could shed some light on that question."

"I don't see the other Reeg. It must have fled after that blast," Dulgin chimed, surveying the room.

"These were summoned creatures from the darkness of abyss itself," the fighter stated, peering back up into the area they came from.

"Damn things came out from that cursed chasm, Kerrith Ravine," Dulgin said in disgust.

They dusted themselves off and began to head deeper into the mysterious, alluring temple. The wide corridor continued, and with every step a magical torch ignited on either side of them. At each burst of light they could see a little further down, until they reached a bronze door littered with ancient engravings in a language long forgotten. They approached it cautiously, and when Bridazak was within arm's reach, the door slowly opened. It swung wide without a creak, to reveal a candlelit sanctuary. Hundreds of small flames outlined the large chamber on different levels of stone shelving. Directly opposite them were steps leading up to a platform, bearing an altar made of marble. A figure, facing away, wearing the purest white hooded robes they had ever seen, knelt near it. It appeared to be of small stature like Bridazak, or perhaps a human child.

"Hello," Bridazak broke the silence, his voice echoing through the room.

The being rose and turned to face them, at the same time pulling the hood away to reveal itself. A male Ordakian greeted them with a brilliant smile that shined from his purple-hued eyes. He was completely bald, with gold earrings laced from the bottom of his lobes to the top. His skin appeared to be soft, without blemish, and slightly glowing. A white ivory staff with a hooked end rested nearby. He had no other belongings.

"We were told to come here," Bridazak continued.

"Yes, yes, the time has come," he responded, excitedly making his way toward them.

"Time for what?"

"I will need a strand of hair from each of you in order for you to enter the portal once it is opened," he calmly stated.

They stared at him with questioning looks. "Specifically, one from your foot Bridazak, one from your beard Dulgin, and one from Abawken's head."

"I don't think so, little-one! How did you know our names?" Dulgin leaned in to the Dak's face to intimidate him.

"I know lots of things." His purple eyes bore into Dulgin. There was an unshakable confidence that the Dwarf had never seen before.

Bridazak could feel a strange connection to the mysterious Dak. There was a peace about him that reminded him of the Orb. Questions started formulating in his mind. *Who is this person? Why is he here? How old is he?*

Bridazak tried to calm his Dwarven friend and reached his hand to his broad armored shoulder, "It will be okay."

He broke from the stare, "I'm tired of going through open portals without knowing—" Suddenly Dulgin flinched backward.

"That will do fine, Dulgin. Thank you," the odd Ordakian said, revealing a red piece of hair pulled from his beard.

"That hurt! How 'bout I punch you in the face, and we call it even."

Abawken stepped up, pulling out one long strand of hair. Bridazak plucked one from the top of his foot and then handed it over. Dulgin stormed off a few feet away, mumbling under his breath.

"We have done what you asked, and I think it is now time for you to give us some answers. To begin with, who are you?" Abawken asked.

"I am Billwick Softfoot, the protector of this temple."

Bridazak and Abawken shot a glance at one another. They spotted Dulgin, his head tilted slightly sideways, a preposterous look on his face.

"Yeah, well tell that to the dead guy outside this temple of yours. You are an imposter. Bridazak, we shouldn't trust this thing, whatever it is."

"Oh, that was me alright, but I am more alive now than ever before."

"What do you mean?" Bridazak motioned to his Dwarven friend to keep quiet, though he knew Dulgin and Abawken stood attentive and ready for action.

"I was sent back here to ensure your next step, as per the prophecy spoken over the realms."

"Next step?" Bridazak coughed in surprise.

Abawken interjected, "Spoken by whom?"

"He has many names. He is the King of all Kings and the Lord of all Lords. It is the appointed time of the prophecy. There is an awakening inside of all mankind and the dawn of truth approaches."

Dulgin stepped forward, "Well, if you are the protector, then you're not doing such a good job."

"You might see it that way, but I will reveal my strength through weakness."

Billwick's response brought Kiratta's words to both of their minds. Abawken caught their peculiar exchange of glances, "What is it?"

"Kiratta, the one we told you about, said we would know the Prophet when he spoke those words."

"So, that must have been you who blasted that light into those Reegs that attacked us in the corridor," said Dulgin.

Billwick suddenly displayed a concerned demeanor, "Reegs? Then we don't have much time."

"What do you mean we don't have much time? Why?"

"They have discovered where you are, and they will be coming."

"How is that possible? No one should be able to find us."

"Yes, you are correct, but the Reegs have reported back to their Master."

"They report to King Manasseh?" Dulgin questioned.

"No, someone much more sinister and evil than him, or any of the known realms. It rules Kerrith Ravine and has orchestrated the tyranny sweeping across the land. They *will* be coming. We need to begin."

"Great, another portal, I can't wait. Where are we going, anyway?" Dulgin huffed.

"Come in. Come in. No more questions." He waved them to enter and the door behind slowly closed.

Several minutes passed and the group settled in as the mysterious Ordakian began to gather items; everything from an unlit candle to a chip of white marble was placed by the altar.

"Might I have a word with the keeper of the Orb?" Billwick peered at Bridazak, continuing to arrange the objects. "You have questions, there is no doubt."

"The Orb told us to come here, but I thought we were bringing it to you."

He laughed, "Dear child no, not me. You were called, Bridazak, to bring the truth within the Orb back to its people."

"But why? What is it?"

A smile of joy washed over Billwick's face, "Imagine you learned the location of a great treasure but you did not own the land. Would you sell all you have to buy it?"

"Of course."

"Then sacrifice all you have Bridazak, and press on toward the prize." Billwick reached into the right sleeve of his robe and pulled forth an ancient parchment, edges frayed and tattered.

"What is that?"

"This is the Scroll of Remembrance, and it was written just for you."

"For me? How is that possible?"

"The One that was, that is, and that will always be, knew of you before you were even born, and knew you would be here at this time, in this place, for this reason."

"What does it say?"

"That is for you to find out." Billwick handed him the scroll. Bridazak timidly took hold of it and then unfurled the thick paper. He looked at the blank page and before he could say anything, he noticed faint writings seeping through. The blue ink strengthened and the words seemed to jump off the page as he began to read, *"Bridazak Baiulus, you have been chosen from the beginning to carry The Truth. Though you feel you are weak, my strength will shine brightly for all to see. I was despised and rejected by men. Full of sorrow, I am familiar with suffering. I long to be in the hearts of men once again. Though you travel not fully knowing your destination, know the God of All has heard your heart's cry. My thoughts are not your thoughts, neither are your ways my ways. My Word will not return to me empty, but will accomplish what I desire and will achieve the purpose for which I sent it.*

Awake and behold The Truth for it will be the bridge to the Holy City of God. Everlasting joy will crown the heads of those who seek righteousness. My Truth will be crushed for you and for all. The Tree of Death's roots have spread deep and wide, but I will uproot it and its deadly branches will no longer cast their shadow of darkness over the realm. I will cover the transgressions of those who believe." The writing slowly faded as he finished. He saw Billwick proudly smiling.

The golden Orb appeared before them all and rose to eye level. Light from the candles in the room began to intensify as it bounced off of the sphere. Then it spoke aloud.

"The stars of heaven and their constellations will soon conceal their light. The rising sun will be darkened, and the moon shall not cause her light to shine. The realms will be punished for its evil, the wicked for their crimes. I will put an end to the arrogance and humble the pride of the ruthless. All the stars of the heavens will be dissolved and the sky rolled up like a scroll; all the starry host will fall like withered leaves from the vine. My sword has drunk its fill in the heavens, it now descends in judgment. The nobles of the land will have nothing to be called a kingdom; all the princes will vanish away. Thorns will overrun the citadels, nettles and brambles the strongholds. And it shall be a habitation of dragons, and a court for owls.

The people walking in darkness will see a great light. To those living in the land of the shadow of death, a new light will dawn."

The Orb disappeared, and once again Bridazak could feel the weight of it back in his pocket. A strong heaviness inside his soul also accompanied it, as he was overwhelmed by the impactful words. It was hard to believe he had come all this way, for this moment, at this time, but was there an end in sight? He thought it was done when they found Billwick and the temple, but he says there is more. *Haven't I given enough? Sacrificing all I have, for what? I know that if Spilf was here, he would want me to go to wherever this crazy adventure ended. Am I willing to lose more of my friends; to lose myself?*

"What does this mean, Billwick? What are we supposed to do?"

Billwick placed his hand onto Bridazak's shoulder, "You are now to go and find a healer called Xan. His pain is great and he has been out in the wilderness for a long time, waiting for you."

"Why? What happened to him?"

"He, much like yourself, awaits answers to his deepest longings, and when you find him you are to tell him: 'The time has come and has already come.' Once he hears this message, he will show you what to do next."

When Billwick finished this last message there was a sudden shift within the room. A gust of air burst forth behind them, causing their hair to cascade over their faces and several hundred candles to be extinguished. Grey smoke drifted and then began to swirl together next to the bronze door. A portal appeared. It was filled with darkness, and strange whispers came from within.

"If this is the portal we need to go through, then you can forget about it!" Dulgin yelled.

"No, this is not the way. We must hurry. They have found you and are coming through."

He grabbed his staff and spoke a single word, "Lishno!" A wall of brilliant colors shot forth from the staff, separating them from the opening. Bright and vibrant, it swirled about, humming with electric energy. Billwick turned and focused on the altar with his gathered items. He knelt down and began a ceremony. His hands were raised up toward the ceiling and he spoke a language they could not identify.

From the dark gateway came the black-leather armored men they had encountered in Oculus' lair and Lonely Tear; they were King Manasseh's men, and the same red-robed mystic accompanied them. Dulgin's anger erupted, and he charged. There was nothing that Bridazak or Abawken could do, but Dulgin soon found out that he could do nothing himself, as he slammed into the prismatic wall; he was shot backward and fell to the ground. His friends were by his side, quickly lifting him back to his feet. The men on the other side were trying to get through the wall, but without success, as each of them were also launched backward. Colors swirled about in agitation and sparked toward anyone approaching. At least ten of them had gathered, with more coming through. A sudden burst of light came from behind the heroes, and they turned to see a brightly lit opening just beyond the marble altar.

Billwick Softfoot stood and turned toward them, "It is time, heroes of Ruauck-El."

"Come with us!" Bridazak pleaded.

"It has been an honor, Bridazak. You must see this quest through to the end. Stay clear of the Reegs. Adon cahl-raw." His final words spoken in Ancient Ordakian.

Bridazak was awkwardly compelled to embrace Billwick, and felt a rush of warmth as the affection was returned with an even stronger grasp. The moment in the quiet folds of the old one's white robes brought peace to Bridazak. The mysterious Dak finally separated from him and then threw the hair samples he'd gathered earlier into the open doorway of light. A blue aura erupted; the alchemy of the final components. The smell of mountain air blew into the temple.

"Well met, Bridazak!"

Dulgin and Abawken walked through together. Bridazak entered the brilliant opening backward, slowly taking each step, keeping his eyes on the grandfatherly Dak as he disappeared into the blue light. The wall that had kept Mannaseh's forces at bay came down. Billwick knelt and lifted his eyes toward the ceiling once again, with his arms outstretched and a smile of victory on his face. The darkly clad humans apprehended the Ordakian and the mystic leader commanded others to give chase and enter the portal. Swords drawn, two approached the lighted doorway; as they entered their flesh sizzled and they watched themselves dissolve before their own horrified eyes. Screams faded as their ashes spread throughout the chamber.

The gateway snapped closed like a bolt of lightning. A thunderous crack resounded.

The staff of the wizard began to glow. An emerald hue revealed the twisted outlines and partial faces of Billwick's captors, who turned the Ordakian to face the mage.

"Where are they?"

"Beyond reach. You are too late."

"Who are you?"

Billwick responded with silence. The mystic leaned in, "We have ways of making you talk, so I suggest you be forthcoming, Halfling."

He did not speak, but instead smiled brightly.

"Fine! Take him away!"

The two militia tried to push him forward but they were unable. Their hands, gripping his softly glowing skin, began to slip, finding nothing to grasp. More men came in, but the mystic gestured for them to hold. They stopped and watched the mysterious halfling transform into pure white light and ascend beyond the ceiling above. Each man raised his arms to shield his eyes from the brilliance, and then the darkness returned. Billwick Softfoot was gone.

Out of rage, the mystic pointed his staff and a searing jet of fire ignited the two who had failed to retain their captive. The others backed away from the human bonfire.

"Manasseh will not be pleased."

The trio now stood in a rocky valley with mountains on either side of them, near a small creek running through the sandstone. The land was bare, with little vegetation growing in the warm and dry terrain. The sunlight was already waning as it descended behind the mountain.

"Well, I suggest we follow the creek and see where it takes us," Abawken suggested.

"I'm glad you guys are here with me. I couldn't imagine doing this alone," Bridazak professed.

"Ah, don't get all sentimental on us now, ya blundering fool. My axe is getting hungry so we best be finding it some food, if you know what I mean. That damn mystic would really hit the spot right about now."

"Master Dwarf, you are one amazing individual. I pray I never encounter your equal."

"Not to worry about that, Huey, I'm the only one left in my family."

They began their descent into the valley, following the creek in search of someone named Xan. Bridazak stretched open the Scroll of Remembrance and thought about his name, Bridazak Baiulus, which felt both foreign and familiar at the same time. Could this artifact really connect him to his unknown past? He laughed inside; this was not about him, it was about the Orb. He walked alongside his friends, an old one, and now a new one, and refocused on finding the peculiar healer who somehow managed to live in pain. He smiled as he thought of Billwick Softfoot, and couldn't deny the strange feeling inside, the stirring of deep emotions he had buried for so long. It felt like hope.

10

The Puppet King

"How many times must a King see failure in his subjects before he says 'enough'?" King Manasseh's words lingered in the slightly drooped heads of six mystics in the circular, marble-floored tower. The Tower of Recall harbored four open ledges leading to the view outside. He menacingly approached the lead mystic, who dodged making eye contact with his master. The feared King scanned around at the other red robed subjects. The room remained deathly quiet.

"How does an Ordakian continue to elude my best?" There was no response from anyone.

"ANSWER ME!!!" The King shouted at the top of his lungs. Spittle flew from his enraged lips into the face of the wizard in front of him.

The trembling voice crackled to life, "My King, it has had some help."

"A Dwarf and a human? That is what you consider help? That is what's besting my best? Then perhaps I need to find better!"

"My liege, there is something different about this group."

"Different? Explain yourself."

"Your magnificence, I have sensed a power that radiates from the Ordakian. It is something that I have not felt before. Perhaps it is a magical item. We have discussed this amongst ourselves, and—"

"Discussed?" the enraged King interrupted him. "I am the one who gives permission to discuss, Constable! Your group of misfits sicken me!"

"Forgive us, King Manasseh."

"Three times they were in your sights and three times you failed to retrieve for me the lowliest, the weakest, the most insignificant creature in all the realms! I will not stand for this, Vevrin!"

"Yes, my King. I will not fail you again."

Manasseh laughed aloud, "I decree upon your words that any further failure will result in your immediate removal from existence. I will see first-hand to the torture of your body and soul for a hundred years."

"Yes, my—"

"Get out of my sight! You disgust me! All of you!"

Each head bowed to the sound of shuffling feet quickly exiting the sparse room. The walls were made of a black stone and the grey marbled floor had veins of red that swirled in random patterns. In the center of the chamber was a large, five-foot-wide pedestal with a silver basin at the top, filled with murky dark water. Manasseh walked to the southern balcony and leaned his hands on the black stone railing. He stood on the highest point of his castle and gazed upon his vast kingdom, but all he could see was the gaping wound of failure left behind by incompetence. There was no more room for error; he would take no further chances on Vevrin. It was time for him to take matters into his own hands.

For a moment he watched the laborers working on a new section of his castle expansion below. The hammering and chipping of stone spoke to him of progress. A training arena to groom better soldiers was being pre-pared. He had already started to gather the young men from the villages, towns and cities.

Off in the distance, his pet dragons and their riders practiced maneu-vers over the desert. The grey sand, like ash from a volcano, was the endless marker for those travelling toward Kerrith Ravine. This castle was one of a dozen throughout his land; a military deployment center. His men trained in a place feared by all, The Desert of Guilt. The deadly and mysterious Reegs from Kerrith Ravine roamed the dunes.

He spotted one of his commanders sending out a group of ten training soldiers into the ashen terrain. This was their final test, after all of the com-bat techniques were ingrained into their bodies. Half would return, hope-fully, and become part of his elite. In months he would be ready to start invading the other Horn Kings, and then nothing would stand in his way, if only he could find this elusive Dak, and gain the favor of the Dark Lord.

"What are you doing Halfling? Where are you going?" He whispered the questions as he looked out onto the horizon.

King Manasseh turned to face the empty room. His black cape caught the wind as he walked back inside to approach the waist high pedestal in the center. The cloudy liquid was still—he stared at his reflection. It was time for him to gain information to help him track down this fugitive.

He plunged his face into the magical Pool of Recall, gripping the rim of the basin. Bringing Vevrin to mind, and then the Halfling, he was shown the three encounters that had transpired—the lair of Oculus, the town of Lonely Tear, and then finally, the temple in Everwood. He waited for the pool to show him anything more he might have missed, bitterly viewing the temple scene—the site of his greatest disappointment so far—again and again. The Dark Lord, whose taunting tone still rang in his ears, 'Another chance, my son,' had come to inform him of their whereabouts. How had he found them when his mystics could not? Once given the location, Vevrin had embarrassed him with his failed attempt at opening a portal into their position. The Dark One stepped in and completed it with his own power, but Vevrin had still allowed them to escape. Where were these insolents now? He demanded the pool show him what he could not see—how could he reach them? He pulled himself upright, the murky water leaving dark tracks as it ran down and soaked into his tunic. His face wore a menacing grin of satisfaction.

He winced in pain as his senses returned, realizing he must have passed out, again. It was dark as night in the dungeon hole. He began the arduous task of attempting to learn the status of his own body. Blood dripped from his chin and he barely heard the sporadic splash as it hit the cold floor below him. His wrists and ankles were completely numb, which he was thankful for, as he remained suspended in the air by manacles chained to the wall. Uncertain if he was capable of wiggling his toes, he remembered his hair-patched feet and his head of hair being pulled out in clumps at his last torture session, bringing with it rips of skin, like weeds pulled from a garden. That brought on the nausea once again.

His left eye was swollen shut, and his right ear had been chewed to pieces by one of the tormentor's pet rats. His nose and several other bones were broken or shattered, and intense pulses of sharp pain periodically shot through his broken body.

Spilfer Teehle had seen better days. He hadn't told them about the box with the strange writing that only Bridazak could understand. Keeping him alive long enough to give them all the information they needed was their goal, but he wished his last breath of life would leave his body. Enduring all the pain and long stretches of silence was beyond any Ordakian. He missed Bridazak, and even Dulgin's dwarven tirades. Spilf's split lip curled with a slight smile as he realized he even longed to be called 'Stubby' again. It seemed it would be a miracle if he got out of this one. They were wearing his will down. He was running out of hope.

Spilf was suddenly jostled. He could barely hear through his damaged eardrums; everything sounded so far away. His good eye fluttered open and shut, but he couldn't assemble his wits enough to grasp just who was in front of him. One of his shackles came undone around his wrist, and half of his body slumped forward awkwardly, but was caught and balanced mid-swing. Another shackle released around his broken right ankle. He was being freed, but by whom? The person was saying something to him, but he only heard garbled sounds. Seconds later he was lying on the ground. He cracked open his eyelid and was blinded by torch light. He fought through the stinging pain as his eyes slowly worked to focus on the blurry form hovering over him. A liquid of some kind was poured over his face, and the healing began as the magic of the potion was released into his body. His vision cleared, and the once-deadened sound returned as his ears popped open to the voice of his best friend. It was Bridazak standing over him. He couldn't believe what he was seeing, and reached up to grab his cheeks.

"Spilf! It's me!"

"Bridazak! It's really you. How?" Spilf coughed.

"We came to rescue you."

"Where is Dulgin?"

"He is guarding the portal we need to go through."

"I didn't tell them anything, Bridazak."

"It's okay. Are you able to stand?"

"They broke my ankles. Do you have another healing potion?"

"I found the potion inside your cell. There was only one. What did they do to you, Spilf?"

"They asked so many questions."

"What do they know about us?"

"They tracked us using the mystics, and they wanted to know who was helping you escape. They lost contact and were unable to scry your location several days ago."

"I know."

"Does that mean you opened it?"

"Not yet. What else do they know?"

"They kept asking me how you were blocking their magic, but I never told them about the box, or the prophecy."

Bridazak paused, "That box is nothing but trouble. It is what caused this entire mess."

"Don't say that, Bridazak. They didn't kill me, so it must be significant. Even after all of this, I still believe there is something important about it. It chose you, and you must find a way to open it. Remember, you are the only one who can decipher the writing."

"I won't do it unless I have you by my side."

"Bridazak, Kiratta said to protect it at all cost. You shouldn't have come."

"It will be okay. Let's try and get you out of here."

Bridazak tried to lift Spilf up, but the dead weight of his body was too much for him.

"I will have to get Dulgin to help carry you out. I will be right back."

"Can I see Lester and Ross? I miss them so much."

"They are standing guard at the portal with Dulgin."

Spilf's body jolted to Bridazak's strange response. His longtime friend suddenly let him drop to the floor, carelessly. Spilf watched as Bridazak transformed before his eyes into King Manasseh. His heart sank, and his last wisps of hope dwindled as he realized he had failed his friends and given his enemy all that he knew. Death was imminent. Soldiers entered the room; the sound of the dragging chains being gathered to shackle him echoed in his healed ears.

"I'm sorry, Bridazak," he whispered.

"Thank you, Halfling. You have been very helpful," King Manasseh spoke.

"You can't stop him."

"And what makes you think that? This box he possesses?"

"A day is coming when—"

"When what?" he chided.

"When people will speak of you no more and your kingdom will fall. I won't rest, even in the afterlife, until that day comes."

"We will see about that," the puppet King said while walking out of the cell to leave Spilf trapped within his guilt.

Vevrin stood before his King once again. They were alone in the war chamber, on opposite ends of the large, wooden, central table. Several maps of the realms laid scattered across the top. The walls of the room were adorned with large tapestries, depicting past battles of King Manasseh's victories, and he looked forward to adding more. Vibrant colors and masterful stitching told the tales of his conquests, but all that mattered in his mind was finding one-lowly-little Halfling.

Manasseh rolled out a map of his lands; sliding his hands and extending his arms to smooth it out, "Here is where we have seen and encountered this, 'Bridazak'. There is no pattern, so it is a waste of time to try to strategize where he will appear next. Also, you are still unable to scry his location," he accused, "so, we must entertain this prophecy that our captive mentioned. What do we know of a prophecy?"

"It is fragmented, cryptic and not tracked by any of our historians; it's more story and myth than a recorded or known prophecy, my King. The stories now seem all but forgotten."

"Well, I suggest you start remembering these stories, because somewhere in them we will find the halfling and his destination."

"It revolves around The Holy City, the ancient city lost to Kerrith Ravine. No one has ever seen the city since it was separated, five hundred years ago, from the rest of the realm. Some even say that the city is pure myth and never existed, though we do have sparse writings and occasionally the rare, long-living creature that gives testimony to it."

"Perhaps this place has something to do with where he is going. But, how will he get through Kerrith Ravine? I think our scope is too grand; we need to simplify our search. The halflings are friends—good friends. I believe I know how to bring out our missing Ordakian. It's an old method, but highly effective when dealing with people who have a heart."

Vevrin understood what he wanted, "I will have riders set to go before the day's end."

"I want to see something within an hour. There is no time to waste, as I don't know what I'm racing against, exactly."

His longest serving mystic saw another opportunity to pet his master's ego, "Your intelligence and wisdom are great, my Lord."

Manasseh leaned back with steepled hands under his chin, "Vevrin, I can feel another addition of a tapestry to my wall forthcoming. Don't you think? Once we have captured this Halfling, we will be launching our offensive against the Eastern Horn King, but in order for that to take place, I need you to make this happen. Do not fail me again. Continue your research into this prophecy, and go as far as necessary, even if you have to reach out to your brother in the West."

Vevrin cooly glanced at Manasseh's countenance at the mention of his sibling, and checked his own before replying, "As you wish. Would you like me to dispatch the prisoner, since he has given us the information we needed?"

"Dispatch? That is such a clean word, Vevrin. I like, 'maimed till he goes insane,' or, drain his blood for the dogs, or even leave him to be eaten to death by rats." A dark thought washed over the King's face and then he continued, "No, let's keep him alive for the time being. You may go."

The King sat down at the head of the table, put his left hand to his clean-shaven chin, and pondered the situation. He had intentionally withheld the mention of the mysterious container that was in Bridazak's possession, and possibly the key ingredient in blocking the magic of his mystics. Such power must be his. He retrieved the necklace gifted to him from the demon god, and gazed into the swirling smoke trapped inside the crystal shard; the same medallion used to transmit his team to the dilapidated temple in Everwood.

"You are after this box, aren't you?" he whispered into the empty room. "What is inside, I wonder?"

The thuds of a galloping horse increased. A single rider thundered down the lonely dirt road. He pulled on the reigns, and the steed snorted as it slid up to the wooden pole informing weary travelers of the miles marked to the town of Gathford. The young soldier yanked free a wanted poster to make room for the new announcement. The older parchment swayed to the ground and the ugly face of a cocky gnome was quickly saturated with muddy water. *Trillius, also known as Silly Samuel,* was now replaced. The new posting showed a sketch of an Ordakian, his name, description, and known accomplices. There was another drawing at the bottom, depicting the one they had captured. Bridazak's face was being plastered across the land on every wooden post possible. Once the misfit leader saw that his friend Spilf was alive, he would come out of hiding. The largest sum of gold ever offered adorned the page: 5,000 gold pieces. This would surely awaken the dregs of the land in an all-out search for the soon-to-be infamous Bridazak.

11

Lost and Found

As the sun descended behind the ominous mountain range, the heroes recognized their location. The Moonrock Mountains were legendary in their own right, as this range of glowing rock was visible in any direction from miles away. The natural phenomenon illuminated the valley, and made evening travel commonplace in this channel of land. The mountains absorbed the sunlight and then transformed it into an amazing radiance of soft moonlight. This also brought unique creatures out at night, and the adventurers could hear the rumbling of rocks crashing into each other in the distance, the occasional roar in declaration of territory, and scuffling through the brush and rubble nearby.

They decided to hunker down between two larger sandstones in a cluster of earth-toned rock, in hopes of concealing themselves. Thankfully, the night had passed uneventfully in this strange valley, the temple portal's destination. The sunlight finally revealed itself, alighting a rather still, quiet morning—no birds, no insects, just their own voices and the melodically trickling stream moving through the rock bed. They ate their dried rations and packed up their gear once again, to continue their journey. Further down the valley they encountered clusters of trees, which grew thicker the deeper they went. They were still many miles away from the greenery, and they estimated it would take a day to reach, as the terrain was not easy to navigate.

Several hours had passed when Abawken stopped the group. He cocked his head slightly, intently listening to something. Bridazak and Dulgin did the same. They all heard it together; a sound of metal hitting metal echoed up to their ears from further down in the valley. The beginning of the forest was before them.

"A blacksmith?" Bridazak asked innocently.

"Nah, no smoke to indicate a fire," Dulgin responded.

There it was again, and this time, it sounded more distinct.

"Combat," Abawken said. "Let's go."

They hurried toward the sound of swords clashing. The stream intensified in this area, and larger rock outcroppings funnelled the widening stream, causing it to pick up speed. The crashing sound of water cascading over the lip of a ridge ahead informed them of the sudden change in the terrain. They slid along the large, flat stone until they could peer down below. It was a grand spectacle that none had expected. Twenty feet down the clear water tumbled into a larger pool, but the liquid below was an intense red, as Orc blood was being spilled by an enraged male Elf. Eight slain Orcs floated face down in the shallow puddle near the clamor, with still more further downstream, already being carried away. The Elf was currently battling four other Orcs, with more trying to navigate closer to join in the battle. On either side of the banks, there were at least thirty more blood thirsty, pig-like creatures, jockeying for a position to be next to try to kill the woodland Elf.

Skillfully, the Elf swung his long sword and slayed another opponent; it splashed back into the water to join his other dead kin. The pointy-eared male yelled in triumph, and again launched an assault onto another Orc next to him. Each slash was accompanied by a growl as the wild Elf ferociously attacked without relent. His hair was knotted and nasty, with dirt and leaves entwined. He wore leather armor that bore several cuts and slashes, and his face was covered in smudges of dirt, blood, and scraggly hair.

"Not a very happy Elf," Dulgin whispered.

"Indeed."

"Should we help him out?" Bridazak asked.

"I kinda like this Elf," Dulgin said, entranced by the gore below.

"He might know about Xan."

"Yeah, and I don't want him to have all the fun," Dulgin added, backing away from the ledge and preparing to head down with his axe.

Abawken also backed up, and they both started to move to the right, searching for a trail to lead them below. Bridazak stayed where he was, pulling out his quiver of regular arrows; a handful of mindless Orcs was not worthy of the magical ones he found in Everwood. He notched his first arrow, and waited for his friends to give him the go-ahead. It didn't take long before a strange guttural roar came from behind the Orcs. A rock elemental, completely formed of the surrounding earth, emerged, breaking a veritable hole in the tree line. Bridazak was startled at first, but then realized it must be from Abawken's Sword of the Elements. It immediately engaged the pig-like creatures. The legless body of the earthen creature moved through the ground like water. Its glowing white eyes tracked its next victim, pounding at its enemies with its massive arms. As it roared, dirt and debris bellowed out of its mouth. Several Orcs scattered away to the sides, while the bulk of the group was pushed toward the enraged Elf in the bloody pool beyond.

Bridazak noticed that the Elf was not phased by the event in the slightest, and continued his onslaught. He let loose his first shot at the Orcs on the opposite side. The Seeker sought its victim with great accuracy, and Bridazak was surprised by the ease of the pull. The shaft of his next arrow seemed to align itself as he notched and aimed. The impact of the arrow launched his target back several feet, and another arrow quickly whistled in to deliver its death punch to one more Orcasian.

The Elf finished off the other Orcs within the pool. No others engaged him, as they were now focused on the newer threats. Orc blood and water dripped off of the Elf as he slowly looked up on the ridge of the waterfall above. His deep, lavender eyes connected with the sight of the halfling. The sounds of combat faded around them as they continued to stare at one another. Bridazak realized he was caught inside a trance that the Elf was expelling from himself, and his mind was being intruded, triggering emotions of anger and hate. The bombarding waves of fury suddenly ended, and Bridazak gasped for air; he had unknowingly held his breath within the mind-battle. He saw that his good friend Dulgin had rushed the Elf and broke the mind link.

"Now what seems to be the problem, Elfy?"

He growled back at the Dwarf, then uttered an Elven word, "Jossume," and magically sprang the twenty feet up the falls, landing right next to Bridazak. Several Orcs charged Dulgin, while the other pig-kin were in melee with the giant rock creature on the other side of him.

Bridazak was quickly on his feet, backing away from the Elf, "We don't mean you any harm. We are here to help."

"I've heard that one before," he replied, walking toward the Ordakian. Water splashed around his strides and he brought up his long sword, preparing to strike Bridazak, who was still foggy from the trance. He fumbled with another arrow he had extracted from his quiver, but it was too late, as the Elf disarmed his bow and arrow out of his hand with great skill. He was now defenseless.

"I've waited a long time for this, Bridazak." His sword came down to strike.

"Looks like you will have to wait a little longer," Abawken flew in and blocked the Elf's sword with his own, just in time.

"It's you," the wild Elf responded in shock and disgust.

Just then, Abawken's eyes widened in recognition, "I've seen you in my visions."

"Then you must have seen your death as well." The Elf violently swung his sword, and the human parried the flurry.

Bridazak retrieved his bow just before it plummeted over the edge of the waterfall. The roar of the elemental that Abawken had summoned caught Bridazak's attention; the creature was smashing another Orc's skull wide open, like it was a watermelon. Dulgin was doing his dwarven battle dance, chopping one after the other with his axe as he went deeper into their ranks. Some began to break away and flee the scene.

Clashed swords rang in his ears and brought his focus back to the Elf and human fighting as greatly matched warriors. He had never seen such skill in all his years. The sword masters were now in a stalking position, trying to find an opening for another assault.

"Why do you protect the halfling?" The Elf asked as they circled one another in the water.

"Why do you seek to kill him?"

"I never understood the visions about you, until now. I didn't know that you would be together," the Elf said.

"Who are you?" Abawken asked.

"I'll let you know after I kill you."

The Elf launched into another tirade of attacks. Abawken quickly parried them, but had to back up in defense. Sparks began to fly off the magical weapons, and the clanks of metal intensified. Back and forth they exchanged blows, trying to find an opening, but this round also ended in a standstill and they continued to circle one another. Abawken seemed to be more defensive about the situation as he tried to figure out the Elf's reason for attacking.

"What did Bridazak do to you that has caused you so much pain?"

"I will be taking that up with him shortly."

"You will not defeat me, Elf."

He laughed at Abawken's statement, "I know something that you don't, Human."

"What is that?"

"My visions showed me your death." A self-assured grin prominently revealed itself. He launched into another offensive flurry.

Bridazak watched the spectacle and heard all the Elf's comments. He must do something to help his friend. Dulgin was occupied with the Orcs below and was handling himself well, but it would take him too long to finish what he had in front of him, and then climb the rocky hill, to be of any help. He pulled out an arrow and notched it. Aim was critical when two combatants were engaged; there was no room for error. His eyes focused on the end of the arrow tip as he pulled the bow string back. Even with his new magical bow, his confidence wavered. He wanted to wait for another break in the fight but he couldn't risk it, as Abawken could be killed at any moment. The arrow was set loose. In an instant the battle changed as the Elf, with a confident smirk, anticipated the shot and leaned quickly out of the way. The human never saw it coming as it slammed into his midsection and he flew back several feet from the impact of the magic, yelling in pain. Bridazak's eyes widened in horror.

"Now it is your turn, Bridazak!" he yelled as he trudged over the few steps in the water and towered over him.

"Why are you doing this?" Bridazak asked as his glassy eyes looked up at the Elf.

"I only wish it was your father instead of you."

"My—my father?"

There was a pause before he spoke, a pause before he struck. The Elf's eyes narrowed, "He destroyed my family!" His sword stabbed through Bridazak's leather armor, then his skin, and finally penetrated through to the other side. There was no more sound. He could see Dulgin coming back up from below and running towards him. There was no pain, and he wasn't sure he was even breathing. The Elf stood over him, showing no emotion in his revenge being fulfilled. He slid his sword out of the Ordakian's chest. Bridazak's hand went to the wound instinctively but it rested on the medallion around his neck instead. A strange warmth exploded throughout his body and he could see the Elf's face shift uncomfortably as he began to back away from him. There came a bright aura and within seconds, a spirit form stepped out from the Ordakian.

The ghostlike figure turned around, and he recognized that it was not his spirit form, as he supposed at first, but instead Ember. She materialized into flesh before everyone. Her milky skin glowed in the sunlight and her red hair was ablaze. Silver silk clothing wrapped around her body and fluttered in the breeze. Bridazak reached up to grab the hand that she extended to him. He was alive, and noticed now that the medallion crumbled to dust within his other hand.

"You saved me."

"I protected you. Someone else has saved you."

"Who are you?" The Elf questioned with his sword raised towards her.

"Bridazak, I believe you have a message to deliver to this Elf."

"This is Xan?" he asked in unbelief.

"Tell him your message."

Her words faded along with her body. The Elf stared blankly with his sword, still shakily raised. Dulgin was uncertain as to how to proceed, until he heard the human groaning in pain several feet away from him. He trudged through the water to wait by his side.

"Xan, the time has come and has already come," Bridazak delivered the cryptic message as instructed.

He could see the impact of the words on the Elf. His knees buckled and he fell back into the water, stunned. The tears welled up and freely streamed out of his eyes. A minute went by without a word spoken.

"Please help us. Abawken is hurt."

The Elf seemed to come back slightly, and then turned to see the human bleeding profusely from the arrow embedded in his stomach.

"Billwick said you are a healer. Please help him."

He slowly stood up, leaving his weapon in the water, relinquishing the darkness that had captured him, and approached the fallen human.

"Please—" Xan began to speak.

"I forgive you," cutting off the Elf, Abawken replied.

"How did you know what I was going to ask?"

"In my own visions this is what I saw, but never understood," he said through his gritted teeth.

Xan raised his hands in the air, closed his eyes, and began to mumble words that none of them could understand. He knelt down beside him and placed his hands around the arrow shaft. Abawken felt heat inside. Xan pulled slowly and the burning intensified, but surprisingly there was no pain. Abawken's grimaced face lessened as the discomfort steadily decreased every moment. The barb of the arrow was now completely out, and the puncture closed behind the exit of the tip, leaving behind no trace of a scar—completely healed. Dulgin helped him to his feet.

"Thank you," the human acknowledged the Elf.

"I'm the one who should be giving thanks."

"Yeah, yeah, thank you and thank you, now what in dwarven hell is going on here?" Dulgin demanded an answer.

"I will take you to my home, and we will talk there."

Bridazak handed the Elf his sword and gave him a smile along with it. They gathered their belongings and headed off into the forest. Abawken's rock elemental stood ready down below, surrounded by dead Orcs. He dismissed the creature with a wave of his sword and it fell back into the earth, a cascade of rock and dirt.

An hour passed as they followed the Elf in single file until they reached a cave entrance. Nestled amongst the trees was a hill with huge boulders of granite and a large opening that perhaps once was residence for wildlife in the area.

"This is your home?" Dulgin asked.

"Do you like it?"

"I've never heard of any Elf living inside a cave. I can't wait to hear this story," the Dwarf continued on as he followed everyone inside.

Xan led the group through a narrow, mineral scented tunnel until they reached a strange, reinforced wooden door. It was heavily fortified with iron strapping and rivets on almost every square inch of the dense entryway. The Elf waved his hand and whispered a word that the heroes couldn't discern, which unlocked the magical entrance. The door silently swung open on its own, to reveal a luxurious mansion beyond. Grey marble covered the bottom level floor, and the large, open plan was decorated with fur rugs, rich tapestries, solid oak tables and chairs, and plush couches; rivaling the interiors of any palatial villas in the kingdoms. A staircase ascended along the right wall to an opening above, with several doors leading to additional rooms behind the railing on the second level. Rich aromas of sweet vanilla mingled with the scent of porridge as they heard the slow bubbling coming from the iron pots hanging over the fire.

"This is not a cave," Dulgin said in shock.

"Come and sit. We have much to discuss."

Anticipation of a hot meal, after days of dried rations, consumed their minds as Xan distributed bowls to each of them. Dulgin scarfed down the most, and trails of semi-crusted porridge streaked down his red beard as he scraped his fifth helping clean and licked his lips. The Elf had tied his knotted hair back into a long ponytail. He still bore some of the Orc blood that had dried on his face. The trio had relaxed and shared the details of their recent adventures leading up to this point. Bridazak had also revealed the Orb, which brought noticeable tears to Xan's eyes, but the Elf waited patiently for their story to come to a close before starting his own.

"My name is Xandahar Sheldeen," he began.

"Sheldeen Elves?" Dulgin asked in disbelief. "They have not been seen for hundreds of years."

"You are correct. I am the last."

"What happened to your people?" Abawken asked.

"They were lost in the Holy War at the time of the Separation."

"The Separation? Just how old are you, Elfy?"

"I'm approaching my seventh century."

"How do you look so young? You don't look a day over a hundred," responded Dulgin.

He exhaled deeply before going on, "Let's get to the heart of the matter, shall we?"

"Like, how you knew my father?" Bridazak asked.

"Yes, let's start there. You probably don't remember him."

"No, I grew up an orphan. I can't remember anyone or anything before that time. I spent several decades looking, but gave up and just thought it wasn't meant to be. Here," Bridazak pulled out the Scroll of Remembrance and pointed to his last name as the magical ink revealed itself once again, "Does this name match my father's?"

"Yes, Hills Baiulus. I had partnered with your father to find a way back to The Lost City, to save my wife and son from what had entered into our world. He told me they would be safe amongst the Ordakians while we went off to gather information. When we came back we found everyone was gone; killed or missing, and the homes all burnt to the ground. Two of the Horn Kings had decided that the battle ground would be right there. We could not find our families, but the carnage on that day will forever haunt me, and we assumed they were killed. He, however, had a strange feeling that you were still alive since you were so young and the militia had taken the surviving children with them. We fled the area and came here to the Moonrock Mountains."

Hesitantly, Bridazak braved his next question, "Did he look for me?"

"Yes, he did. We carried our loss differently, however, and we drifted apart from one another. He eventually came back, after a long journey of looking for you and gathering information, with a message." Xan paused; the anticipation of his words held everyone in the room captive. He composed himself and continued, "He told me that he found my family, and they were waiting for me to unite with them. He went on to describe a prophecy, and that I was a part of that prophecy. I needed to wait for the one who brings hope back into the world, and I would know it was near when I heard the words, 'The time has come and has already come'. He instructed me to hide in these mountains and wait, and here I have waited ever since. The years turned to decades, decades turned to centuries, and my hope dwindled, and my hate grew. You being here has changed everything. I can now see that my mind worked against me, hardening my heart toward the world and everyone in it. I thought I would never see my family again. I thought he lied to me about the message, so when I heard you say those words, it—" he stopped and looked at Bridazak.

"What happened to my father?"

He cleared his throat, "He went off in search of the Tree. I never saw him again, and don't know what happened."

"The Tree? It mentions something about a Tree of Death and branches in here, is it real!?"

Again, Xan took in a deep breath and proceeded, "The Tree was a gift that has now turned into a curse. It was never meant for mankind to touch, because it was pure and Holy. This tree gave us insight, knowledge, and wisdom, by just being in its presence and gazing upon it. It was an act of selfishness and greed that separated us all, as someone wanted to become like a god. The individual was fooled by a voice from another realm. Without the connection to the source of all that is good, the Tree began to poison the land, the people, our hearts, and Kerrith Ravine formed, releasing evil itself. The realm of Ruauck-El and all its inhabitants were separated from the Lost City, but it was not just a city; we were separated from the one who created this world, who lives there—the creator of creation itself. Darkness fell on the land."

"My brother, El'Korr, spoke of this Tree, but I thought it was a myth."

"Xan, how do you know so much about this?" Bridazak questioned.

"I've seen the Tree." There was silence in the room and Xan went deep into the recesses of his memories, from a time before his great darkness, "It had petals of sparkling crystal. Branches of silver and purple weaved together in perfect unison. It drew me in with its beauty. The power that emanated from it would heal the sick, answer questions, or bring favor to a family. Upon each answer or gift, a single glass-like leaf would fall and disintegrate into glittery rainbow colors and then vanish before reaching the ground. A new leaf would unfold to replace the fallen one. It was breathtaking; it was life-changing. Nothing in all of Ruauck-El compared, and my description does not do it justice."

"What did the Tree do for you?" Bridazak inquired, mesmerized by the beauty of the story.

"It gave me a son. My wife was barren and it was my only wish in life to have a child. I will never forget the crystal leaf falling after my request. I almost couldn't believe it would happen."

"How did one know not to touch it?" Bridazak asked.

"Do you remember when or how you knew right from wrong? God placed inside each of us the knowing in our spirit, and the closer you approached it, the stronger the push of this insight. There was a story of a human who came so close he was able to see his reflection in the crystal petals, and he was blinded by the beauty of what he saw."

"What happened to him? What did he see?"

"No one knows. The Legend of Bakka says he was escorted by the Shimmering Monks of old to an isolated temple on top of the Mountain of Gold, where he still remains to this day."

"Bah, now you talk of tall tales, Elf! There is no such place."

"I cannot disagree with you Dulgin, but this is the legend."

Abawken brought the conversation back, "Why did Bridazak's father have to search for the Tree? Didn't he already know where it was?"

Xandahar rose from his chair and went to a desk along the back wall, where he pulled out an old parchment. He unrolled it before them to reveal a map of the lands. He pointed to a place called Black Rock.

"This is where we suspected the Tree would be located. Before the time of Separation, The Tree would teleport randomly throughout the land where everyone could share in its beauty and knowledge. Black Rock was the last place that it was recorded to be."

"What is Black Rock? I've never heard of it before," Dulgin inquired.

"It is a secret castle of King Manasseh's, at the edge of the Desert of Guilt."

There was a long pause as everyone stared at the map. Bridazak broke the silence, "Does Manasseh know about the Tree?"

"Oh yes, that is the source of his power. That is why he has not aged as a human, and has ruled for over three centuries. He has become a dark and twisted soul."

"But where does the Tree get its energy from, now that it has fallen?" Abawken questioned. "It must come from somewhere."

"Not somewhere, but someone. The Dark Lord is the master of Ruauck-El now."

"Do you know who that is?"

"Whispers of his true name are forgotten echoes within the realm. We know he is the ruler of the bottomless pit, the father of the Reegs, but his identity remains unknown."

"So my father intended to destroy the Tree?"

"I believe so."

"How do you destroy something like that?"

"Bridazak, how does one defeat darkness?"

The Ordakian looked at the Elf in contemplation, and then it hit him, "With light!"

"Exactly. You now possess that light."

It dawned on him, "The Orb."

He nodded in confirmation of the revelation, "It is the bridge back to the one true God of all creation. It is our only hope."

Dulgin and Abawken stirred uncomfortably around the table, as they understood what the next step must be.

"This is insane, Bridazak! We can't be marching right into Black Rock. It would take an army," Dulgin blurted out.

"I have to agree with Master Dulgin. It will take us years to possibly gather enough strength to attack. Years we don't have."

There was another pause in the conversation. Bridazak wandered to the fireplace, trying to process the information all at once.

"There must be a way," Bridazak said.

"There is," Xan responded.

Everyone turned toward him, "I know of an army."

"Where?"

"They have been hiding and waiting for a very long time. We will start tomorrow at first light. I will take you to them."

"How far?"

"Several days from here. We have a long journey ahead of us, so tonight, we must rest. Let us retire and awake with fresh eyes and minds."

Everyone slowly disbanded and headed upstairs to the bedrooms. Bridazak and Xan were the last to go up, and before opening the door the Ordakian turned to the Elf with yet another question.

"Just curious, how did you know my name when you first saw me? Or was that in your visions too?" he teased.

Xan reached inside his cotton tunic and pulled out a folded paper, handing it over to Bridazak. He then walked to his bed chamber without a word. Bridazak quizzically watched him close the door, and then entered into his own room. Several lit candles gave light as he unfolded the parchment. It was a 'wanted' posting, featuring a picture of his face. They would not be able to enter any village, town, or city with his mug memorized by every bounty hunter and mercenary network out there. Dulgin and Abawken were listed as accomplices, which added more guilt onto Bridazak's already heavy burden. He scanned further, and spotted an odd word, "CAPTURED." Next to it was a face he loved. He gulped as he began to comprehend what he was seeing.

With labored breathing of panic and excitement he began to yell, "He's alive! He is ALIVE!"

Dulgin busted through the door with his axe readied, and Abawken was right behind him.

"What's going on, ya blundering fool!?"

"He's alive!"

"Who's alive?"

"Spilf!"

12

The Burning Forest

"We are almost there," Xan announced.

"Good, 'cause my feet are killing me from travelling for days on this god-forsaken volcanic rock," responded Dulgin.

Bridazak tapped his dwarven friend on the shoulder to get his attention, "Perhaps we should have gone through another portal to speed up the process."

Dulgin gave him a squinty-eyed glare, "Unless there is Dwarven Ale involved, you can forget about it. The next portal I see better have someone else coming through, cause I ain't budgin'."

Abawken and Bridazak chuckled as Dulgin continued to march on with a little extra stomp in each of his steps. In the distance they could see smoke filling the sky, but were unsure as to the source. Their last thirty miles were tread over volcanic rock, with sulphur smells dominating the atmosphere, but there was no volcano in sight. Xan had remained fairly elusive as to where they were going, so they suspected it was somewhere very dangerous, considering the current environment was already harsh; the obsidian stone was cutting through their boots. Luckily, the Elf had provided a pair of thick sandals for the barefoot Ordakian, knowing the terrain they would be facing. They could feel the cracking of skin within their nostrils as the dry sulphurous heat absorbed the moisture in their bodies; an occasional nose bleed forced them to stop and take a much needed rest.

Several hours of difficult trekking passed before they first spotted the flames sprouting out of the land. As they came closer, they could make out what appeared to be the remnants of some kind of forest, ablaze. Pops and cracks warned them of the impending danger of entering this consuming, fire land. Hundreds of stubs of the long-gone trees in various clusters lay before them. Each stood four feet tall with spires of flame licking toward heaven, as if trying to reach higher, having burned away all the height and branches of the former forest, but somehow neither dying out, nor finishing off what remained. The blaze burned with an intense roar, and a strong smell of toxic fumes surrounded the surreal scene.

"We've reached the Burning Forest."

"I've never heard of this place before. What is it?" Bridazak asked the question on everyone's mind.

"It is where we will be getting you an army."

"I don't see how there could be anyone in there," Dulgin responded.

"Do you mind informing us where we are, and what we need to do, Master Elf?"

"Indeed, Abawken. This used to be a great army. They were cursed by evil itself, and now burn eternally. Those are not trees, but warriors."

"What? You're kidding, right?" Dulgin blurted.

"When did this happen?" asked the Ordakian.

Xan looked directly to Dulgin before answering, "The Kerrith Ravine crusade."

The information stunned the Dwarf. He took a step backward and then pivoted to look at the cursed land. These were his people. In there, somewhere, was his brother. Through gritted teeth, he asked "What do we need to do, Elfy?"

"Anyone who enters the forest will be consumed by the fire and fall victim to the curse. I have prepared a spell that will protect us for one hour."

"But how do we battle this curse?" asked the human sheik.

"A beast of fire controls this forest. My guess is that once it is destroyed, the curse will fall also."

"That is a pretty big guess Xan—and a big risk."

"I know, Bridazak—but long ago, someone told me to think of risk as faith."

"I'm in," Dulgin quickly interjected.

"I'm with you!" Bridazak announced. He knew the sooner they procured an army, the sooner they would be on their way to rescue Spilf.

Xan looked to Abawken for his answer.

"There is a saying where I come from; 'A curse waits to be broken.' I am with you also."

They each prepared for the upcoming battle with a creature they knew nothing about. Xan readied his magical protection spell, while the rest of the group ate more of the simple dried meats and fruits, and drank plenty of water. Just what was in there none could imagine. The cleric dwarves of long ago came to this place to battle evil, and here they had been for hundreds of years, suspended in fiery torment.

"How is it that you know so much about this place, Elfy?"

Xan wasn't surprised by the question, "I knew of the battle plan, and about what had happened."

"How?" Dulgin now seemed to be interrogating him.

There was no response, but Dulgin pushed further, "If there was no one to tell about it, then how did you come up with this information?"

Abawken and Bridazak now came closer to the conversation.

"Well?" Dulgin raised his voice.

"Because I was there," the Elf finally disclosed.

"You were there—I mean, here?" Bridazak fumbled for words.

"Yes. There was nothing I could do except save myself, but now it is time to restore what was lost."

Xan moved away, continuing his preparations in silence. Bridazak noted the phrase again, the same as the one in the dream he had back in Gathford, *"It is time."* It couldn't be coincidence.

Abawken stepped over to intercept Bridazak, "Have you consulted the Orb about this place?"

"No, but that is a good idea." He withdrew it from his pocket and held it in his palm. "What can you tell me about the Burning Forest?"

The Orb of Truth rose into the air, and the gold surface of the perfect sphere rotated hypnotically. "Do not be afraid. I will bless those who bless you and whoever curses you I will curse; all the people of the land will be blessed through you." It then rested on top of his palm, and each of them took a deep breath as they understood the importance of their mission, and the battle ahead of them. Bridazak spotted Xan wiping away tears, his back to them. He could see a subtle change within the bitter Elf, and he knew the Orb had something to do with it. Bridazak began to understand the healing that Xan needed was far beyond any normal healer of Ruauck-El.

Xan's spell of protection worked incredibly well. They were immersed inside the flaming landscape, without any harm to their bodies or belongings. It was a protective, invisible shield that surrounded each of them. The Elf had also added another incantation, which he called 'Breath of Fresh Air'. Inside the shield they inhaled fresh air from around them, instead of the thick ash and sulphur. Moving deeper within the ranks of the cursed dwarven army, Dulgin scanned each of the torched kin with a determined focus, in hope of recognition among some of the trapped soldiers. Deep inside each holocaust was the barely distinguishable shape of a person. No details were obvious, but in this proximity, they could clearly identify these trees as individual dwarves, with a few numbers of other races scattered amongst them. "We are ten minutes in," Xan announced, with no sign of the creature. The sound of the roaring flames intensified the further they went on. There was a rage to these fires; the flames lashed out at each traveler as they passed by. Another ten minutes had gone by when they reached a cleared area of volcanic rock.

"Why is this area clear?" Bridazak yelled the question over the sound of the flames.

"We might be at the center. I remember a large, luminous eruption amongst our army, but I never knew what it was," Xan answered.

The area expanded a hundred feet in all directions, forming a perfect circle of black rock. They began to walk inside this expanse to investigate, and as they did so, the noise of the fire diminished greatly.

"How much time remains?" Abawken asked.

"I don't care! I'm not leaving without my kin!"

"Twenty minutes have elapsed," Xan announced.

Abawken nodded his approval toward Dulgin's glare, and they proceeded further into the open area. A larger glow on the opposite side stood out to them all. They cautiously approached, but quickly realized that caution was not necessary, as a huge beast of flame launched from the forest beyond and landed in front of them. It bellowed a blast of fire at the group, but the heat harmlessly reflected off each of them. The creature resembled a large dog. It was fifteen feet long, more than twice the height of Dulgin, and stocky, as though he were made of boulder mountain rock itself. It had a mane of fire around its head, and its eyes glowed a brilliant red. Each foot-long tooth dripped molten saliva. The canine's infernal tail whipped around as the beast lowered its head toward the heroes and growled. Veins of lava showed through its black skin, and the volcanic rock melted with a hiss at each of the creature's steps.

The heroes fanned out, with their weapons ready to strike. This was going to be a battle like no other. Bridazak took several steps backward to get some distance, notching an arrow on his magical bow, the Seeker.

"Time is a wastin'!" Dulgin yelled, charging with his axe.

The monster stood its ground as it brought its scorched fangs down upon the Dwarf. Dulgin was quickly captured within its jaws. He was protected from the heat damage but not the physical penetration of the teeth—they clamped down and sank into his armor. He yelled in pain, but used the agony to bolster his dwarven resolve. Half of his body hung outside, and he swung his free arm, holding his axe, at the beast's jaw, burying it into its black flesh. There was an ear-splitting, guttural yelp as it released the Dwarf. He plummeted to the ground. Armor pieces fell off of him with a clanking sound as he hit the rock below. He winced, but got back up with the help of his axe, and glared back at the creature.

"Bad dog! Now I have to put you down!" Dulgin said.

The beast roared once again to intimidate them. A volley of arrows sailed in, but they instantly melted upon impact, with no effect. Xan began to circle to the left to try and find an opening, while Abawken went the opposite way to flank it. Dulgin stood in front brazenly, not willing to budge from his location. The three of them moved in closer and the canine hunched its back, ready for the encounter, baring his teeth and growling. Xan was the first to come in, but he was quickly thrown aside when its tail whipped in and slammed him. He sailed several feet away. The fire once again did no damage, but the impact cracked one of his ribs.

Dulgin swung his mighty axe at its lowered head, but it lifted just in time and he missed. Abawken, on the other side, tumbled in and found himself underneath the creature. He sliced the hind leg, and his blade administered extra damage when he yelled out a command word to release the magic within; his sword instantly shot out a blast of water at the same time he struck the beast. Steam erupted everywhere from the combination of heat and water colliding. The human tumbled and flipped from under it, and once clear, he looked back to survey the damage. A scream of intense torment bellowed from it and its back leg barely held on. He knew the creature would be susceptible to water. It lunged at Abawken, who dodged the bite but not the immediate retaliatory head swing to knock him back. He sailed through the air but landed smoothly on his feet, thanks to his Sword of the Elements once again. The beast growled in disdain and hobbled toward the human on its three good legs.

More arrows flew in from Bridazak's skilled aim, but they were no match for the beast. Frustrated, he set his backpack down to try and find something creative he could do to contribute to the battle. He paused when he noticed three shafts glowing within his quiver of magical arrows. Slowly, he deliberately pulled one out—it began to pulse within his grasp. The ancient, Ordakian writing engraved on the shaft read 'Magical Beast'.

Another yelp came from the dog monster when, in pursuit of Abawken, Dulgin chopped at its front leg. "Did you forget about me?" he chastised. The Dwarf was immediately slapped by its tail, and again he was tossed back to the ground. He grunted in pain, but stood up nonetheless. His axe remained wedged in the creature's leg. Abawken moved in to engage it, but was grappled by the fiery tail. It wrapped around his sword arm, lifting him high in the air. He jerked his legs, trying to break free of the grasp, but the strength of this canine was beyond imagination. He was lowered right in front of its jaw, its gaping mouth opened for the kill, but it flinched away, looking to its right when Xan plunged his long sword into its side. Lava flowed out from the wound. The Elf retracted his blade, but the magic of the shield around him could not help his weapon any further, and it melted. He dropped the hilt, a clank of metal sounding as he began to back away. Another blood curdling roar erupted from the creature.

Dulgin and Xan were now both without their weapons, and Abawken was still grasped by the tail, suspended in air, defenseless. The magical beast snarled, and refocused his attention back to the human in his grip. It brought Abawken closer to its face so it could get a good look before devouring him. The human fighter peered around for something he could do, but without his hand free to use his weapon he was in trouble.

Bridazak pulled back the bowstring with ease, closing one eye while the other locked on his target. The arrow was released. The light of the magic intensified as it sailed through the air, igniting in a brilliant flash as it impacted into the chest of the fire beast. The smoke dissipated and Bridazak saw the creature dead, its chest wide open. Xan and Dulgin were launched back from the explosion, but they quickly stood up and stared in disbelief at what lay before them. They looked around to find where Abawken had gone. He was nowhere to be seen.

"I'm up here."

The human slowly floated down from above, his sword in hand. The explosion had sent him hurtling up, but the magical power within his weapon saved his life, as a summoned current of wind gently brought him to the ground. Now gathered once again, they surveyed the land. Dulgin retrieved his axe which Abawken had spotted while floating down.

"Master Bridazak, you used one of those special arrows you found, right?" asked Abawken.

"I noticed it glowing. My other arrows had no effect."

"It was a great shot. You saved my life. I am once again in your debt," he bowed.

Dulgin quickly changed the conversation, "Why isn't the curse broken yet?"

"Perhaps it takes a few moments," Xan proposed.

They waited another minute, but nothing changed.

"Something is wrong, Elfy. We must have missed something."

"We tried, Dulgin."

"Dwarfshit!" Dulgin stormed off toward the fallen enemy. The rest of the group followed.

The short, stubby fighter yelled out in anger from behind his red beard, "RELEASE MY KIN!"

There was a rumble under their feet.

"Did you feel that?" Bridazak asked, looking around. No one replied. Then it came again.

Thirty feet away, the group spotted a small, dark, hovering cloud, that seemed to be growing. Dulgin slowly made his way back to join the others, never taking his eyes off of the spectacle. For a moment they were hopeful that this phenomenon had something to do with breaking the curse, but as the dark mist began to expand more than twenty feet in all directions, flashes of lightning within it, they weren't so sure.

"This is strange," Bridazak stated.

"I'm not thinkin this is good," Dulgin responded. They could hear the faint crackle of the bolts beyond.

"The sound of that thunder seems too distant, and faded. This could be a portal," Abawken added.

"I'm not going through anymore portals!"

The lightning flashes intensified and the ground continued to rumble. Then, something appeared. A creature beyond anything they had ever seen or heard of stepped out of the mysterious cloud—a twenty-foot-tall humanoid with bronze colored armor plating. Its head was the shape of a dragon with spiraling tendrils of black skin at the back of the scalp and neck. It had brilliant red eyes, a protruding jaw with razor sharp uniformed teeth, and smoke billowing out of its nostrils. Each claw on its hands was the length of a long sword. Muscles bulged in all areas of its body and the armor plating moved like it was its natural skin. It growled with rage at the adventurers.

"Holy mother of all dwarven mothers!"

"Spread out! I will summon help through my sword."

"*This* is the protector!" Xan shouted.

"Then that other thing was its pet!" Bridazak realized.

"Great, this is going to be fun." Dulgin slightly limped into position, hoisting his father's axe into his battle stance, ready for action.

"We have twenty minutes remaining on my spell," Xan warned.

Bridazak started to back up to gain some distance. The others resumed their positions, Dulgin remaining firmly planted as the swordsmen spread out to flank once again.

"I'm givin ya one more chance to release my kin," Dulgin declared.

The behemoth suddenly produced, out of thin air, a huge, two-handed sword of fire. Flames dripped off of the blade like oil as the keeper of the Burning Forest towered over the Dwarf.

"Time to make you bleed, big boy!" Dulgin charged the monster with reckless abandon. The flaming steel came down to meet the small intruder, but the Dwarf side-stepped the assault at the last instant to avoid the deadly strike. Large chips of rock flew out from the impact of the sword and littered the ground. Dulgin countered, striking the monstrous forearm. His axe clanked off its armor, doing no damage. The short fighter continued his run between its legs. The beast watched the Dwarf's movement, and then lifted its sword and turned around.

Dulgin was close to Xan when he finally reached the other side. "I suggest not getting hit. He moves slow, but that damn armor or skin of his is hefty."

"Thanks. I will keep that in mind," replied Xan. The Elf knew he would not be engaging this beast in melee, especially without his sword, but he had some other ideas of how to contribute to the battle.

Abawken yelled another command word, "EREZ!" The familiar Rock Elemental creature formed out of the ground beneath the giant, and instantly began to pummel it with its powerful fists of earth. Rock pieces flew off in all directions from the impact as it bellowed out a roar of discomfort. Its attention was now on the immediate threat. The human went in for an attack, striking its left achilles tendon while it was distracted. His sword of the elements penetrated through its thick armor, and a black, acidic ooze poured out of the wound. Its voice boomed in pain, but it still descended on the summoned earth creature.

The behemoth pinned the Rock Elemental to the ground under its right knee. With one hand free, the Burning Forest protector ripped the head off, killing it instantly. Still on one knee it threw the rock piece at the human. Abawken was clipped in the shoulder and was forced to release his sword. He fell to the ground in agonizing pain. His shoulder was broken. His cry could be heard by everyone.

Bridazak simultaneously released a second magical arrow. It slammed into the lower right side of its back and erupted into another powerful blast, like before. The giant was pushed to the ground, but it was still alive. It stood and turned toward the Ordakian. A large, gaping wound was very evident to the others when it turned. The black blood now began to flow freely.

Meanwhile, Xan went quickly to Abawken's side and cast a spell. He placed his hands on the shattered shoulder, which caused the human extreme pain, but he relaxed and received the healing power. His bones were mended.

"You are not out of this combat yet, my friend."

"Thanks," Abawken said, getting back to his feet and gathering his weapon.

Dulgin prepared to charge but was halted by the Elf, "Wait, Dulgin. I have something for you that will help." The Dwarf hesitated and almost ignored the request, but decided to investigate what the Elf had in mind.

"This better be good, Elfy."

The monster was now focused on Bridazak, but was stopped by yet another Rock Elemental that sprouted below him and began to attack. The

Protector lifted its giant foot high into the air, squashing the rock creature below him. Debris went sailing in all directions, and a fine, powdery dust enveloped his foot. The heroes heard a huge sound of grinding rock and the thud of the impact that followed. The beast roared in triumph, and then set its attention back on the Ordakian.

Bridazak grabbed his last magical beast arrow and notched it. He zeroed in on the head and unleashed the magical bolt. At the same time, the creature breathed a jet of fire from its mouth to intercept the arrow. Magic collided with the intense heat, and an explosion resulted. A huge ball of flame and magic blasted both Bridazak and the monster. The Ordakian was knocked back several feet, and hit his head hard on the volcanic rock. He lost consciousness as blood began to sprawl out from behind his skull. The beast withstood the blast, but not without taking considerable damage itself. Its chest and face bore deep, open gashes.

Abawken flinched from the intense heat and light of the explosion, and saw that Bridazak had fallen. The pressure to destroy their opponent quickly increased, as there were no signs of Bridazak getting back up. He was only able to summon one additional elemental for the day, as the power of his blade was being diminished; like him, it needed to rest. He wished there was a water source so he could bring that kind of elemental to combat this being. Just then, he saw Dulgin charging with his axe, but instead of running on the ground he was running in the air.

Dulgin had received the powerful spell from the Elf. He needed to get to that gaping wound in its back to do valid damage with his axe. Xan had given him that opportunity.

The creature had just taken the blast from Bridazak and was gathering himself when the Dwarf arrived. Before it turned around, Dulgin had swung his mighty axe and embedded it into the raw flesh that was exposed. It flinched intensely, twisting away from the assault, and bellowed in pain. Dulgin held on to his weapon shaft and went for a ride as it shook him violently, while trying to reach its hand around to pull it free. The stocky Dwarf kept jamming it deeper and deeper inside, and wiggling the axe blade back and forth as he was able to brace himself in the air with the magical spell in effect.

Abawken sprinted over to the Elf, "Are you able to produce a water source?"

An eyebrow rose up at the question, and then he smiled.

He suddenly began waving his arms while speaking a strange tongue to create the spell's effect. A large amount of water poured out of his hands onto the volcanic rock. Steam was rising but before it evaporated the human yelled out another command word, "Mem!" The water formed into an elemental and Abawken brandished his sword in the direction of the giant. It glided over the rock like a wave.

Dulgin was finally grabbed, and then tossed away. He couldn't hold on to the axe and had to let go. Still able to walk on the air, he was not injured by the toss. As he stood back up, the wave of water impacted the legs of the giant. A blast of steam ignited the area, and the group could no longer see it. They felt the ground shake violently beneath them, and heard the creature roar a blood-curdling yell. The steam faded, and lying before them was the slain pet and now-dead monster. From its knees down, it was disintegrated. Black blood gushed out from the stumps and washed over the rock. Its eyes were now dull and lifeless, and black smoke billowed out from its mouth and nose. The fire sword had disappeared and all was quiet.

The group of heroes were by Bridazak's side, and with another healing spell from the Elf he was back on his feet, but still groggy from the encounter. They were all exhausted and tired.

"Look!" Dulgin yelled, pointing across the former battlefield.

They all marvelled at the spectacle. The flames began to die down and within minutes, the Burning Forest was no longer. A dwarven army now stood before the heroes, and they all smiled in victory and embraced one another. The vacant circle where they stood filled in with the living army. Dwarves surrounded them, and cheering erupted throughout the area. Suddenly, one of the dwarves broke through the ranks. The orange-bearded clan member's eyes made contact, and tears welled up instantly.

"Dulgin?"

"El'Korr!"

They ran to each other, colliding armor clashing as they fell to their knees and embraced.

13

On the Move

The new army consisted of a thousand dwarves, a hundred humans, and a handful of the Sheldeen Elves. Every one of this military force was an experienced fighter with clerical spell-casting abilities; this was a very formidable group to launch at King Manasseh. They did not don the same armor or shields like regular infantry, but instead, each wore their own unique vestments in colors ranging across the rainbow. Some were armored in plate mail, others wore woven chain. The dwarves came from several clans throughout Ruauck-El, but none so noteworthy as Hammergold. El'Korr, Dulgin's lost brother, was the leader of the operation, a highly respected commander, and he wore the grandest of any armor. The brilliant plate mail gleamed so brightly that everyone blinked away from the shine of it. There were no blemishes, dirt, smudges, or any marking, as the magic of the armor prevented it. He wielded a dwarven war hammer which dangled at his side, and a shield with his gold hammer crest emblazoned on the front.

El'Korr's second in command was a Dwarf known as Rondee the Wild, due to the wild magic he and the others of his clan, called Smasher, often released—though unpredictably, and not always beneficially, most stayed clear of them. Rondee was the oddest Dwarf the heroes had ever encountered. His speech was erratic with broken common and dwarven intermingled, and his jerky mannerisms would interrupt his movements or speech. He was like a puzzle missing several pieces, but this rare Smasher clan member had earned his rightful position beside Dulgin's brother. Rondee's brown hair and beard were both gnarled and knotted. The only weapon he wielded was an extra small golden hammer that was fastened to his pockmarked leather armor. It was so small Bridazak wondered if it wasn't a weapon at all, but rather, some kind of trophy.

Rondee's group, made up of other Smashers, were the wildest and most tempestuous of all dwarves. A handful of these could deal damage equal to a hundred fighting dwarves; with their chaotic nature, their insatiable determination, and the pure instability of the magic they could release. There were twenty of them here, ready to serve and assigned to protect El'Korr at all costs.

There were a lot of questions going around, as the warriors had been held in stasis for hundreds of years, but they waited patiently for their next move and began to set up camp in newly formed groups, ready to receive instructions. Bridazak and Dulgin sat across from Abawken and Xandahar around a small campfire, ready to council El'Korr, Rondee, and several other commanders, eager to discuss their position. Joining them was Raina, a mysterious Elf mystic in lavender robes, wielding a wooden staff with etchings burned into it from top to bottom. Her face was pale and delicate, with a noticeable scar on her chin, and her whitish-yellow hair was tied back. She had high cheek bones and her ears were pointier than the other elves. Her appearance, at first glance, might communicate frailty, but her emerald eyes and gold pupils told a different story. Many soldiers approached her but none held her gaze, not because of her beauty, but in genuine fear. No other leader stood out more than she.

"We are in your debt," El'Korr addressed the heroes who had freed them, "and we are ready to take on this King Manasseh."

Xan stood and spoke to the gathered, "We believe the Tree resides at Black Rock, and is the power source for the King and his army."

"We did not realize the Tree was the source when we gathered years ago," El'Korr interjected.

"Bridazak's father, Hills Baiulus, suspected it was, and went off alone. He has not been heard of since," Xan continued.

Bridazak looked down to the ground, trying to avoid their stares. His father had died trying to undertake the mission it seemed they were about to attempt.

"The prophecy alludes to the Truth being the foundation of life. The words 'life' and 'the tree', translating from the forgotten language, are interchangeable. It is possible that the Orb of Truth will be the key in destroying the Tree." The Elf paused so everyone could absorb this new revelation.

"Can we see the Orb, Master Bridazak?" El'Korr asked.

Bridazak was lost in his thoughts, recalling the dream he had endured for centuries, picturing an Ordakian family he had conjured and longed for his entire life. He heard someone call his name and peered up at the meeting attendee's stares.

"The Orb? Can we see it?"

"Oh, yes. Of course," he fumbled to get his hand into his pocket, but it wasn't necessary, as the Orb appeared before them all. They stood in awe of the beauty and power that emanated from it, and the sense of peace that penetrated each of them. The flames of their fire flickered high as ever, but they seemed to dim in contrast to the bright glow of the golden sphere, as it spoke in the same booming and authoritative voice.

"I am the Spirit of Truth. He that has ears, let him hear what I am saying. The cities of Ruauck-El have become like harlots. They once were full of my justice, but now murderers abound! Their silver and gold have become dross, their choice wine diluted with water. The rulers are now rebels, companions of thieves; they love bribes and chase after gifts. They do not defend the cause of those without fathers, and the widows in need do not come before them. I have turned my hand against them and will restore the days of old. The City of Righteousness, the Faithful City, will be redeemed with justice, and my penitent ones will rise again. The self-proclaimed mighty men will become tinder, and their work a spark; both will burn together, with no one to quench the fire.

Behold, the day has come to fight for Truth. Strengthen your feeble hands, steady your knees that give way, and say to those with fearful hearts, "Be strong, do not fear; your God, the true God, will come." You will be my hands and feet and through you, the eyes of the blind will be opened and the ears of the deaf unstopped. The Way of Holiness will shine once again and the redeemed will return and walk out the destiny that rightfully belonged to them. Gladness and joy will overtake them, and sorrow and sighing will be no more."

The Orb fell silent, and El'Korr dropped to his knees, stretching out hands toward it. "I have heard the voice of God this night, and vow my allegiance."

It disappeared and Bridazak could feel the Orb back in his pocket. *Could El'Korr be right, and this entire time he had actually held the voice of God?*

"Where is this God, El'Korr?" Bridazak broke the silence of the reverent moment.

The Dwarf stood, "I met him, Bridazak, and that is his voice. I entered the temple at the Holy City early on my path as a cleric, and had a vision during my initiation. He came to me in the form of a Dwarf; one that I cannot describe to this day. In that vision, he told me many things and brought to my memory lost dreams. I continued to hear his voice, until the time of Separation; until the silent years fell upon us. There is no doubt, you hold the voice of God in the Orb of Truth."

Rondee the Wild slammed his gauntleted fist and forearm into his armored chest, "El'Korr spoke tiente beh-moshu death." His randomness snapped everyone out of the heavy conversation. His right leg spasmed like a dog having a nightmare.

"What did he say?" Bridazak whispered to Dulgin.

His dwarven friend shook his head and answered, "El'Korr spoke truth, kiss of death. That Dwarf is one strange individual."

El'Korr smiled and then looked at everyone around him, "It is time to make our plan of attack. The Tree must be destroyed in order to bring this rebel King down. We will have the element of surprise. Our army will march to Black Rock and bust through their front door. They will not know what hit them!"

"There is another way," Xan broke in.

El'Korr's speech to bolster his leaders seemed to dissipate at the interjection from the Sheldeen Elf. "Share your thoughts with us Xandahar. What other way?"

"The Dragon Caves. They lead underneath the castle."

"Impossible for our army to get inside. We will be slaughtered."

"No, but a small group can go, while the main force distracts the enemies above. If we can get to the Tree and destroy it, we will weaken Manasseh's forces enough for the main force to launch their attack."

130

The proposal lingered in the air and the Dwarf leader looked at everyone for a long moment.

"I think this might work Xandahar. Who do you have in mind for this small group?"

"Hills Baiulus suggested that the caves would lead him to the Tree so it would be best to have Bridazak take the Orb. I cannot force anyone to go. It is only my suggestion."

"What say you, Bridazak?" El'Korr asked.

"I'll go," he said, standing up.

"Where Master Bridazak goes, I follow," Abawken responded.

"This blundering fool can't go anywhere without me," Dulgin came to the Ordakian's side and brought a smile to his face.

"I wish to accompany the Orb," Xan added himself to the group.

El'Korr studied each of them intently. "I am appointing Rondee to this group as well."

The Wild Dwarf leapt into the air where he stood, waving his arms around frantically, as though a bee was attacking him. He was saying something but no one could understand him. El'Korr grabbed his shoulders to settle him down. Words were finally discernible as he spoke with loss of breath, "We cannde separate. Chicken banshee!"

El'Korr paused, "You speak truth, te chaver."

As odd as it was to wonder about the erratic tongue of Rondee, they all understood the main point; El'Korr would be joining them.

"Who do you place in charge of the army, then?" Raina finally spoke.

"You will lead," El'Korr stepped closer to her and gave her a smile.

"It will be an honor," she bowed. Everyone seemed to approve the dwarven leader's choice, except Xan, Bridazak noticed. The Ordakian was adept at reading people and there was definitely a disconnect between these two Sheldeen Elves, not worth bringing up to anyone, but something to make note of moving forward. *"Perhaps they were once lovers,"* he thought to himself.

The dozen leaders disbanded with El'Korr's instructions to rest and be ready at first light to start their journey. Bridazak intercepted El'Korr in private.

"Sir, I wanted to let you know personally that I intend to rescue my friend Spilf, who is being held captive."

"I heard from the others that you might. Bridazak, you can't be sure that he is still alive. Manasseh could have just planted that information to bait you and draw you out."

"I know, but I have to find out for sure. I'm hoping to have your support."

"Of course you have it, but our main goal is to destroy the Tree, and then afterward we can set a rescue in motion. Agreed?"

Bridazak hesitated a moment, and then nodded his agreement. He knew if the opportunity presented itself, he would find his friend first, with or without anyone's help. El'Korr strode into the darkness while Bridazak lingered by the campfire for several minutes, contemplating the future, and the words that Xan had said to him; *"I tend to think of risk as faith."*

On the move, the army marched through the barren volcanic rock with resolve and determination. Bleak surroundings of dead terrain were ignored by the men; being locked up for hundreds of years had only strengthened this fearsome medley of troops. Their steady movement resounded like the thundering of horse's hooves—the cacophony of different colors shimmered like a cascading rainbow as they marched, each warrior so individual in appearance but all moving as united. Lines of ten Dwarfs walked in perfect unison, and were only a day away from their goal. Their quest of battle was halted a few centuries ago, but now the leash of bondage was broken and they moved with a righteous fury.

Over the course of their march, the wild dwarves discovered an added bonus that each member of the infantry now possessed—due to the curse they had endured, they were now immune to fire, and could summon it at will.

On the third and final day of travel, they reached the departure point. The main army would approach the castle at sunset and then begin their assault. El'Korr's group was ready to split off and head toward the Dragon Caves; it would take them a few hours of travel to reach the opening.

"Raina, you are now in charge. Rondee has instructed his elite to guard you as if you were me. Let Manasseh and his men pay. Do not hold back and by the grace of God, we will meet you inside."

"They will feel it and you will hear our arrival."

El'Korr shouted to his men, "It is time!"

"There it was again," Bridazak thought. The message he received in his dream those many days ago are now coming to fulfillment.

A cheer erupted, loud voices thundering in triumph, as weapons clashed against shields and boots stomped the ground. A chant slowly birthed itself amongst them, "Malehk El'Korr! Malehk El'Korr! Malehk El'Korr!" A sign of honor, the remaining Dwarves of Ruauck-El increased in volume, to announce to the world their new king.

"You ready, young Bridazak?" El'Korr asked while the united chorus continued.

He sighed, "Ready as I ever will be."

El'Korr returned his attention back to his loyal army, but Bridazak stared off into the distance of the arid, volcanic, rocky terrain, and spotted black smoke rising many miles away. The gloomy environment so different from his days of adventuring in cities, towns, and villages while he navigated marked pathways and roads.

"What have you gotten yourself into?" he thought to himself. He pulled out the Varouche feather to remind him of Spilf. A slight smile came upon his face at the thought of rescuing his lost friend and showing him the Orb of Truth. *"Spilf, I was able to open it. It is the voice of God."*

14

The Dragon Caves

They headed toward the rising smoke in the distance. Once they found the source of the grey soot, it was immediately identifiable as the legendary Dragon Caves.

"We're going in there?" Bridazak asked in a concerned tone, though he already knew the answer.

"Were you expecting a warm inn to greet your hairy feet, ya blundering fool?"

The cave entrance looked menacing and everyone could feel the cold chill of evil in the area. It didn't faze the fighters in the group, compared with the uneasiness that Bridazak felt. There before them symbolized the ultimate step of faith—entering the mouth of the beast. He was glad his comrades were by his side, until he remembered Billwick's words—he was told he would have to sacrifice all. He looked around at them and realized each of these friends he had come to love had signed on for this assignment because deep down they all believed in something bigger than themselves. He carried the Orb; they had all seen the power of the voice of God displayed. Everything seemed so surreal, thinking back to the night he received the mysterious box that cradled the then—unknown Orb, and now they steadily marched toward fulfilling an unknown destiny, where each step brought them deeper into danger. Spilf could already be dead, for all he knew, and more of them... he pushed the thought from his mind and instead said a silent prayer, *"Oh, God, please help us all."* Warmth cascaded down his arms and then wrapped around his entire body, and a peace beyond understanding infiltrated his heart and mind.

The cave entrance had the rough appearance of a dragon's head. Small crags represented the eyes, while the open mouth displayed jagged pieces of obsidian, to reflect the teeth. Smoke slowly wafted out from inside the massive mouth. The band of heroes nestled between the lava rocks in one of the many small crevices throughout the area, waiting to see if there was any movement before heading inside. It was midday when they arrived, and sparse clouds blocked most of the sun's warming rays.

"There," Abawken keenly spotted and pointed it out to the others.

"Sneaky bastards," responded Dulgin.

"Dragon-kind guards. Small reptilian spawn—very well hidden. Look at the rock teeth at the entrance and you will see them move slightly," El'Korr added.

Bridazak spotted them next. "How do we sneak past them?"

"Who said anything about sneaking?" Dulgin retorted.

"We should try none the less, Master Dulgin," Abawken responded.

"I have an idea," Xan grinned.

The dark shapes of the Dragoons, as they are called, stepped out from their hidden positions sooner than Xan expected. There were six of them in all—three on each side of the entrance. Abawken, in shackles, walked next to him as they approached, with El'Korr and Dulgin to the right and left of them and Bridazak and Rondee bringing up the rear. The illusion spell was working perfectly as the Elf had designed. The dwarves and Bridazak were magically transformed to look like the dragonkin, while Xan and Abawken were shackled as their prisoners. They just needed to get close enough for the element of surprise.

Now twenty feet away, the guards called out to them in their native tongue; a slithering hiss sound. The heroes couldn't understand the dialect and did not respond, nor did they stop, but continued to march closer. Bridazak heard scratching noises and glanced over to Rondee. The Wild Dwarf's hand was shaking violently across his chest, distorting the illusion. One of the Dragoons brought up his spear, quizzically watching the unannounced party arriving, slightly bending his head in bewilderment. The spell could no longer cloak Rondee's spastic movements—the guard quickly advanced as the illusion dissipated and the Wild Dwarf's true appearance was suddenly revealed. The remaining disguises vanished as the group sprang to action to respond, though for the rest of the dragonkin, the surprise was mostly intact.

El'Korr's hammer whirled through the air and hit the alert sentry, still fifteen feet away. The creature's chest caved in at the impact, like a wicker basket at the mercy of a rock. The mighty hammer flew magically back into his ruddy hands, where he unleashed it once more—another fell as it smashed into its skull.

Dulgin charged the one in front of him, quickly cleaving its leg off, and continued to sprint, slamming his head into the next Dragoon's gut. It fell to its knees with a grunt and loss of breath. Dulgin's one-limbed victim was barely able to let out a scream as Abawken's scimitar beheaded it. Brownish-red blood spewed out of the separated head and leg.

"Xan!" Bridazak yelled.

Xan realized very quickly Bridazak had an arrow ready to launch, and released it just as the Elf dodged out of the way. It zipped by his head, and he watched the tip and shaft bury itself into one of the remaining creatures. Bridazak reached into his quiver when he saw Rondee hit the ground on his stomach and reach out with his hands. He aimed his next arrow in search of the attacker, but realized the Dwarf's body stretched out three times his usual length. This small, bulky mass of a Dwarf miraculously thinned the further he stretched. Rondee grappled the Dragoon's legs and brought him down to the ground.

There were two remaining enemies—one with the air knocked out and the other entangled in Rondee's grasp. Between Dulgin, El'Korr and Abawken, it didn't take long to dispatch them. The last gurgle of life expelled from their bodies and then all was quiet.

Rondee remained in his thin, elongated form on the ground. El'Korr looked down at his proclaimed bodyguard, "How are you supposed to guard me like that?"

Rondee looked up, "Ruffled feathers dankosh biesto?"

"Come on. Let's pick him up and bring him inside. We don't want any flying dragons to spot us," El'Korr commanded as he helped Rondee up.

Having pulled the Dragoons inside, they hid them among the rocks, and began to move into the considerably cooler caves, each booted step echoing down the immense passageway. The occasional sound of steam pockets releasing pressurized vapor from deep in the darkness gave them a hint of the danger before them. Black, shiny rock lined the cave walls and path as it twisted beyond their vision.

Ten minutes had passed when finally Rondee's body reverted back to his normal size. The group was now ready to traverse the Dragon Caves in search of the Tree. A burst of flame was produced as El'Korr raised his war hammer up like a torch. "This fire trick is pretty handy," he mused, beginning to descend.

"We have five to six hours before Raina and the army reach the castle. The Tree should be directly underneath, and once it is destroyed, we will make our way to the surface and meet up with everyone to finish the battle," El'Korr laid out the plan as he walked, "and," he emphasized, "we will be rescuing Spilf." That brought a smile to Bridazak's face, but it was quickly wiped away when they all heard a large roar echoing down the fifty-foot-wide cave. There was no telling how close it was.

"What exactly is down here, Master Xandahar?"

"Well, I've heard it's black dragons, but no one knows for sure."

"Acid, then." El'Korr nodded.

"Yes. I've prepared a spell for us to help endure it if one was to breathe on us, but it is not able to withstand the full force of its power."

Dulgin chimed in, "Cast away, Elfy. We will take all the protection we can get, at this point."

"Dragons are crafty—very intelligent, very powerful. We must be careful," El'Korr said. Xan took a step back as the group gathered together to receive the benefit of the incantation. Dulgin questioned him after he finished.

"How do we know it works?"

"I would suggest not finding out to begin with," Xan replied. Each of them took the effect of the spell in faith and they continued on with their weapons ready.

Three hours had passed as they made their way deeper into the Dragon Caves, discovering several pockets of lava tubes branching out from the main cave along the way. They suspected those led to the Dragoon's various lairs. An occasional distant roar of a dragon resounded, but the only other sounds were the drips of calcium-filled water onto the rocks. They finally reached an opening to a chamber that was beyond measure. They stood on the ledge overlooking an underground valley, awestruck by the breathtaking scene. Fingers of light from above penetrated the darkness with sharp distinguished lines, fading as they reached toward the floor below them. Clusters of crystal shards in various heights littered the cavern floor—some as tall as a horse, a few rivalling an inn. Echoes of flapping wings resounded further in the darkness—dragon wings.

El'Korr dismissed his flame. The light coming in from above was sufficient, and they didn't want to attract the scaly creatures to their location. Abawken jumped off the ledge and floated down by the power of his sword. It was at least a five-hundred foot drop.

"Does anyone have rope?" Bridazak asked.

"We won't need any," El'Korr responded.

"How are we planning to get down then?" The Ordakian's face contorted a bit.

"We are jumping, just like the human." El'Korr pulled out a bone scroll case and slid out the parchment that was rolled inside. He began to repeat the holy words that were inscribed on it. Each of them suddenly felt as light as a feather. Rondee and El'Korr jumped from the ledge first, and Xan right after them. Dulgin waited for his friend.

"We will go together," the Dwarf said.

"You mean you're scared of heights and wanted me to hold your hand?"

"I don't know what yer talkin about, ya blundering fool. Let's go."

Bridazak and Dulgin edged closer, and the Ordakian noticed his friend stiffen, his hand squeezing his forearm as they floated down together. "You can open your eyes, Dulgin."

"Just gettin' a little shut eye. Now leave me be."

At the bottom, they inspected the huge crystal rock groupings throughout the area. The natural light from above met the stones and refracted out, sending colorful patterns in all directions. Deep blues and greens splayed across the volcanic rock. With such beauty it was hard to imagine that evil dragons infested the area.

"I suspect there will be another opening across from here, so be on the lookout," Xan said as they began to head out.

Two more hours of exerted travel in the dimly lit environment had passed when they came to the edge of a large pool of dark water. Several formations of obsidian rock jutted out of the surface. Any view of the other side was blocked, so they agreed that moving along the edge of the underground lake would be the best option. Bubbling water gurgled in several spots, releasing the strong smell of bitter minerals.

Bridazak's long history of mastering his thieving instincts told him they were being watched, and he repeatedly checked behind them.

Dulgin noticed, "What is it?" he whispered.

"A strange feeling that something is behind me, but I don't see anything."

"It seems quiet."

"That's what worries me. I haven't heard the scurry of any animal for quite some time. Just the echo of dripping water."

Dulgin noticed three of Bridazak's magical arrows, which were slung over the Dak's shoulder, pulse a soft red aura. "Your arrows. They are glowing."

Bridazak withdrew one, and Ordakian writing he had not seen before sprang to life. "Dragon," he whispered.

The Dwarf alerted the others ahead of them with a quick snap of his stubby fingers. Each of them put their backs to the rock crystal they had been edging along, looking in all directions. Bridazak moved to one of the jagged gem structures and silently notched the magical arrow. Dulgin backed into an obsidian formation directly across from him.

The light from the arrow intensified, and the Ordakian saw a slight movement in the reflection of the crystal. He looked closer—a black dragon head was coming out of the dark water just behind him. It took in the air to unleash its mighty breath weapon.

"Look out!" Bridazak screamed, diving behind the crystal. A blast of misty acidic steam poured out of its gaping maw. Dulgin witnessed Bridazak engulfed, but when the rock he was leaning against started to move, he realized it was not a rock at all, but another dragon, camouflaged.

"Ah great, just my luck," he said under his breath, bringing his axe around to chop away at the monstrosity.

These pearly-black monsters stood forty feet tall. Their indeterminable length melded into the shadows as they prepared their assault. Two sets of ebony eyes and large, two-foot-long horns adorned their heads. Leathery, translucent wings with menacing claws stretched wide as they puffed up their darkly scaled chests to intimidate their prey. Their hind legs were muscular and their thick, charcoal tails slithered around, waiting to strike with the barbed end.

Water fell like a violent rainstorm, cascading from the dragon rising up behind where Bridazak had once stood. They focused their attention on the beast in the water, each hoping for a sign of what happened to the carrier of the Orb.

El'Korr launched his dwarven war hammer, impacting the side of its massive torso and causing it to flinch. The hammer was back in his hands ready to be hurled once again. The dragon's head turned to face them.

"Continue on with that one!" Xan yelled aloud. "We need to put it down quickly!" He moved toward where the second monster engaged Dulgin.

Rondee the Wild ran directly toward the one in the lake while pulling forth his tiny golden hammer. Before he reached the edge, he jumped straight toward the darkest water, and instead of plummeting into the unknown depth, his foot landed on a magically conjured stone step. With each stride another step appeared, until he finally closed in on the monster. The black dragon turned just in time to see the Wild Dwarf approaching in reckless abandon, but it was too late for the beast, as Rondee's weapon miraculously enlarged to a maul worthy of a titan. Everyone heard the crack as his hammer slammed into the left side of its head; the horn broke off and the eye gruesomely dangled from the socket, blood pouring from the opening. Rondee continued his stride and was now sitting on top of it, as it reeled back and gave a horrific bellow from the pain of his blow.

Abawken was also on the move. Blade in hand, he ran on top of the water. His first attack cut through the initial protective layer of scales.

Xan easily located the second dragon, following a trail of shattered crystals and the sounds of its agitated roar, and Dulgin's taunts at every miss. He knew the Dwarf couldn't keep on the defensive forever, he rushed to help him.

Seconds had elapsed, but it already felt like an eternity. Bridazak was still nowhere to be seen. They longed to assist him, but knew the only way for that to happen was to take out these formidable threats as quickly as possible. They secretly hoped the Orb had protected him beyond what the acid protection spell could do.

Another thwap of El'Korr's powerful hammer caused several scales to shatter. The partially blinded dragon began to flap its huge wings to fly away from the painful onslaught, quickly wrapping its tail around the human fighter and flinging him away with tremendous power. Rondee was trying to balance himself enough to get another strike in, but the dragon, in a panic, moved too erratically. Huge gusts of air washed over El'Korr and Abawken as it gained altitude within the cavernous underground valley. Rondee was almost bucked off, but the wild magic ability that raged inside him involuntarily sprang large metal spikes from his legs. They impaled the scaled monster at the top of its neck, which triggered a guttural hiss, and finally granted the Wild Dwarf some stability. He was getting ready to swing his mighty hammer, but before he could, the tail yanked him from his established position. Rondee's spikes ripped out of the beast's neck and caused another painful outburst. He was flung away and splashed into the dark water below. The black dragon was now high above, and again began to intake the air around him.

"He's going to breathe!" Abawken shouted, running for cover.

"Dammit!" El'Korr responded while also taking refuge.

Before it unleashed its deadly mist, Bridazak rolled out from behind a crystal shard with his arrow notched.

"My turn," Bridazak whispered as he released the special arrow.

It struck the chest and exploded on impact. There was a violent screeching as the dragon plummeted into the water below. A mighty splash caused waves to roll into the dry chamber. Smoke from Bridazak's powerful blast billowed up, and parts of the dragon could be seen sprinkled on jutting rocks or floating atop the water.

El'Korr and Abawken came out of hiding to see the aftermath. The human sprinted out on the water to retrieve Rondee who thrashed wildly on the surface, as he could not swim.

"We need to help Dulgin!" his brother shouted.

Bridazak turned, beginning to notch a second dragon arrow, to start making his way toward them, but quickly spotted Dulgin coming their way in a slow walk. The lumbering behemoth trailed right behind him, moving cautiously.

"Dulgin, are you alright?" Bridazak asked, never taking his determined eyes off of the dragon, his arrow trained carefully on its every move.

The others had caught up now, only to discover what Bridazak already saw: the approaching dragon had Xan captured inside of its mouth. The Elf was pinned down between its teeth; the slightest pressure would mean certain death. The massive black beast brought its head low so they could verify Xan was still alive, and then rose back up again.

"Thank you for taking care of that bitch!" The dragon spoke inside each of their minds.

"If you let him go then we won't kill ya," El'Korr retorted.

"I have no intention of killing him, or any of you for that matter. I want to make a deal."

"I had him good and tired until Elfy got too close," Dulgin said in defeat.

"What do you want then?" El'Korr asked.

"I will give you back your Elf once you agree to parlay with me."

"Parlay about what, Blacky?" Dulgin scoffed.

Its grey, massive teeth pressed in ever so slightly, causing Xan to groan under the tremendous pressure.

El'Korr stepped closer, "Fine, let us talk, but release him now."

The black dragon lowered its scaled armored head and opened its jowls. Xan scrambled out and hustled to his friends. The creature raised its long serpentine neck and sat in confidence.

"Are you okay?" El'Korr questioned Xan.

"Aside from its bad breath, I am fine."

El'Korr returned his focus back to the dragon, "What is it you want to talk about?" The group was ready for any hostile reaction. Bridazak kept his arrow at the ready.

"I want to make a deal."

"We're listening," El'Korr responded.

"In return for safe passage through my domain, I require you to kill the Guardian."

"Guardian? What guardian?"

"The one who guards the Tree. I will take you to it."

"What's in it for you? How does killing this guardian help you?"

"Once the Guardian is taken care of, I can take my rightful position as leader of the dragons—the Doonkah."

Bridazak jumped in, "What is it, and why don't you and the other dragons kill it yourself?"

"You keep those arrows ready, Halfling. Impressive, for such a small creature. As far as the rest of us, we are unable to attack it due to the power and protection of the Tree. I will tell the other dragons in the area to back away, so you can deal solely with the Guardian. You must be quick; do not delay once you see it."

El'Korr was thinking about the deal. The rest of the heroes waited for the dwarven king's response. Bridazak took a bold step forward with the Seeker and magical arrow trained on it, "El'Korr, we don't have to agree to anything. We know what this arrow can do."

Surprised by the Orb carrier's challenge, El'Korr stood next to Bridazak, "We have the advantage now, and if you value your life then you will lead us to the Tree. We don't make deals with dragons."

It laughed heartily inside their minds, *"Fools. I give you what you are looking for and yet you still resist me."*

"You no longer have any leverage."

"Oh, leverage is what I need? Well then, let me present to you my full leverage. I can teleport to Manasseh's door and warn him of your little army of dwarves."

El'Korr warily narrowed his eyes. He peered back at his band of heroes and then into Bridazak's eyes, who waited for his response. El'Korr returned his focus on the black dragon, "Once this guardian is killed and you have taken over as the leader of the dragons, I want your kind to pull out of the battle above. You believe we are capable enough to handle the Guardian, so I want to sweeten the deal for us."

"Hah! Now it is you that has no leverage! But, I have been under Manasseh's hand for far too long. I will take your request into consideration. Do we have a deal?"

"Not much of a deal, but we have one."

15

The Guardian

"The army will be engaging King Manasseh's forces anytime now. I suspect we are right below the castle. Blacky, as my brother calls him, says the Tree is in the next chamber, and anyone approaching it will summon the Guardian. Any thoughts?" El'Korr asked the huddled group.

"We need to protect Bridazak and the Orb, so he needs to stay behind us, preferably at a high point with his arrows, while we take on the critter," Dulgin suggested.

"Agreed. The protector of the Tree must be a dragon of some kind, as the black dragon alluded to Bridazak's arrows," Abawken added.

"It's going to be one dead dragon after we're done with it," Dulgin clenched his fist in anticipation.

"Rondee will go first and trigger the Guardian to show itself, while the rest of us spread out through the chamber. We don't want to be caught in any dragon breath situation. Hit it with all you have, boys. Don't hold back."

They all nodded in agreement and began to walk further down the large rock tunnel, Rondee in the lead. Everyone was on high alert, looking side to side, turning back to look behind them, and peering up towards the ceiling. A short hundred yards later, they reached the opening.

As they entered the massive chamber, made entirely of the same obsidian rock, they each felt a distinguishable sense of foreboding that caused their skin to tingle. Cut columns carved from the walls rose beyond their sight into the darkness. In the center stood a stone pyramid twenty feet tall with steps on one side leading to the pinnacle. On top was the Tree—a black, gnarled, leafless skeleton, its branches twisting out in all directions. An oily, opalescent sheen wrapped around the trunk and branches, like a disease. An eerie blue mist hugged the ground at the base of the Tree, and traversed the stairs, surrounding the structure it was planted on. The mystical vapor weaved through a graveyard below, and gave off an occasional flash of light accompanied by a muffled crackle. The smell of death and decay was prevalent.

"Are those..." Bridazak hesitated to state the obvious.

"Skeletal remains," El'Korr barely answered, as his focus was on the horrific, defiled gift to the world of Ruauck-El. The fallen state of the once glorious tree churned his stomach. He felt violated at its sight, anger beginning to boil inside.

"Looks like Manasseh made this a sacrifice site to the Tree," Abawken surmised.

"Or this guardian has been well fed," Dulgin added.

"Dear God Almighty," Xan was the last to enter, and whispered at the sight of the disgraced relic atop the pyramid. It pained him to see it in this state. The petals of crystal were no more, the life was drained, and he felt the cancerous evil inside of it as waves of dark energy bombarded his heart.

"Stay focused, Xan. Everyone spread out. Rondee, kel-forteh," El'Korr commanded. "Bridazak, stay back and cover us. Make your arrows count. Xan, you will support us with your spells."

Bridazak continued to stare at the endless pile of blanched bones. Had his father come this far in his quest? Had he... met his end, here? *"Bapah,"* he whispered, surprising himself. He couldn't remember ever having used that word—the Ordakian for Father.

Suddenly, breaking him from his thoughts, the earth moved beneath them. They heard loud thuds and noticed dust falling from the darkness above with each concussion.

"What was that?" Bridazak asked.

"That was Raina, saying hello to King Manasseh. Give them hell, Raina. Now, let's do our part." He refocused his attention and moved away from the Ordakian.

As the explosions continued above, they all focused on Rondee near the base of the pyramid, stepping on the many skulls that littered the floor surrounding it. The mist shifted with every step he took. It chilled his skin, and the smell of death intensified. He fearlessly took the first step onto the stone stairs leading to the Tree. From behind him he heard the rattling of the bleached white bones.

"The Guardian is here," the black dragon said within their minds.

A dozen skeletons reformed as they stood, and then moved toward Rondee.

"Skeletons, bah!" El'Korr laughed, pulling forth his holy symbol—an item he had received at the Holy City temple. He yelled, "Shaubiste," holding the clerical piece toward the walking dead. An unseen pulse of power waved out, hitting and shattering the skeletons into bone shards.

Another group of skeletal remains sprouted up, and then another. Rondee was still on the first step, but now completely surrounded by the undead. He revealed his yellowed, chipped teeth in a snarl, and then began casting a spell.

"Look out!" Bridazak signaled above them. The Ordakian spotted a distorted movement within the mist behind Rondee. He could not make out what it was, but he was sure it was descending the stone steps. The others looked around at each other to get confirmation of Bridazak's alert, but saw nothing. The arrow in his grasp was glowing brightly and giving the strongest vibration he had yet seen from the magic. He quickly notched it and lined up his shot. He knew instinctively it was there. A voice inside his head settled his mind. It was the Orb saying, *"Trust me."* He released his arrow. It soared through the chamber and ignited into the brightest light the heroes had ever seen, but was somehow soothing to their eyes. The light illuminated the entire room, and there before them they could all now see what Bridazak initially spotted. The once invisible dragon hovered above the Tree—a dragon like no other.

"It's a Dracolich!" El'Korr yelled.

The arrow had launched into the sternum of the skeletal body and exploded on impact, so only Bridazak noticed its invisible bone tail had stabbed Rondee from behind. Blood shot out of the wound as the tip penetrated cleanly through the Dwarf, leaving behind a gaping hole under his left shoulder, but narrowly missing his heart and lung, thanks to Bridazak's timing. The wild magic contained inside him burst as he flailed to the ground. A sudden rain cloud appeared above the skeletal warriors, and as the water droplets hit the dry bones, they began to smoke and hiss, like water striking a hot surface. The undead felt no pain, but they soon collapsed from the holy effect of the acidic rain pummelling them. Rondee flinched at each pelt of the wild magic he released; he was fortunate enough to be on the outside edge of the caustic torrent.

A chilling roar echoed throughout the room, filling their ears. The non-living dragon was still active, though several pieces of its bone structure were now missing. A bluish flame surrounded it, with intense light flaring from inside the empty eye sockets. It was a dragon larger than the black ones earlier, except it had no flesh. Its leathery wings were shredded, dangling from the cartilage.

"It's too powerful for me to turn it!" declared El'Korr.

"Somebody get to Rondee!" Bridazak shouted.

"I'm on my way," Xan responded, running to assist the writhing, bloodied Dwarf.

Abawken flanked the Dracolich by utilizing the power of his sword to walk on air. El'Korr cast a spell which caused him to rise up in the air. An aerial combat was their best chance to take the advantage back from the undead monster. The human fighter was soon dodging several attacks from its claws, wing bucks, and the powerful maw filled with sharp and broken teeth. A deafening snap of the ossein jaw rang throughout the chamber. Abawken spent his time defensively with no counter strike, and El'Korr understood the reasoning: his mighty warhammer was more effective in smashing bone than a scimitar slashing at it; they had found their strategy. Another crushing blow came when he hurled it while still moving higher into the air. Several fragments from the dragon's neck fell to the ground below.

Xan reached Rondee just in time. He quickly summoned healing powers and laid his hands upon the life-threatening wound. The gaping puncture soon began to fill in with flesh, tendons were repaired, and it was sealed with a new layer of skin. His left arm and part of his leg were pockmarked by several acid burns, but he would survive those for now. Rondee appeared to be himself again and said, "Fhelp rocks glin glitter." Xan cocked his head; he couldn't grasp the jumbled jargon, but understood the gratitude behind the Dwarf's smile.

As Xan helped Rondee back to his feet, one of the skeletons attacked, raking the Elf's back. He turned in pain to see several more of the bleached figures coming toward them. He shouted out the same word El'Korr had said earlier, "Shaubiste!" His clerical training had given him the ability to turn and destroy the lesser undead. The skeletons were blasted back and exploded into dust particles.

Bridazak held his last arrow, made specially for dragon-kind, waiting for the best shot possible. He scanned the battle below; Abawken and El'Korr still engaged it head on, Dulgin battled more of the skeletal army, and Xan put down another group of them with Rondee back up on his feet and by his side. Bridazak suddenly felt very alone; an inexplicable chill of separation caused his heart to race and his breathing to become more sporadic, until a garbled voice snapped him back into focus—Rondee was casting a spell. His torso swayed from side to side and his arms waved sporadically in all directions. There was a low groan coming from him that became louder each second.

"Shaza bocktel geesta!" He finally shouted. An eruption one-hundred feet up along the wall sent huge fragments of volcanic rock coming down. Massive pieces of the columned wall now descended.

"Look out!" Xan yelled to them.

Abawken and El'Korr scurried and dodged the larger rock, but were grazed by several other smaller debris. The Dracolich was hit multiple times, as it was too large to maneuver away. One of its wings completely snapped off, like a huge branch cracking off of a tree. The behemoth pitched sideways and was hit by another large piece of rock, which caved in its torso. It was pushed further down by each impact, but it still remained in magical flight, showing no signs of weariness.

"What in dwarven crap is going on?" Dulgin scrambled around the falling rubble. Large chips destroyed several of the walking bone warriors that had sprouted around him.

Another roar from the Dracolich sounded in the cavern as the rock pieces shattered. Bone and rock dust enveloped everyone on the ground below, and rose up into the air like a billowy cloud. Bridazak's vantage point allowed him to see the dragon turn invisible again while the others battled the dust now around them. He suddenly noticed a protective, blue-hued force field around the Tree, brightening a bit with each impact as the rocks bounced away harmlessly.

Abawken and El'Korr pushed higher into the air to be able to see the area more clearly. Xan and Rondee could only wait for the dust to settle. They had their hands over their mouths, their eyes squinting against the powder. The smell of rock and bone infiltrated their noses and they couldn't see more than five feet in front of them.

"It's not dead yet! It went invisible!" Bridazak shouted to them.

Some of them were coughing. Dulgin was closest to Bridazak but still deep into the room. "We've got it on the run!" Dulgin yelled.

"I don't think so," Bridazak whispered quietly, arrow still readied, eyes carefully peering through the dust. "Where are you?" he whispered.

A slight shift in the dust behind Xan and Rondee drew Bridazak's focus, but it was too late. A blast of electrical energy shot out from the Dracolich as it became visible once again. The Elf and Dwarf convulsed wildly; blue and white sparks shot out from them like arcing static, too charged to have been extinguished by their bodies alone. A bright light once again filled the room at the release of Bridazak's arrow. It slammed into the eerie eye socket and then detonated, splinters of bone launching violently in all directions. Then it was quiet. Remnants of electrical shock intermittently crackled over Rondee and Xan's crumpled bodies. Bridazak held his breath. The Draclich now laid motionless, but he did not feel at ease.

Bridazak lowered his bow. Dulgin yelled back to him, "Good shot!"

"*Yes, a fine shot indeed, Halfling,*" came the voice of the black dragon again inside his head. Before he could turn around, the scaled beast had him inside its mouth, the same way he'd held Xan.

Dulgin responded to the sudden attack, "Let'em go, Blacky!"

The black dragon pulled Bridazak back into the darkness.

"*I changed my mind. The Halfling, once presented to King Manasseh, is a bigger prize.*"

The group hustled, Rondee and Xan still sluggish, to the open cavern perch to intercept it, but it was too late, as the dark betrayer blinked from sight and teleported itself, along with Bridazak, out of their reach and directly into their greatest enemy's evil hands.

Dulgin screamed as he continued to charge the vacated location. He fell to his knees and raised his father's axe while yelling uncontrollably in pure rage.

"He's gone. Dammit! We need to get the Orb back," El'Korr stated.

"We need to be gettin Bridazak back is what you meant, right brother?" Dulgin snipped.

"But how? Manasseh will have him," Xan questioned.

El'Korr responded quickly to soothe and control the volatile situation, "Then that is our new target. Our only option is to infiltrate the castle and find Bridazak and Manasseh."

"It's time to go for the head of this serpent," Dulgin proclaimed as he stood back to his feet.

"But Manasseh is getting his power from the Tree. Without the Orb we can't defeat him," Xan added.

"I don't care!" Dulgin retaliated. "Abawken, back me up on this."

"Master Dulgin is right. We must try. I would lay down my life to rescue him."

"Bridazak didn't come all this way on his own. We must have faith that the Orb will protect him, and hopefully grant us a little luck along the way. An answer will reveal itself in due time," the Dwarf leader finished.

"During the battle, Master El'Korr and I spotted a narrow stairway on the other side. We suspect it leads into the castle somewhere," stated Abawken.

Dulgin headed out, mumbling as he passed, "Somewhere is a great start; let's go."

They crossed the chamber to the stone steps. El'Korr came alongside Dulgin as they walked. Dulgin walked hurriedly and paid his brother no attention. El'Korr kept in step with him and there was an awkward silence until finally El'Korr began, "...Brother?"

"He's my best friend and we need to be gettin him back, Orb or not."

"We will, but we have to be smart."

Dulgin abruptly stopped and glared into El'Korr's eyes to show his bitterness behind his words. "I don't have time to be smart! He is—" Dulgin's voice started to crack with emotion, "a brother I didn't have."

"I'm still your older brother," El'Korr finally broke the intensity, "but because of you, I'm alive and I'm back. Things will be different now Dulgin, and I hope you can forgive me." Dulgin paused, noticing the others moving further away, as he wondered what to say or do next.

"Bah, older my ass. You never aged in that damn curse you fell into. I look older than you now."

"When our father left us in search of the Mountain of Gold, I took on the role of protecting you. I never imagined I would, in a sense, wind up doing the same as our father. I never wished to abandon you for anything. Now though, I see that in trying to shelter you, I have done you a great disservice. You have become a mighty fighter on your own. I no longer walk in front of you, but instead, walk beside you, my brother. Your pains are my pains, your goals are my goals, your victories are my victories. Let us unite, and let nothing separate us again."

Dulgin held his gaze until finally embracing him. The two mighty warriors walked side by side, and caught up to the others soon after, both seeming a little taller, now. Abawken stared at Dulgin's moist eyes.

"Cave allergies," the Dwarf retorted as he walked by.

Abawken smiled.

16

Black Rock

Raina stood, dauntlessly surveying the area from the precipice above the expansive ravine they had been traveling through. Before them waited Black Rock Castle, the menacing tower rising hundreds of feet above the obsidian walls. The base of the fortress appeared to have been fashioned from the lava rock itself, and indeed showed the great power of King Manasseh. There were thousands of men in training outside the walls along the edge of the Desert of Guilt. The ashen grey stretched for miles—the marker for those insane enough to enter Kerrith Ravine. Several small, black, mounted dragons practiced maneuvers in the distance. Only a few hundred yards of open terrain separated her army from Manasseh's. The odds were against her; they were outnumbered ten to one. *"Perfect,"* she thought to herself.

"I am ready," she said aloud to one of the wild dwarves standing beside her. "Direct the men to engage once my spell has been cast."

She stepped up onto the lip of an opening that led down into the ashen desert. A slight breeze caused her hair to flutter back and her robes to push into her sleek, elven body. She raised her wooden staff into the air above her head and began to whisper words of the arcane. "Kel vas torak-vue sheltite ke-ahmbet!" Sparse clouds overhead quickly gathered together and became dark. A flash of lightning struck from within. Her eyelids fluttered as the sky opened up, revealing a wrathful hailstorm of fire. The initial stares from the humans below turned to yelling, then screaming directives to take cover. Raina opened her eyes to witness the beginning onslaught coming for King Manasseh and his army. The humans were forced to take cover and be spread out or be showered with the ignited meteors pouring out of the sky. Hundreds from the ground and air now writhed on fire, and the smell of burnt flesh and sulphur reached Raina's nose.

"Geetock! Begin your assault!"

"Yes, Master Raina. It will be our pleasure," the Wild Dwarf responded.

"Do not move to the walls until I give you the sign," she added.

"Understood, my lady."

Geetock gave a shrill whistle to alert the dwarven army to move into the region. The booted footsteps poured out from the ravine into the Desert of Guilt. Twenty-two formations of warriors in groups of fifty, plus a group consisting of just the wild dwarves, fanned out and made their way to their enemy. Fifteen of El'Korr's personal bodyguards charged in as the tip of the arrow. The remaining four dwarves stayed with Raina along the ridge.

"It is done, my lady," Geetock informed her.

"We will have King Manasseh's attention with our first strike, and then my full destructive might will fall on his castle door," she claimed.

The firestorm subsided but the clouds and mystical energy above remained. Dwarves flooded through the ranks of King Manasseh with their killing blows. A thousand men fell at their hands.

"My Lord, we are under attack!" Vevrin quickly announced as he barged into King Manasseh's personal chamber.

Manasseh was shirtless, wearing only black leather pants. He turned in surprise to face Vevrin, rising from his seated position upon his mock throne.

"What! By whom? Which of the Horns dares to attack me?"

"Not the Horns, my Lord; it is dwarves."

Manasseh's eyes narrowed in contemplation of this unexpected scenario. "Meet me in the tower with your other mystics. I will assess what we are facing from there."

"Yes, my liege." Vevrin turned and promptly left, his red robes flowing behind him.

Two guards sealed the door and Manasseh sat on the edge of his chair, stroking the smoke-filled medallion gifted to him by the dark deity. *"Could this have anything to do with the halfling?"*

"I think we have his attention now," Raina declared. "Alert your team to move toward the gate."

Geetock nodded and then moved to the three others of his clan. They closed their eyes in unison, only to open them moments later.

"It is done, my lady. Our message was received by the others."

The storm clouds above the battle began to swirl in a vortex. Lightning bolts hit the ground in several areas, each releasing a deafening crack. Raina stretched out her staff toward the sky and labored to bring it down, as though she were pulling on something tangible. Out of the formed eye of the clouds a huge meteorite of fire burst forth with a sonic boom, streaming down toward the fortress. The battle below stopped to watch the ball of flame soar in and strike the front gate of the castle. A gigantic crater lay behind as splinters of the former door and shards of the surrounding stone were sent flying in all directions. Smoke and debris littered the area, with the strong smell of burnt wood, stone and flesh mingled together.

"Knock, knock!" Geetock yelled. "I'll bet our King El'Korr below heard that one!"

"Indeed. He will know we have arrived."

Several smaller meteors fell from the sky and pelted along the wall of the castle. Archers fell in scores, brick tumbled, timber split.

Several minutes went by before one of the other wild dwarves pointed, "Look—dragon!" A colossal black dragon suddenly appeared at the top of the highest tower and hovered there.

"This is the first large one we have seen. I will target the tower next," Raina said with a smirk.

"Where did these dwarves come from?" Manasseh demanded, looking out of the Tower of Recall.

"We are not sure my Lord. There has been no—"

"It doesn't matter," the King cut him off as he returned from the balcony. "Once we regroup, we will crush this minor speck of an army. Send out the giants to push them back and then have our commanders gather what is left of our men outside the wall. They have no siege warfare to penetrate our defenses."

"Yes, my King," Vevrin responded with a head bow. Suddenly they heard a boom, and watched a soaring meteorite hit the front gate. They grabbed hold of something to steady themselves as the tower swayed.

"They have a mystic! Find it and kill it!" he raged. Vevrin signaled to a group of red-robed wizards standing behind him, waving them out.

King Manasseh composed himself, "I have always hated that front gate."

"I am sure this mystic is not able to summon another of that magnitude. It has never been heard of that one could summon two meteors," Vevrin tried to console his leader.

"You are sure? I would suggest you make damn sure right now Vevrin, because you stand where they will most likely strike next. Do something for a change."

Vevrin moved to the balcony and cast a spell. His mumbled words were not discernible and then he walked back inside. "The tower is protected, my liege."

"Good. I feel perfectly safe now," he sneered. "Now somebody tell me just how an army marches right up my ass."

Manasseh walked to the balcony to view the battle below, watching more of his men fall. He knew the group of dwarves were more than regular fighters. They were different—more powerful, but still no match for what lay directly beneath him. He could feel the strength of the Tree pulsing through the very ground he walked on as it radiated its power throughout his conquered land.

Suddenly, a huge black dragon manifested right before his eyes. He retreated back from the opening along with Vevrin.

"I have the halfling you seek," it said telepathically while displaying the caged Bridazak.

Manasseh moved closer to get a better look, his mannerisms starkly altering to that of a gracious host, "My gratitude, Barawbyss."

"I don't want your gratitude."

"I know that we have not always seen eye to eye, but we might be able to come to some agreement."

"You have waited too long to move on the other Horns. I have run out of patience."

"So have I. We were building an army with your help, but it appears we are currently losing some men, if you haven't noticed. This halfling, however, has something that will change the tide."

"This is your last chance Manasseh, and this will be my last gift."

He released Bridazak and two guards grabbed him.

"Where did you find him, Barawbyss?"

"He was in the caves. Alone." The dragon then disappeared.

"I see. So this army is yours, perhaps. Where did you find so many dwarves? Most of this race is dead and scattered."

Bridazak courageously looked into King Manasseh's eyes and responded with silence.

"Where is it?" the King asked, in a sickeningly sweet tone, but still received no answer. "Search him," he commanded.

They tore through his backpack and bedding to find nothing. Then they felt around his clothes until discovering the lump in his pocket, finally producing the Orb. No longer was it gold, but instead a blood red. Bridazak's eyes widened at the unexpected change of the voice of God, and silently waited for it to reveal its true power and nature, but nothing happened. The King took it and inspected it closely. It was warm to the touch, and he could feel a slight pulse like the beating of a heart.

"What is it?" He looked over to Vevrin for the answer, knowing that Bridazak wasn't going to divulge any information.

The wizard held it and then cast another spell. "I don't know. It is certainly magical, but I'm unable to identify it."

"Perhaps it's the source of this dwarven army's power. I had thought that I might try to wield this myself, but I think if we destroy this orb..."

"No!" Bridazak cried out.

"So, it is the power of your army." Dripping in hypocritical grace, he continued, *"This* little trinket, *this* is what was contained inside the coveted box? Well, thank you for answering all my questions. Vevrin, prepare this orb to be sacrificed, and get this halfling out of my sight."

The Wild Dwarf brigade waited at the gate after receiving the telepathic message from their brothers. Several giants stepped out of the smoke-filled, destroyed entrance. Each towered at the height of a village building, with muscles bulging, and wore only a loin cloth. Sounds of battle echoed all around them. Manasseh's men backed away from the dwarves when the giants came into view.

"Saddle up, boys! Time to change some diapers!" One of the dwarves yelled.

They tumbled together and a few climbed on top, forming a dwarven pyramid. A chant began in unison.

"Kaba teekseh bo!" "Kaba teekseh bo!" "Kaba teekseh bo!"

Their skin began to meld together as the spell was released, and soon the group of dwarves became one and continued to expand. Popping of bone sounded along with the stretching of skin, like rope tightening. Within a minute, there stood before the giants a fifteen-foot-tall mega-Dwarf. The new creation laughed heartily and then smacked their hands together. As they pulled their hands apart a shaft of a weapon materialized: an enormous war hammer was birthed.

The giants hesitated a moment, confused, but then charged. Immediately, one of them was launched back as the hammer swung and connected. The others came in and began to grapple and pummel the Dwarf monster. Fire suddenly encompassed the monstrous humanoids as the colossal, bearded being released the power they received from the broken curse of the Burning Forest. Several giants fell to the ground ablaze, writhing in pain. The mighty hammer came down and was buried into their skulls one by one. Flesh smoldered, and the blood flowing from the cracked skulls bubbled from the intense heat emitting from the blazing Dwarf creature. King Manasseh's men ran from the scene and stayed away from the hulking fire Dwarf.

Suddenly, a bolt of lightning struck from above. The hood of a crimson-robed mystic flew into view. A magical rune tattooed on his forehead glowed under the shadow of its cowl. The wild dwarves pointed their hand at the mage, shooting forth a jet of flames. A second mystic, under summoned magical power, flew in and protected the other with a spell. The fire splayed around the target as it hit the invisible shield now in place.

Lightning hit the dwarves again from a third source. Pain wracked the gigantic body. A fourth bolt struck. There were too many of the mystics.

The stormy sky opened once again and another huge meteorite streaked down. Screaming out of the heavens, it shattered upon impact on the magically shielded tower. The embers of rock fell like a firework, causing only minor damage to the castle structure surrounding the tower. Raina's eyes narrowed as she thought, *"Manasseh's mystic acted more quickly than I expected."*

"My lady, several mystics have engaged us at the front gate," Geetock said, after receiving a telepathic message.

"It is time that I personally introduce myself."

The tower swayed once again, but Vevrin's protective spell saved it from the mighty blast. Bridazak was being directed toward the staircase by two guards. Another soldier carried the Ordakian's weapons and belongings in front of him. Bridazak noticed a faint aura coming from the quiver he'd found in Everwood—some of his magical arrows were glowing.

"Make sure this one is isolated. Give him our best suite," Vevrin said.

"Yes sir," one of the guards responded with an evil grin.

Vevrin then tapped his staff on the stone floor and suddenly disappeared. The arrows' telltale glow faded away.

"It's barred from the other side," Dulgin announced.

"Anyone have a way to get through barred doors?" Xan asked, looking at each of them. No answer came.

"Great, we can handle the most powerful monsters in all the land, and yet we can't open one damn door!" Dulgin scoffed.

"Rondee has an ability to meld himself into stone, but it is dangerous," El'Korr finally chimed in.

"I can summon a rock elemental, but it will make quite a bit of noise bashing the door down."

"Can't it just open the barred door instead of breaking it down?" Xan asked.

"It is not able to grab things like that. It is a creature formed from rock."

"Well, it looks like Rondee is the only way," the dwarven king said while looking at his bodyguard.

Rondee nodded, and everyone backed away from the reinforced door. The Wild Dwarf placed the palms of his hands against the wall just next to the entrance. He braced his legs and began to push on the rock. His muscles bulged and then he whispered a chant with his face up against the rough cut stone. Rondee's eyes were shut and his neck veins strained as he continued to push.

"Nothin's happening," Dulgin whispered to his brother.

"Shhhhh. Let him concentrate."

Several more moments went by until finally Rondee's hands began to meld into the rock. Each push with his legs sent him deeper within. He was now consumed by the wall and the heroes could no longer see him. They waited in anticipation of Rondee opening the barred entry. A minute elapsed with no indication from the Wild Dwarf.

"He should be on the other side by now," Xan surmised.

Abawken moved to the door and tried to listen. "I don't hear anything, but it might be too thick."

"Something's wrong. I can feel it," Dulgin said.

"Abawken, summon your creature," El'Korr commanded in haste.

Before he could pull out his magical scimitar, everyone heard a thud on the other side. Then it was silent again. Seconds ticked slowly by, and then the door popped open to reveal Rondee, smiling. Just beyond him were several human guards lying dead on the ground.

"I coombre stop chenko for directions." Rondee said.

Another thunderbolt just barely missed the dwarven giant as it dodged out of the way. There were now five red-robed mystics shuffling about in the air. The Wild Dwarf fired several blasts of flame at the mages, but they were all protected, and beyond the reach of the massive war hammer. Five glowing missiles made of magical energy slammed into their back and knocked them to one knee. The other wizards began to cast more spells to finish off the Dwarf.

A dark bolt of energy suddenly erupted and blasted one of the evil mystics back into the castle wall with tremendous force. The human fell to the ground dead—robes ablaze. They all looked up to see a female Elf hovering in the air before them.

"Kill the wench!" one mystic commanded.

"What amazing manners your King has taught you," she responded playfully.

Two mages launched more force missiles. All ten of them soared in, but dissipated once they hit the protective shield that Raina had in place around her. The energy dispersed harmlessly. Another wizard shot lightning from his ornate ivory rod. It sizzled in with a bright flash of light only to be absorbed into Raina's wooden staff.

"I think this belongs to you," she said. The same bolt re-launched with a thunderous crack and hit the dark mystic in the chest. He flipped over in the air and then slowly descended to the ground, blue sparks arcing sporadically over his lifeless body.

The fifth mystic conjured a large ball of fire, and rocketed it into Raina. Fire engulfed her. The mystic smiled in triumph until he saw her come out of it unharmed. Raina released another incantation that instantly dispelled the mages flying power. He fell to the ground but was able to land softly after releasing a quickened spell before impact. The last thing he saw was an enormous war hammer coming down on his head.

Two wizards remained.

"Who are you?" one asked.

"I'm the Sheldeen Elf mystic," she announced.

"Impossible! She has not been seen for centuries."

"And yet, here I am. Look around you. King Manasseh's reign ends today."

They took a moment to look at the battle field. The dwarves had decimated the King's men. Ten thousand lay dead, and yet the bearded clan pressed further in, and were now amassing at the front of the castle with minimal losses.

"Surrender."

King Manasseh remained to watch from his high tower as the unresolved battle below continued to challenge his defenses. A second powerful fireball hit, smashing into the protective shielding that Vevrin had just put in place, shattering the burning rock on impact. He took in a deep breath and exhaled in frustration; Vevrin had mistakenly underestimated an enemy, again.

"Yes, use your magic, Mystic, while you can, because soon your feeble attacks will end," he spoke softly and confidently to himself. He briskly exited the tower.

Minutes later, Manasseh was inside the familiar circular room, where blood stains covered the stone bed, laced with etchings of the ancient tree. Torches and candles adorned and outlined the chamber. Vevrin placed the deep red colored orb onto the tablet, a place normally reserved for the living, rather than a simple object.

"Good, I see that we are ready."

"Yes, everything is in place, my liege."

Vevrin pulled forth an ornate dagger made from the same obsidian rock as the castle.

"A dagger? How am I supposed to destroy a round, two-inch object with a dagger, Vevrin?"

"My apologies, Lord."

The King flipped the blade and the sharp end landed flat in his palm. He stepped toward the Orb and struck it squarely with the bludgeoning hilt. The stone handle cracked and then crumbled. Frustrated, he grabbed the blood-red sphere and tried to crush it with both hands. Vevrin had seen his master crush the skull of a human with his power, but now, with gritted teeth and veins bulging in his neck, he labored for several seconds until finally releasing his grip. He slammed it down onto the stone slab and then turned sharply to Vevrin, "Your turn."

The mystic bowed slightly and turned to face the Orb. He hesitated a moment, then pointed his skull-topped staff at the innocent item and uttered a command word, "Zanthumbeh!" A tight beam of intense energy flared out, but the Orb absorbed the magical heat force. He was amazed at the resiliency.

"Is that it? That's your best?" Manasseh bellowed. "Get a hammer! We need to crush this thing!"

"Yes, my Lord." Vevrin quickly exited.

Manasseh stared at it for a brief moment, then felt the pull of the Tree directly below him. The sacrifice chamber was not built above it by coincidence. He snapped his fingers and magically teleported to the Tree. From atop the pyramid he surveyed the chamber. Things had changed since he was last here—the Guardian was destroyed, rock shards from the walls were scattered everywhere, and the dust from the struggle lingered as it continued to settle. Barawbyss had told him the Halfling was alone, but a solitary Ordakian couldn't possibly have done all of this on his own. Manasseh pushed his thoughts aside for the time being and knelt at the base of the twisted stock.

"Help my army. Let the defilers see your true power."

The bluish glowing mist cascading down from the Tree began to intensify with sparks of light.

Bridazak was thrown into an enclosed, damp cell. The claustrophobic space, not much larger than he, smelled of feces and rotting flesh.

"Enjoy, sunshine," one of the guards mocked.

"You must not know anything about Ordakians," Bridazak sputtered as he stood back up.

"We know enough of your kind," the guard responded as he started to close the door.

"Then you would know it would be unwise to leave without tying me up," Bridazak said hastily.

"And why would we do that?"

"Nevermind. I don't know what got into me."

"Hey Ghent, the King has the other one tied up," one of the guards chimed in.

Ghent smacked him, "Shut up. This one is just messing with us and will probably try something as soon as we go in with rope. No one said anything about tying him up." He slammed the heavy door shut.

Bridazak heard the sound of multiple keys locking him inside the dungeon cell. It was pitch black, but it didn't matter. He'd confirmed Spilf was here, and most likely still alive.

Thousands of men remained barricaded inside the heart of the castle. Raina addressed the army of dwarves while she hovered above them.

"Our fight is not yet over. It is time to deliver the final blow!"

A cheer erupted from the eight hundred dwarves, the handful of humans, and elves.

"Be swift, strike true, and make them pay!" Another cheer went up, but Raina's attention was caught by something out in the gruesome battlefield. An eerie blue mist seeped from the ground and hovered over the dead.

The dwarves turned to follow her gaze, and spotted movement.

"Undead!" Someone yelled, while more of Raina's men confirmed the sightings. King Manasseh's fallen army was rising.

17

Inch by Inch

"*L*ester, what is going on?"

"*I'm not sure Ross. We are in a dungeon, from what I can tell.*"

"*Where is Bridazak?*"

"*I don't know Ross. The humans are going through his belongings on the table above us.*"

"*He abandoned us, Lester. We are doomed,*" Ross squawked in his high-pitched voice.

"*Stop it Ross. No one abandoned us.*"

"*How do you know that? We are certainly doomed. It was a nice thousand years, Lester,*" he began to cry.

"*Stop being so melodramatic, Ross. I can hear the humans talking. Just shut up and listen.*"

"*Why are you being so mean to me?*"

"*Just listen!*"

"*Okay, okay, I'm listening.*"

The human guards were rummaging through Bridazak's backpack.

"Halfling's don't carry anything worth a damn!" One said, while throwing down a child sized tunic.

"Ghent, what about the arrows and bow?" Another gruff raspy voice asked.

"Vevrin told me we can have anything *but* those."

"Of course he did. He knew there was crap in this halfling's bag."

165

"Well, we have a couple items to divvy up. Who wants the flint and steel?" Ghent asked, trying to divert his men's frustration.

"I'll take it," one said with a resigned sigh.

"Okay, how about the dagger?"

"Yeah, sure. Why not?"

"About time you replaced that old knife of yours, Bosh!"

"It's still good enough to run you through, Rudd!"

"Knock it off you two! I guess I'm stuck with the whetstone."

The others chuckled. None of them had made out with anything great. "You can always take the feather, Ghent," they laughed as Bosh waved it in his face.

"Real nice, guys, but I will stick with the whetstone."

"Whoa, what do we have here," Rudd discovered a small leather pouch hidden inside Bridazak's pack. He untied the wrapped string around the top and then poured the contents into his open palm. The beautiful diamond ring, formerly belonging to Lady Birmham, was revealed. Their bedazzled eyes were held captive by the sparkling bauble.

"Now we're talking," Ghent whispered. He took it from Rudd's hand and inspected it closely.

"Yeah, I hope the boss-man brings us more Ordakians now."

"We will have to sell it when we are off duty and then split it," Ghent suggested. "I will hold on to it for the time being."

"What about the coin bag he had?" Bosh asked.

"We will put the coin up at our next card session as the prize money, but right now we all need to do our rounds."

"Yes sir," they said in unison.

"I'll check on the Ordakian," Rudd proposed, taking a step towards a barred door.

"No, Rudd. Vevrin was very clear, no one goes inside," Ghent responded.

The humans in their black leather garb went through another door. The room was now empty. Crackling flames from torches hanging on the wall were the only sound remaining.

"He didn't abandon us after all, Lester!"

"Our master needs our help, Ross."

"What can we do?"

"You know."

"Know what? I don't know what you are talking about."

"C'mon, search inside that thick pick-head of yours and figure it out."

There was a pause as it dawned on Ross what his brother was referring to, *"No, Lester. You know that I hate doing it."*

"It's important, Ross—and it's only a short distance to the door. Our master is right behind it and once he is freed, he will take us out of here."

"You promise, Lester?"

"I promise."

The magical thieves' tools began to vibrate on the stone floor. The tinkle of metal on rock intensified, and within seconds they morphed into a pair of vibrant green worms. Inch by inch, they made their way to the barred portal.

"Just a little further, my brother."

"I'm tired, Lester. I don't think I can make it. Go on without me."

"Oh stop it, Ross! The lock is just a foot away, now suck it up, soldier."

"Why do you continue to torture me?" He began to cry again.

"Ross."

"What?"

"Look!"

Looking up, he saw that they had arrived. *"We made it, Lester! We didn't die!"*

"I know. Now let's get to work and set our master free."

"Thank you for believing in me, Lester. You saved my life."

"I'll remember you said that, for next time we have to do this."

"Oh god, I hope there isn't a next time."

"Calm down, Ross. I'm sorry I said that. Let's just focus on getting this door open."

The brothers morphed back and forth between worm form and pick form in order to unlock the multiple contraptions. The last obstacle was the door that was still barred; they were too small and weak to push something that heavy.

"Well, it is all up to you now, Lester."

"Yep, our creator was so clever to think of everything. Now inch back, my brother."

Ross clung on the wall and watched Lester work. The bar began to rattle, then jerk an inch, as Lester mentally pushed, then another inch, then another, until finally it fell to the ground with a loud clank, and the door popped open slightly. They eagerly waited for their master to burst through the threshold and embrace them tightly. Seconds elapsed, and their joyful faces began to sag back to disappointment.

"Where is he?" Ross asked.

"Perhaps he is tied up and can't get to us."

"You promised, Lester!"

"I did, and that promise is still intact. We need to go in and help him."

"You go first. It's dark in there."

They worked their way down, inching into the gloomy chamber. There were several stone steps and an open room beyond. A faint blue aura was the only light source; it emanated from a glass vial on top of a wooden table just to the right of the stairs. It was damp, cold, and moldy. A slight rustle of chains echoed from further back in the dark recesses.

"Based off the looks, I believe it smells in here."

"Ross, we can't smell. We don't have that sensory ability."

"That is what I said; based off the looks, get it?"

"Oh, yeah, I get it now and I agree. It looks like it smells bad in here."

"I think I am going to cry, Lester."

"Why, what happened now?"

"You finally agreed with me for once."

"Oh, brother. Just keep your eyes open for our master."

They crawled further inside. Ross stayed right behind Lester for fear of being separated. Drips of moisture falling onto the stone floor could be heard echoing inside the area.

"I see something, Ross."

"What is it?"

"Looks like someone hanging from chains, but I can't make anything out accept that it looks bald."

"Our master isn't bald."

"I know, Ross. I need to get closer."

"Closer? Are you sure that's safe?"

"I don't see how we have a choice. You can stay here if you like."

"I like."

"Okay, I will be right back. You stay here and keep a look out."

Lester made his way up the mildew covered wall, and then to the anchored chain. He traversed the metal links and was soon hanging above Ross.

"Psst. Hey, I'm up here."

"Oh, there you are. I'm glad I didn't go. That looks frightening."

"It's fun, Ross. It's like we are on our own adventure."

"Oooo, don't say that word. That is a scary word."

"Adventure, adventure, adventure."

"Stop it, Lester!"

"You are so boring, Ross!"

"I'm not talking to you anymore."

Just then, Lester spotted something moving in the darkness, and coming closer to Ross. He squinted with his tiny worm eyes until he finally realized what it was.

"Ross, look out! Giant rat!"

Ross instantly looked up at Lester in shock and horror but then he turned away without a word, thinking his brother was teasing him once again and trying to frighten him. He was scared, but he wasn't going to show Lester.

The ferocious rodent came in for the kill. Its fur was wet and slimy and its glowing red eyes were locked on its next meal. Ross was instantly scooped up into its dirty claws and then swallowed whole by the ugly beast.

"No!" Lester shouted.

The rat began to move away, but suddenly stopped. It's stomach convulsed, and it began to heave repeatedly until finally it spat out the metal object, which lightly clinked on the stone floor. The rat gave a shrill shriek as it scurried back into the darkness.

"Damn you, Lester! Why didn't you tell me I was going to be eaten?"

Lester let out a sigh of relief after hearing his brother's voice.

"I did. Remember, 'look out, giant rat', does that ring a bell at all?"

"I'm still not talking to you, Lester."

"Oh, just hold on. I'm going to see if this is our master so we can get out of here."

Lester inched his way until finally reaching the shackle, which held a bloody wrist. He moved along the arm and was now on top of the shoulder of the unknown individual. He decided to take a risk. There was no way to see the face as the head hung downward.

"Can you hear me?"

The body shifted slightly, and a low moan of pain escaped out from its mouth.

"Use your mind to talk," the magical pick said.

"Lester?" A shaky voice asked.

"Yes, that's my name. How do you know it?"

"It's... Spilf." He finally was able to get it out.

"Spilf? You are alive!"

"Help... me."

"Yes, of course. I will release the manacles right away."

Lester went to work on the locks and within minutes Spilf fell to the ground, semi-conscious. Ross crawled over to investigate the individual his brother had released. He wormed his way up to the face.

"Spilf? Is that you?"

"Yes," came the groggy response.

"I thought you were dead! Oh no, does that mean we are dead? Lester! Lester! Where are you? You abandoned me," he squawked.

"I'm right here, you worm-brain!"

"Oh thank goodness! Look, it's Spilf."

"I know. I'm the one who released him."

"Why isn't he getting up, Lester?"

"I think he is too injured. Spilf, can you hear me?"

"Yes, I need to get to the healing potion on the table. Just give me a minute. I'm trying to gather myself," he said, gaining more strength in his mind.

"Take as long as you need, former master," Lester responded.

"How long is that?" Ross asked.

"Not sure."

Another minute went by until some movement from Spilf alerted the magical picks.

"He's moving," Lester stated.

"Where is Bridazak?" Spilf asked, lifting his cheek up off of the wet, cold stone.

"We don't know. He's been captured. We thought we were rescuing him when it turned out to be you," Lester responded.

"We will find him shortly, my friends. I just need to get that potion."

In pure determination, Spilf fought through the agonizing pain as he slid his broken body over the rough cobblestone. Streaks of blood smeared the floor as he crawled toward his prize. With each forward movement, Spilf gritted his teeth. His sweat mingled with the dried blood on his grimaced face. All of the beatings, all of the torture he endured, all of the feelings of despair and hopelessness fueled him to push forward. He held his breath for long periods of time to help endure the pain. The wooden legs of the desk were now at his raw fingertips. It was impossible for him to stand, since Manasseh's torturer, called the Hammer, had broken his ankles.

He turned gingerly over onto his bloody, open-gashed back, and then grabbed the two wooden legs. There was no choice—he knew that he would have to catch the vial when it tumbled off the edge. He drew a deep breath to steady himself and pulled the legs forward to tilt the table. He heard the glass tip over and began to roll and slide his way. The blue hue brightened, and then there it was. He pushed the table back up quickly and reacted with his free hand to catch the fragile, falling object.

"Wow! Well I'll be an animated pick! You'd think after a thousand years I would have seen everything, but I've never seen anything like that!" Lester exclaimed in awe of Spilf's superb agility.

Spilf pulled the stopper and then drank the potion. He could feel the healing instantly take place inside his body—bones mending, cuts closing, and his energy returning. He finally stood on his own two hairless feet. He was still bruised and battered, but functional enough to move about. Lester and Ross were scooped up.

"Thank you! You saved my life," Spilf mentally conveyed, strength back in his voice.

"You're welcome," Lester said with pride as he inched higher into the air.

"Good, now save ours. Get us out of here! This place is really scary. They have rats, giant rats!" Ross cried.

Spilf chuckled and then went up the stairs to the ajar door. Light spilled out from the cracked opening. He saw a table with items strewn about, among them an extravagant bow and two quivers of arrows, one set which matched the caliber of the curved wood. A weapon he desperately needed. Spilf peeked out to an empty guard room and freely went for the items. He recognized Bridazak's backpack and clothing. Spilf put on the clean shirt, and as he pulled it over his head, his eyes caught the sight of a peculiar item: a single feather. He slowly grabbed it and lifted it closer, twirling it during his inspection. "This is real," he whispered.

"What did he say, Lester?"

"I don't know. I think he said the feather is real."

"Well, of course it is real. We can all see it is real. Oh no, the brutes hurt his brain function, Lester. He is ruined!"

Spilf smiled, *"No, not ruined boys: set free. It's time to find your master!"*

18

In the Dark

"**M**ove into the courtyard. I will protect you from the arrows coming from the castle. We need to funnel them, so we are not surrounded," Raina spat out instructions to her army.

A wave of the dead rose before their eyes. Manasseh's wickedness had somehow brought his fallen army back to fight once again on his behalf. Ten thousand men versus Raina's eight hundred had been surmountable, but ten thousand undead, with no sense of pain or preservation, against her tiring dwarves, changed things. The army of felled men and giants was one obstacle, but the dragons with their riders, along with the freshly killed mystics, were the greatest threat, as they retained their magical prowess.

"Geetock, have your team keep the undead back as long as possible. I will handle the dragons and the mystics. Use the others to support your efforts."

"We will do as commanded. Should we try to get inside the castle?"

"No, we don't have the resources. Our hope lies with El'Korr and his team. Just hold them off."

The wild dwarves had returned back from their morphed giant state into individuals once again. Nineteen of them engaged the enemy as their troops moved into the open courtyard. Arrows sailed in from the many openings from the interior castle wall but harmlessly deflected away due to the magical shielding cast by Raina.

Several black dragons were now soaring in. Raina pulled forth a small statuette from inside her robes, "I need you my friend," she whispered.

An ancient, deep bronze colored dragon appeared in front of her. The behemoth unfurled its wings to full extension.

"Where have you been, Raina?" it questioned within her mind.

"Long story, but good to see you again, old friend."

The jade-eyed beast looked around at the battlefield. *"Undead? What vile evil caused this?"*

"A human king. No time to discuss now. Will you help me?"

"It will be my pleasure. I have not been in such a battle for many centuries."

"Thank you, Zeffeera."

The red-tipped horns on top of her head and the deep bronze color of her body were highlighted by the sun's setting rays; she was a bright beacon of hope for Raina's army. She propelled away to engage the smaller black dragons. Zeffeera soared into range and then lifted her wings to stop her speedy advance, holding her position in mid-air. A blast of lightning burst forth from her gaping mouth. It forked and struck two of the dragons rapidly approaching. They plummeted to the ground, their lifeless bodies smoking from having connected with the electrically charged breath weapon.

A renewed strength returned to Raina's army after seeing the powerful bronze dragon take down the first two of the flying, animated carcasses. Cheers erupted. Geetock's troops were chopping down the endless ranks of the walking dead as they came in; the hundreds of dwarves behind them supported the effort by launching crossbow bolts and killing any undead that got through. Bodies fell one atop the other, but the greatest mass was still moving in like a tidal wave. The mutilated corpses slowly made their way to the open entrance of the castle. Some still had weapons lodged in their bodies, others smoldered from previous fire damage, but all pressed in to devour the living.

The fallen red-robed wizards were now up and flying toward Raina. She twirled her staff and teleported to the top of Manasseh's tower behind her, releasing a flash of light as she blinked back to alert the undead mages of her new location. Three flew to intercept.

174

"What took you so long, Vevrin?" Manasseh harshly questioned. He had been anxiously waiting for his victory, after teleporting back from the Tree's cavern below.

"I'm sorry, my Lord. I couldn't find any bludgeoning weapons in the dungeon so I brought the Hammer," he moved aside as a large mutant creature stepped through the doorway.

His right hand had been replaced by a hammer plated with steel. The head of the creature bulged out in several spots, like cysts ready to burst open. Dark brown eyes protruded beyond the sockets; neither could focus on the same thing at once. He was seven feet tall and wearing a blood spattered, leather apron over his dirty clothes.

"You are getting more handsome every time I see you," Manasseh half-smiled.

"Shank shoo me Lorg," he spoke in a raspy voice with spit dribbling down his chin.

"Right, I need you to use your hammer, or hand, or whatever you call it, to destroy this," the King pointed at the Orb.

It slurped saliva inside its mouth to try and speak again, but Manasseh cut him off, "No need to speak, just follow the order."

Vevrin closed the door to the circular sacrificial chamber. The Hammer moved his fat, stocky body over to stand beside the stone bed. He looked at his King, and then to Vevrin. The nonchalant movement of the beastly man warranted Manasseh's outburst, "Well, go on! Do it!" The torturer hefted his meaty arm, and with a sudden strike the Orb was destroyed. The sound of a glass popping under pressure resonated in the room, louder than expected. A shimmering, glitter-like material shot out in all directions and then slowly dissipated. He lifted his hammer arm and a red substance remained underneath.

"What is that?" Vevrin asked.

"Looks like blood," Manasseh investigated, moving closer.

The red liquid pooled together like mercury, then all in a moment, the stone tablet cracked as the rumble of an earthquake shook the room, knocking each of them slightly off balance. They watched the blood move to the split in the center, and then descend out of sight.

"It is finished," Manasseh said. "Kill the halflings and then meet me in the Tower."

Perfectly formed blocks of the black rock lined every hallway within the dungeon as the group of heroes made their way slowly inward. It was a maze of identical, interconnected tunnels. Groans were heard within locked cells holding prisoners, and screams echoed off the walls from farther away.

They tried to discern the layout, but the Dwarf King halted their advance, "Finding the Orb without information will be near impossible, so let's find our friends. We'll have a much better chance," El'Korr suggested.

"Agreed," Dulgin said, with a soft gratitude in his voice.

"We will cover more ground if we split up. There shouldn't be too many guards that we can't handle, since Raina started her attack," Xan proposed.

"Master Dulgin and I will go together," Abawken answered.

"Once we find them, we will make our way to the Tower—there is no way we will be leaving through the front entry. With a little luck we might run into Manasseh and get the Orb back," El'Korr said.

Another quake rocked the castle. Dust fell from the ceiling.

"Raina?" Dulgin asked.

"We can only hope. No telling what is going on up there, but with The Tree still active it can't be good," El'Korr responded.

"Tell'im Ghent, before he kills me," Bosh gasped for air.

"For the last time, where is Bridazak?" Spilf demanded, holding the tip of an arrow to the neck of the human pinned to the ground. Spilf was laying on the back of the face-down guard. Beside them lay the dead sentry named Rudd, an arrow embedded in his chest.

Ghent gestured downward with his open hands, trying to placate the angry Ordakian. "Sure. I can show you. Just let him go," he said nervously.

"I don't think so. This is what we are going to do: you will lead me there and I will keep," he paused briefly then continued, "What is your name?"

"Bosh," he replied, trying to be very still.

"You will lead me there and I will keep Bosh as my prisoner. If you try anything, or I suspect anything, then Bosh dies, and then I will fill your body with arrows from this very powerful bow that I'm holding."

Bridazak searched the cramped room high and low for an exit, fumbling around in the dark. He had brought his tunic up to cover his nose from the smell of old blood and decay during the long scrutiny of his pitch black cell. *"I've smelled worse,"* he thought to himself, trying to keep his spirit up, until his eyes started to water, *"Okay, this is bad."*

Finally he resigned himself, "How are you going to get out of this one," he whispered. This would have been the best time to have Lester and Ross with him, but unfortunately they were also taken from his possession.

Time passed unbearably slow as his thoughts swirled out of control and his focus blurred. Feeling stuck in the dank "suite" he'd been placed in began to wear him down, and he soon succumbed to feeling utterly defeated; there was no escape. The Orb was now in the hands of King Manasseh. He had failed.

A cold chill crept through the Ordakian's body. He felt a presence within the dark room. His eyes darted to and fro, but only blackness was found. "Is someone there?" Bridazak murmured.

"He has failed you, my dear Bridazak," a powerful and confident voice echoed within Bridazak's mind. The melodic, resonating tone was like drinking water after a day's travel within a desolate desert. Even so, Bridazak was startled, and placed his back against the wall.

The mysterious voice continued in its entrancing tone, *"What is your heart's desire?"*

"Who are you?" Bridazak asked, trembling.

A smooth, profound cackle filled his mind. Bridazak's heart pounded like a blacksmith's hammer.

"I am the one you have longed for, the one you have searched for."

"No, something isn't right. You are not the voice I know." Bridazak resisted the charm. Sweat trickled down his brow.

"Where is this voice now? My voice is here. I have the power to free you, and not just from this cell."

The invisible entity, with its implied accusations against the Orb, the voice he had trusted and carried so far, made his head spin even more. Bridazak's bottom lip quivered, "I am sorry. I failed you," he barely whispered.

"I can help you, Bridazak. Confess your desire for me, and I will take you away from this terrible place. In the blink of an eye it will be as it was before." His voice had become softer, even more melodic. Bridazak's insides twisted and he felt queasy. He fell to the ground and rolled up into a ball. His arms wrapped around his knees and he pulled them tighter into his chest. His body shivered as he cried in the darkness.

The dark being studied the Ordakian. His alluring and masterfully articulated voice continued, *"I can give you your heart's desires. Jewels?*

Bridazak did not flinch at the suggestion.

"No? I thought surely you had a taste for the finer things. Of course, you want something greater. How about we add in a few slaves to carry your riches?"

The seductive voice answered his silence with another promise, *"Ah, you are wise. A kingdom?"*

Bridazak suspected more than ever that this being was the one Xan spoke of—the antithesis of God's voice. The Dark One, the ruler of Kerrith Ravine. He could feel his will strengthening; this god had nothing for him. As if on cue, the voice presented him the ultimate gift, *"Your family?"* His eyes grew wide. How did he know? The one thing he longed for the most; his entire life had been in pursuit of the family he never had, the piece he had always been missing. He searched again for something, anything, to make eye contact with. If only he could see who was making the offer, see what monster lurked behind the promise.

"Family it is, then. Now all you have to do is bow to me."

Bridazak contemplated, and the battle in his mind and heart raged.

"Such an easy demand for such a wonderful gift—your family. What are you waiting for? Take what you have always wanted, what you have always needed."

Bridazak pleaded within,*"Where are you now God, when I need you most? You brought me here and have abandoned me. You should have sent somebody else from the beginning."* A sudden earthquake rumbled and rattled the stone around him, and one of the many door hinges broke with a loud snap.

Focused beams of light through the tiny pinholes of the hinge hit the Ordakian squarely in the face. He heard muffled voices from the other side.

"What was that?" Ghent asked.

"I don't care—just open the door," Spilf responded.

There was a series of clicks and clanks as multiple keys were inserted and twisted to unlock the prison portal. It swung open awkwardly on its offset hinge. Bright torchlight revealed Bridazak on the ground in a fetal position. Bridazak looked out to see the silhouette of a human.

"Are you hurt?" a childlike voice asked.

Bridazak thought he knew the voice, but it echoed off the walls, and he did not recognize the figure standing in front of him, as it was clearly a human. The voice did not match what he saw.

"No. Who are you?"

"Step aside, Ghent," the strangely familiar voice commanded.

Ghent moved out of the way and another guard came into view, but from his backlit view, it looked like it had two heads. Bridazak squinted through the light that was blinding his eyes.

"I can't see."

"Can you walk? Get up and come out."

Bridazak slowly stood and then hesitantly moved forward while holding one hand to shield his eyes. Then everything came into view.

"Spilf!" He yelled in unbelief.

"Yes, it's me. Okay, Ghent, get in," he directed.

The humans were placed inside the cell. Bridazak stared back into the chamber and a chill came over him, remembering the evil being that spoke to him. Ghent peered up at him with his grey eyes, just as Spilf sealed and locked the door. He turned to his long lost friend; they embraced tightly and held each other as if never to part again. Tears streamed down their cheeks.

"I was the one who was supposed to rescue you," Bridazak said, muffled against Spilf's shoulder.

"I couldn't wait any longer. You were taking too long. See, I lost my hair waiting for you," he smiled, rubbing his bald head as they finally pulled away from each other.

"Spilf, a second hasn't gone by without my thinking of you. I missed you so much."

"You were all I had to hold onto Bridazak—you and Grumpy. Where is he?"

"I don't know. We were separated when I was captured."

"Here," Spilf held out his bow and arrows, "I'm not as good a shot as you."

"Thanks."

"Oh, and these also belong to you," he added as he produced Lester and Ross.

"Master! We missed you," Lester's metallic voice ignited in his mind.

"I missed you too Lester—and Ross."

"You have to get us out of here Bridazak. They have giant rats!" Ross' voice escalated in a panic.

"It's okay. We are going to get out of here."

"Did he tell you about the rats?" Spilf laughed.

"Yes. Did you encounter them?"

"No, but he hasn't stopped talking about them since they rescued me."

"They rescued you?"

"Yeah, tell you that story later. We have to get out of here." They started down the hallway together.

"We have to find the Orb of Truth. King Manasseh took it and was going to destroy it, thinking it was giving my army power."

"Your army?"

"Long story, but there are a thousand dwarves attacking the castle above. Dulgin, his brother and some others were trying to sneak in, but I was captured."

"Wait, you found Dulgin's brother?"

"Yeah, Xan told us about a cursed army and Dulgin, Abawken, and I..."

"Who is Xan, and this Abawken?"

"Oh, Xan was a lost Elf in the Moonrock Mountains and Abawken found us through a vision he had, but I can't go into it right now."

"So, you were able to open the box? What is this Orb?"

Bridazak stopped abruptly and wheeled around, grabbing his friend's shoulders, "Spilf, it's the voice of God."

"What?!" His eyes widened in shock at Bridazak's statement.

"It has everything to do with a prophecy and we are a part of it," Bridazak hesitated for a moment, thinking of whom the prophecy described as their true enemy, and the encounter within his cell he had survived, thanks to Spilf. *"Should I tell him? No, now is not the time,"* he thought. "C'mon, we can exchange our tales later. We need to get the Orb back and find the others."

They continued to move down the dungeon corridor, but Bridazak suddenly stopped and turned toward his friend again.

"Spilf, please take Lester and Ross back. They served me well, but they belong to you." Spilf welcomed the enchanted picks back into his possession.

Vevrin walked in front of the deformed frame of the Hammer as they made their way to kill the halfling prisoners. The confusing labyrinth of dungeon corridors were marked clearly for Vevrin; the torches lining the walls were controlled by one of his favorite spells—Torch Walk. The smell of burning oil increased and each flame released a burst of heightened brightness, directing him toward the destination he wished to find. He turned left at the four-way intersection as the torches revealed the direction, but suddenly halted in surprise when he saw a human and Dwarf walking toward them.

"Well, well, well. Look what we found," Dulgin jabbed Abawken.

A shocked expression briefly flashed across Vevrin's face, "How did you...? No matter, you will soon regret coming here."

"The mystic is mine, Abawken. You get Ugly."

"Dulgin, it is not wise to take on a mystic alone," he whispered to his friend.

"Kill the human, leave the Dwarf to me!" Vevrin ordered.

The Hammer stepped in front. Abawken moved forward to a door on the right halfway down the corridor and opened it. The gigantic, deformed human pursued him with a hobbled trot into the empty guard room. Vevrin and Dulgin remained in the hallway and stared at one another for a long moment.

"No more portals, no more escapes. I've been waiting for this," Dulgin began.

"Is that so? I'm surprised you've lasted as long as you have," Vevrin sneered.

"You've been an itch that I haven't been able to scratch."

"So, is this to be a duel of swords Dwarf?"

"Nah, just me introducing your body to my axe."

"So clever," he scoffed, "but unfortunately your axe will never get close enough."

"We'll see about that, wizard," Dulgin snapped, and began to walk toward him.

Vevrin waved his staff and whispered words of the arcane. Three long swords magically appeared and hovered in the air in front of him. They moved to intercept the Dwarf, as if invisible foes wielded them.

Meanwhile, Abawken stood on top of a wooden table and waited for The Hammer. The grotesque butcher entered and then slammed the door shut behind him.

"I don't want to hurt you," Abawken stated.

"I shwill smashoo," he slurped the saliva that gathered inside his mouth as he stepped in and brought his hammer hand down. Abawken jumped. The table shattered, and The Hammer lifted his arm to see that the fighter was gone.

"I'm up here," Abawken alerted him from above. He was standing on the ceiling.

The Hammer was confused by the illogical feat against gravity, but he reached into a front pocket on his apron to grab something he could use against his out of range target. A clenched fist opened to reveal tiny pebbles of sulphur. "Shire sheez," he said, then let them fall to the ground.

The pebbles instantly began to vibrate on the floor, and then they hatched.

"Oh, 'fire bees'," Abawken realized what they were.

"Yesh, shire sheez." Spittle dripped down onto his clothes.

The hundreds of bees ignited into fire. The buzzing sound intensified as they raced toward Abawken.

The sound of clashing steel echoed down the corridor as Dulgin parried the three magical weapons attacking him. Vevrin laughed aloud as he walked closer. Dulgin kept trying to quickly pass them to get to the mage, but each time he was forced back. He had sustained a few cuts already, so he switched his focus to destroying the conjured swords. The Dwarf soon recognized that the weapons were not defensive, so hitting them was not difficult; breaking them was the real challenge. One lunged in, and he deflected, knocking it to the ground. Before it could rise to formation again, he put all his strength into pinning it down with his foot. The other two swords thrust in at the Dwarfs vulnerable opening, and each one stabbed him—one in his side and the other his shoulder. Dulgin roared loudly as his axe came down on the weapon he had pinned. The powerful impact broke the blade and it disappeared.

Vevrin's smile lessened and he moved forward while casting another spell. He launched a missile of mystical force from his fingertip. It slammed into the Dwarf just as he shattered the second sword.

"One more to go, Misty," Dulgin threatened as he grimaced from the multiple wounds.

"Oh, you have a lot more to go, Dwarf. I will bleed you dry before we are finished here."

Another force missile hit him.

"I hate it when you do that."

"Is there anything that you do like about me?" Vevrin playfully asked.

The last sword finally burst as his axe swung it into a wall, the pieces clanking to the ground. Dulgin fought through the pain and moved toward the mystic. With each step he took, his brown eyes narrowed and his growl increased. Three more of the magical bolts of energy rocketed in and hit the Dwarf.

Vevrin confidently advanced several steps toward the sealed entrance the Hammer and Abawken had gone through, readying his next attack. The door groaned, then suddenly ripped off the hinges and smashed into the unsuspecting mage. Along with it came the Hammer; both landed on top of Vevrin. A screaming gale wind blew out of the room—the source of which caused the door to come unhinged. Dulgin charged his downed red-robed enemy. As he arrived, a force shot the door and deformed human back where they had come from, as Vevrin began to levitate.

"Enough!" the mystic shouted.

He pointed his staff at the enraged Dwarf who was almost upon him with his mighty axe. Suddenly, Dulgin's weapon was pulled out from his hands toward the ceiling. It slammed into the stone, as if magnetized. A glowing incorporeal hand materialized, grappled his throat, and began to strangle the Dwarf, lifting him off the ground. His feet dangled as he desperately tried to find something to help him get his footing back.

The Hammer was propelled back into the windy room, where Abawken had summoned the air elemental. The wind creature had a tornado torso with arms shaped like clubs, stretching out to pummel those in its vicinity. There was no face on the conjured monster, just a mass of powerful air whipping around, grabbing hold of anything loose and sending it flying away.

"Back so soon?" Abawken asked the grotesque looking human.

The Hammer swung at the air creature and connected. Although it seemed made of thin air, even the Hammer could tell that with each strike, its power subsided. He kept pummeling the gust in front of him. Another door leading into the room burst open, revealing several guards with weapons drawn. They crashed to a halt, trying to get their bearings after seeing the Hammer engaged with a wind tunnel, their surprise evident as they shielded their faces from the mighty cyclonic gusts in the confined room. Then they spotted Abawken.

Dulgin repeatedly tried to pull the hand off of him, but there was nothing to grab; his ruddy hands passed right through the ghostly clutch. His voice cracked as the air was being squeezed out of him. There was nothing he could do. He was pinned up in the corner of the wall and ceiling. His weapon within reach; with the little strength he had left, he grasped the handle, but it wouldn't budge.

"I grow tired of you, Dwarf. After I kill you and the human, I will be taking care of the halflings."

"You talking about us?" Bridazak's voice echoed down the corridor.

Vevrin turned his head to see the Ordakians. Bridazak's bow was trained on the mage, a glowing arrow notched and ready to fire.

"An arrow is all you have? You will need more than that, child."

"Release Dulgin, or I will kill you," Bridazak retaliated—a renewed strength in his voice.

Vevrin smirked, and responded with a pinch of the fingers controlling the hand, shoving Dulgin harder into the ceiling.

Bridazak loosed his arrow. It soared down the corridor and then ignited into a brilliant yellow aura. Vevrin's eyes changed from confident to concerned just as the tip hit his shoulder above the arm that wielded his staff. There was an explosion. Dulgin slid down the wall, choking in fresh air. The smoke cleared, and just a few feet away lay the mystic. His arm was gone. Blood spat out of the opening and bone was visible through the shredded flesh. Vevrin's breathing was labored.

Dulgin suddenly heard the rattle of his axe as the magnetization spell wore off. He caught it as it fell from the ceiling, crossed the hall, and triumphantly stood over the fallen wizard.

"I'd like you to meet my axe," he indignantly came down with the killing blow.

Sounds of combat from inside the room Abawken had gone into ended the Dwarf's moment of victory and reunion with his friends. Dulgin fought through the pain of his wounds and quickly made his way to the open doorway. Inside, the air elemental was still battling the Hammer, while Abawken was engaged with two of Manasseh's men. A couple of guards lay on the ground dead. Fire bees were being flung around in the cyclonic air from Abawken's summoned creature, but most of them were now lifeless. Another huge swing from the Hammer destroyed the elemental and the wind suddenly subsided.

The Hammer turned to see the approaching Dwarf.

"You are one ugly boy." Dulgin moved in with his axe.

Abawken felled another guard. The remaining sentry was younger than the others, and his sword was shaking in his hands. The oversized helmet did not move as the boys head shifted easily within to look at the Dwarf and human. Abawken had waited to engage him last on purpose.

"Sheath your weapon, lad," he said. The boy clearly understood he was no match and dropped his sword. It clanked on the ground. A bee burned into his neck and he reactively brought his hand up to squash the intruder.

Dulgin had already given the Hammer a deep cut into its thigh and caused him to fall. He was quite battered now; there was no more fight in him. As much as Dulgin wanted to destroy the deformity, he just couldn't do it. There was something innocent in his brown eyes.

"Ah, you've been misguided your whole life. I can't do it." The Hammer laid there holding his wound, softly groaning. Dulgin pointed his finger at him, "I expect you to change your ways or I will come back." Abawken kneeled down to the fallen torturer and wrapped a makeshift bandage around the cut from pieces of his clothing.

The Ordakians appeared in the doorway.

"Bridazak!" Abawken jumped to his feet and quickly moved to embrace him.

"I had that mystic right where I wanted him. I didn't need your help," Dulgin stubbornly insisted.

"Of course, my friend. My apologies," Bridazak grinned.

"Ah shut yer trap ya blundering fool, and give me a hug."

Dulgin peered up from his embrace to look at Spilf. "Hey, Amazing Stubby."

"Oh, how I have missed your jokes, Dulgin."

"Come here, Baldy!" The Dwarf pulled Spilf in to hug both at the same time.

"You must be Master Spilfer. My name is Abawken."

Spilf looked to the fighter and thankfully acknowledged him with a greeting of, "Hello."

"Well, I hate to break up this reunion, but we need to get to the Tower, as Master El'Korr suggested," the human proposed.

"This place is a maze. It will be near impossible to find it and not to mention we will probably encounter more guards, if we're not careful," Dulgin warned.

"We have a guide," he pointed back to the young man behind him who was still shaking.

"What's yer name boy?" Dulgin asked.

"Uh, it's Jack."

"You are kind of young to be down in the dungeons."

"Um, my father got me in."

Bridazak stepped forward, smiling at the lad. Jack wore the black leather armor uniform. It was scrunched in several areas as it was too big for his stature and his helmet almost covered his grey eyes. The nose shield extended to his mouth; it was quite humorous to see. Bridazak felt a rush of warmth toward this youth.

He sighed slightly, "Your father is fine. He is locked in the cell I was in. Do you know it?"

Jack nodded—half shocked, half confused.

"Take us to the Tower and then go and free him."

Dulgin and Abawken made eye contact, and then looked to Spilf to explain. He shrugged his shoulders.

"Master Bridazak, how do you know his father?" Abawken asked.

"They have the same eyes," he answered, following the boy out to the corridor. "Let's go."

19

The Fall

Manasseh, standing in the circular sacrifice chamber, relished in his victory of capturing the elusive Ordakian and destroying the orb he thought was so important. He wallowed in the strength of the Tree directly below him; he felt invincible. He had done it all on his own merit, without the aid of the dark deity. Truly, the godlike being would be impressed with his accomplishments and reward him accordingly; the entire realm of Ruauck-El was like a ripe apple, waiting for his grasp to pluck it. The other Horns would soon bow to him and he would be the sole Horn King of all. Thoughts of power and conquest rifled through his mind, when he suddenly heard the click of the door release. Manasseh quickly backed up to the wall and magically blended in, to view the unexpected visitor.

"Empty," Rondee said. He started to close the door.

"Wait!" El'Korr held it open. The Dwarf king entered, examining, "This chamber is used for sacrifices."

"I don't see how that matters," Xan followed after him. "Probably one of many."

"I don't know, Xan. I feel something in my bones about this place." He approached the cracked and broken stone bed, and reached down to touch the chipped rock—and was suddenly hit by a vision. The room transformed and there were ghostly images of King Manasseh, a mystic in red robes, and a large, deformed human. The Orb of Truth was placed on the stone tablet and he watched in horror as it was destroyed. The earth rumbled and quaked and the rock altar split. His vision ended.

"El'Korr? El'Korr!" He heard Xan yelling at him. "What happened?"

"The Orb is destroyed," he said slowly, in shock.

"How do you know this?"

"I saw it in a vision. We have lost." The normally sturdy voice of the dwarven King wavered in light of what had transpired. His thoughts caused his stomach to tighten, *"How can evil have triumphed like this? Our beloved voice of God is silenced."*

"El'Korr, maybe what you saw was a trick. Something Manasseh wanted you to see."

"No, I was there; it happened. The Orb is no longer part of the plan."

"Then what is?"

Almost in spite of himself, the dwarven determination rose up in him, "We will not give up! We need to find the others and get to the tower, to give Raina a sign." He left briskly, Rondee and Xan following their leader out of the murderous room.

King Manasseh stepped out from hiding and whispered, "I will meet you there."

Raina stepped safely into the Tower after luring the undead mystics to her new location. Before they arrived, she took in a large breath of air and slowly exhaled, thick fog supernaturally poured out of her mouth and filled the chamber. She was able to see through the mist of her spell as if it didn't exist. As she waited for the risen mages to take her bait, two fireballs suddenly erupted around her. She was immune to the fire damage, but the lich wizards now contained dark energy, too, and that was something she couldn't absorb. Her life force began to drain from her body, but she withstood the assault.

"You will need to do more than that to take down the Sheldeen Mystic," she said under her breath. "Let's see how you will fair against this," she readied her next attack. A spell, shot from her staff, soared out one of the balconies where an undead mage hovered. A javelin of light speared it directly. The energy blasted it backwards, flipping head over feet in the air until it fell out of sight. *"One down, two to go,"* she thought.

A surging, dark bolt of electricity raged toward her location. She fell prone and successfully dodged it; a chunk of cement on the back wall shattered from the blast. The remnants of the electric charge crackled about the room. Another fireball exploded around her. The pain of the dark energy caused her to cry out. She crawled to the wall and positioned herself in the most strategically protective corner. "Come now, Raina. This is nothing you haven't handled before," she said under her breath.

A lich moved to an open balcony, only to encounter another aspect of her spell; it was a blessed fog—it not only hid her exact location, but burned like acid once anything evil in nature entered it. The hiss of seared flesh faded as it escaped the magical mist in haste. The creature was still active, but now they all would know they couldn't enter the chamber.

The battle continued below her—steel clashed against shields, the screams of the dying, and the roar of dwarven war cries. Raina risked moving to an opening to find out how things were fairing, knowing her fog would protect her from the undead's sight, as long as she remained inside. There was only a sliver of a view below. The undead had entered the courtyard. The dwarves had done their best to hold off the overwhelming numbers, but the lines of defense were crumbling. A mound of bodies laid at the gate entrance, impeding movement. She could see her fallen comrades mingled in amongst the dead.

"Where are you, El'Korr?" she asked herself.

"He's on his way," an unfamiliar, raspy voice said from behind her.

There was no time for her to react before the blade entered her back and came through her chest. The whites of her eyes flared and her face contorted in pain; she gasped for air.

"Thank you, Jack," Bridazak said to the young teenage boy. "Now go and get your father and leave this place."

The emotionally torn boy bravely announced to the heroes, "I wish I could go with you."

"It's important for you to be with your family."

"I won't forget you. I will tell my dad that you saved me."

One by one the heroes reached out to Jack and grabbed his shoulder or ruffled his short brown hair. Jack waited and watched the heroes disappear down the corridor toward their goal: the Tower of Recall. He sighed, placed his oversized helmet back onto his head, and then turned to head out and rescue his father.

"How do you know this is the right way, El'Korr?" Xan asked as they rapidly moved down the corridors.

"I am following a strange feeling I have; trust me!" the Dwarf responded. "We need to move quickly."

Rondee stopped Xan, "Best to bienke tomincko fox weather?" He trotted off to catch up to his king.

Xan couldn't understand the Wild Dwarf. "What a strange breed," he said to himself.

"It's here!" El'Korr announced.

Xan came around the corner to see an ornate door bearing golden hinges and an emblem of a castle tower burned into the wood.

"This is it. This will take us to the tower." El'Korr opened the entrance and then began the climb up the stairs.

"Let's hope the others were as successful as we were in finding it."

"We failed, Xan. My only hope now is seeing what I can do to help my people, and get us all out of here, alive."

Abawken was the first to enter the semi-fog-filled room. The mysterious mist was dissipating and he could see some amber light coming in through four openings. His scimitar was drawn. Dulgin entered right behind him while the Ordakians peered through next.

"You have, surprisingly, been quite a challenge, I must say," a voice echoed. They were unable to pinpoint its location.

Abawken waved his sword once, releasing a magical gust of wind to push the remaining fog away. Stepping out from one of the balconies was Raina. The heroes smiled until they realized she was being held from behind by King Manasseh, a dagger blade protruding from her chest, blood melding into her flowing, lavender robes. Some of the skin on Manasseh's face had been eaten away by Raina's acid fog.

"Thank you for ridding us of that nasty spell of hers. She is quite a fighter. It appears she wanted to wait for you before she died. How touching."

"She better not die," Dulgin challenged.

"Let her go, Manasseh!" Abawken blared.

"Let me break down this situation. You tried to destroy my Tree—failed. Your army tried to beat mine—failed. Your most powerful mystic—well, let's just say she failed."

"I don't care about any of that; all I care about is splitting you in two, just like I did your most powerful mystic. That's right, he failed," Dulgin countered.

"You killed my wizard; success for you. I would applaud you, but as you can see my hands are not free to do so," he mocked.

Raina's concentration was focused on her shallow breathing. She clutched her wooden staff tightly with both hands. Her knuckles turned white.

Spilf nudged Bridazak and whispered, "Your arrows are glowing."

He looked at the quiver. There were only five arrows remaining, and all of them were active.

"Her life is fading right before your eyes," King Manasseh mocked. "Have you ever held the life of another in your hands? They are helpless. All the power resides in you to save them. But do you let them live, or die?"

"I always choose for them to live," Abawken responded.

"Ah, yes, the good inside you pushes you to a single answer. Your goodness gives you no choice. I pity you."

"What do ya want?" Dulgin asked taking a step closer.

"I'm just waiting."

"Waiting for what?"

"For your other friends to arrive."

"There is no one else."

"Xan and El'Korr might say differently."

Dulgin growled at the evil man. Abawken then noticed that Manasseh's wounds were slowly healing—regenerating.

Bridazak and Spilf both heard the sounds of armor moving up the circular stairway below them.

"Someone's coming," Spilf whispered loudly to the others.

"Ah, we have more company. Perfect. I was getting bored," Manesseh said.

Another minute passed until finally the dwarven king's brilliant armor manifested around the bend with Rondee and Xan right behind him. They spotted the Ordakians first, but their elation quickly subsided when they saw the horror of the situation.

"Raina!" El'Korr shouted as he entered.

Rondee instinctively held Xan back once he came into view, and for good reason, as the screaming Elf lunged for her.

"We are all here. Now let her go," Abawken said.

"Yes, we have quite a reunion, don't we? All your friends are here, Elf wizard," he whispered into her ear vindictively. The villainous king looked at each of them in disgust. They waited on him. He could feel the power he had in his hands and he thrived on it. "I waited so we could talk, man to man."

"Stop your charades. One way or another, we will kill you," El'Korr declared.

His face was nestled on her shoulder and neck area, "My dear, it appears that I need to have some time alone with these gentlemen. This is a boy's only conversation, and clearly you are not a boy," he began to take a step backward toward the stone railing of the balcony. "Give my love to your army!"

Manasseh spun Raina off the ledge and she plummeted out of view. The heroes rushed the area, but Manasseh turned to face them with his bloody dagger in hand, and they were forced to stop.

"We have some business to take care of, and I hope you won't disappoint me." Suddenly, a black armor phased in to surround him and a wicked, two-handed sword made of dark metal materialized in his hand, replacing the dagger. Both sides of the blade were laced with etchings. The hilt was carved with black dragon heads flaring outward with glowing, ruby gemmed eyes. His impenetrable plate mail armor covered him from head to toe. Manasseh's powerful voice boomed through his helmet, "Let's see what you've got."

A dark bolt of lightning suddenly sailed in and struck Abawken and Dulgin. One of the undead mystics floated into view. The pain wracked their entire body and they fell to their knees. An arrow of light soared from Bridazak's bow through the open balcony, and struck the lich. The daks watched as it shattered into pieces and its crimson, tattered robe fluttered away.

El'Korr and Rondee entered into melee against the wicked king. Xan ran to the balcony in desperation, but he knew he did not have a spell that could save her. He watched her plummet but at the last moment, a huge bronze dragon swooped in and grabbed the fallen Elf before she hit the ground.

"Zeffeera," Xan breathed a sigh of relief.

Bridazak held another magical arrow ready, "Spilf, keep your eyes open for any mystics."

Abawken and Dulgin were back up, and moving in to help the others with Manasseh. Four fighters against one. The king parried the multiple attacks coming in at him, and they moved about the room engaged in the ultimate battle dance.

"Very good. The skill that you all have is incredible. Better than I had imagined," Manasseh taunted while parrying another blow.

Xan stepped back into the room and cast a spell. "Kelloos viamont baruve!" A ghostly figure of a bear appeared over each of the hero's heads and then melded into them. Each of them could feel the power of the spell. They clutched their hilts tighter as their strength increased.

El'Korr's hammer connected squarely into King Manasseh's chest. It was the first strike to hit, and it was a mighty one; the forged mallet and armor collided in an ear-splitting crash. Manasseh stumbled backward a few steps, but recovered just as the others came in hard. The evil human sidestepped Dulgin's executioner style attack and then quickly backhanded the Dwarf to send him flying across the room, grunting in pain.

Manasseh looked at the new dent left behind, then addressed the Dwarf king, "It is nice to see a Dwarf who knows how to use a weapon. I will save you for last, El'Korr."

Abawken stepped back and then issued a command from his sword, "Erez!" The stone elemental instantly manifested behind Manasseh. The titan brought its earthen clubs down upon him. Both connected, and Manasseh's armor clanked hard as he slammed into the ground. Rondee followed up with his devastating golden titan maul, smashing into his back. There was no more movement from King Manasseh.

Just then they all heard the sound of a lightning bolt from outside. Xan stepped out to see an undead mystic launching his dark crackling energy spell at Zeffeera in the distance. It clipped her wing, but she continued to fly away.

"Bridazak!" He yelled back into the room.

"Oh, there you are," the Ordakian said as he spotted the remaining lich.

His last Crimson Hand arrow, as the glowing writing on the shaft indicated, flew true. Cheers erupted from below as the hundreds of dwarves witnessed the death of the mystic. This was the first time Bridazak had seen the outside battle. The thousands of undead pushed in. There was no escape for El'Korr's men. One by one the heroes came out to see, and their hearts dropped.

"This is not good," Dulgin whispered.

Battered, bruised, and bleeding, they watched helplessly. They had just defeated Manasseh, but his wicked power raged on without him.

"It's that damn, cursed tree!" El'Korr spat.

"What can we do? The Orb is lost," Xan stated.

Bridazak wheeled around at the Elf's statement, "What did you say?" Xan, with a dire face, didn't answer him. Bridazak's eyes narrowed, "What do you mean, lost?"

"I'm sorry, Bridazak," El'Korr confirmed what he never thought could be.

His knees buckled and he collapsed to the ground. Spilf intercepted him halfway down, grabbing hold of his long time friend to comfort him. "I failed, Spilf. I truly failed God. He told me that I would have to sacrifice everything, but I never thought it meant this."

Spilf consoled him, "You didn't fail, Bridazak. You rescued me, and that means something. We have not lost everything yet."

"This is not how it was supposed to be," Bridazak whispered through burning tears.

20

Sacrifice

"*Where do you think you are going?*" Zeffeera's powerful claws snatched the Elf, barely clinging to life and still clutching her wooden staff, as she sailed through the air above the battle. Zeffeera rose back up in elevation.

"*I need to get you to Xandahar. You need his healing power,*" the dragon communicated within her mind.

"*There is no time, my friend. Fly to the heart of the undead army.*"

"*Raina, you are too weak to take them on.*"

"*Just clear an opening and set me down carefully.*"

"*I won't be able to hold them off, Raina.*"

"*I know, and that is why you will need to leave the area.*"

"*Raina—*"

She cut the bronze beauty off, "*Trust me.*"

A blast clipped her left wing from behind her. She wavered in flight and then recovered.

"*Hurry, Zeffeera. My time approaches.*"

"*I don't like the sound of that, but I will do as you wish.*"

Reanimated warriors flew back as the gigantic female dragon breathed an electrical discharge and she came in for a soft landing. She laid Raina ever so gently on the charred ground.

"*Now go quickly!*" Raina commanded.

Zeffeera's wings came to life and her powerful hind legs launched her up into the air. She hovered fifty feet up.

"I will miss you, Raina."

"The Sheldeen Mystic is not one to be rid of easily, my dear Zeffeera. I will rest in the annals of legends forever."

She soared away. Raina's eyes were focused and resilient like her spirit, gazing at the heavens above. She had no strength to look around at her surroundings, but her elven ears could hear the muffled, haunting moans of the evil creatures sensing her life force; they soon would be upon her. The elven mage raised her wooden stick into the air. She was holding her final breath of life. There was no more pain. Her senses were now dull. Her lips instinctively moved as she spoke her magic word to release the power of her staff.

"Korban," the word and her spirit rushed forth from her body.

The heroes watched the immense explosion. It raced through the heart of the corpse army and incinerated all in its path. A bright flash of light rivalled the waning sun in the distance. The shockwave finally hit the castle and shook the very foundation. Thousands of King Manasseh's army fell.

"What has Raina done?" Xan fought back tears.

"She has given us hope," El'Korr responded solemnly.

"Well, I *hope* you weren't planning on leaving," King Manasseh announced from behind them.

His black, two-handed sword sliced through the rock elemental. The earth creature crumbled before the human king as he began to supernaturally grow. His armor expanded with his bulk, and a massive, towering version of himself stood before the heroes.

"That was a good first round," the deep voice behind the helmet spoke.

"We are getting out of here, boys!" Geetock yelled, cutting down another walking corpse.

The dwarven army rallied and began to push through. Raina had given them a miracle and punched a hole large enough to give them a chance. Now that their wizard was gone, they lost the protection they'd had from Manasseh's army, who continued to unleash volleys of arrows from within the castle; Geetock was losing dwarves by the second. The loss of many of his brethren was inevitable, but their escape from the guaranteed kill zone was forthcoming. Eruptions of intense light summoned through the divine clerics of old, blasted the undead as they surged through the weakened ranks. Jets of fire streamed from outstretched hands and burned the decaying flesh of the walking dead. Dwarven priests yelled out the same spell command El'Korr and Xan had used. Celestial power penetrated flesh and bone and shattered the vile, lifeless puppets. They moved in unison further away. The back ranks held up shields to protect themselves from the relentless arrows, and every man pushed on until finally they emerged, outside the range of the distant shafts of death.

Geetock stood on top of a larger mound as his men pushed past on both sides, like a raging river. The soulless beings continued to pour into the vacant wake of the army's march. The automatons sensed and pursued the life inside each of them, like insects attracted to light. He breathed a Dwarven prayer for his dear King El'Korr and the others, that they would find a way to join them. The battle was far from over as the undead knew nothing of pain or tiring, and would continue to attack relentlessly.

Manasseh had been more powerful than they had imagined was possible. Abawken summoned another rock monster but it was quickly destroyed. All of the fighters were hard pressed to protect themselves from the evil king's devastating sword. The slim openings that came along didn't do much to damage the malevolent king.

Menacing laughs erupted from within the armored fiend. "You cannot defeat me!" He bellowed proudly.

Abawken used the power of his blade and soared above him. Manasseh's eyes followed the sheik fighter. Dulgin went in while he was distracted, as did the others. Hammers and axe plowed into him. He stumbled back from the impact of all three weapons and grunted in pain. Then he roared back with a counter attack of his own. His black sword came down upon Dulgin. The Dwarf brought up his axe to block it. His axe shattered and he fell back to the ground.

"That was my father's axe!" He cried.

"When you see your father, tell him I said hello," Manasseh mocked.

"You bastard!" Dulgin charged, weaponless.

The wicked enemy let the Dwarf grapple him with open arms. Spikes magically sprouted out from the armor. Dulgin was impaled. He fell backwards as the spikes retracted, making the sound like that of a weapon being pulled from a scabbard.

Xan caught Dulgin as he stumbled back. The Elf slid the dwarven fighter away from the battle zone.

A magical arrow sailed between the fighters that remained and slammed into the chest of King Manasseh. There was a loud explosion. Smoke engulfed everyone, and the smell of burnt metal intensified. Manasseh stepped through. He was still standing. His black armor had a gaping hole in the chest and they could see his charred skin underneath. Melted metal sizzled and vapors escaped around the edges.

"That hurt! You die next, Halfling!"

El'Korr and Rondee stepped in his way. Abawken flew in from behind him and slashed at the back of his neck. It was a good hit, but it still didn't put him down.

"I grow tired of you, pests!" A caustic green mist began to come off of his armor.

"Acid!" El'Korr alerted the others.

Spilf tapped Bridazak on the shoulder to get his attention. He pointed to the bronze dragon flying in. Its head was enormous and it hovered before them.

"*Climb on!*" Zeffeera said aloud inside their minds.

Spilf looked to his friend and waited. Bridazak pushed him to go first.

"Xan! Grab Dulgin. We need to get out of here." The Elf was already carrying the Dwarf to the balcony.

El'Korr and Rondee continued to fight defensively, backing themselves toward the dragon.

The glow of the Tree pulsed as Manasseh pulled on its power. The bluish, hovering fog stretched throughout the cavernous chamber. A flash of the protective domed shield ignited as small rocks and dirt fell from above. The sound of the debris clacking amongst the rubble and bones echoed as they skipped and ricocheted.

From a crack in the ceiling, a single drop of blood fell. The Spirit of Truth descended upon the evil. A sizzle of intense heat resounded as it bore a hole in the shield, and the first drop struck the highest of the gnarled branches. Then another, and another. Blood oozed down the limbs and the roots began writhing within the ground. Faint and distant, a haunting shriek bellowed within the spindly frame. The smooth, dark wood of the trunk began to split and crack. The root system popped and snapped as it shriveled beneath the ground. The once mighty tree toppled over and fell down the steep incline of the pyramid it rested on. It's aura slowly faded, the power severed, and soon the room was cast into utter darkness, silenced once and for all.

King Manasseh drove the dwarves further back with each of his powerful swipes. There was no way that they would escape together. Rondee stepped forward to try to push his assault away. El'Korr understood what his loyal friend was attempting to do, but he couldn't abandon his sworn protector.

"Go, my Malehk!" Rondee yelled.

"We do this together," he insisted.

They pressed in as a unit. Hammers swung with rage as they knew this would be their last fight. Weapons connected into Manasseh's right leg. It caused him to fall to one knee.

"I knew you would bow to me, Manasseh," El'Korr jabbed.

He roared back in anger and fought through the pain he suddenly felt in his leg as he stood. The dwarves noticed that his height had lowered.

"Coming down to our size, eh?" El'Korr taunted as he came in with another blow.

"Yit, yit, yit!" Rondee said in a high pitched voice. The Wild Dwarf grew taller and now matched the seven-foot frame of the diminishing human.

Another slash came from Abawken's scimitar, but Manasseh quickly grabbed the fighter.

"I've had enough of you!" He tossed him out the closest balcony and then waved his hand to cast a spell that never came to fruition. There was a noticeable confused turn of his head within the dark helmet. Abawken quickly flew back into the room.

Another reduction in his size occurred and Manasseh was now back to his original height.

"What is happening?" King Manasseh panicked. He began to feel pain inside his body, his right leg throbbed and the back of his neck stung as sweat and blood intermingled from that scimitar slash he had absorbed earlier. The sudden taste of blood inside his mouth intensified.

The dwarves delivered another punishing blow simultaneously, and the malevolent king fell onto his back. Manasseh bellowed in agony as his black armor and sword faded out of existence.

"He is losing his power!" El'Korr announced.

The dwarves both brought their weapons around for the kill, but relented when they noticed a pool of blood forming around Manasseh's body. The former king's eyes stared blankly as his vital fluid poured out from underneath. Slash marks suddenly materialized on his body, dark purple bruising in his flesh came to light, and then the sound of his breastbone cracked as his chest caved in. The wicked king was no more. The Elf broke them from their gaze of the gory aftermath.

"Hurry, get onto Zeffeera!" Xan yelled from the back of the dragon.

"Go!" The giant Rondee commanded as he pulled on his dwarven king. El'Korr relinquished his stubbornness and climbed aboard the dragon.

Troops suddenly emerged from the stairway chasing two individuals. It was Jack and his father, Ghent. A crossbow bolt stuck out of Ghent's leg. His son was helping him hobble along.

"Jack! Over here!" Bridazak yelled.

It was an all-out hustle to get to the Ordakian, but three of the King's men bent one knee, lined up their shots, and clicked the release trigger on their crossbows. Ghent suddenly positioned his back to protect his child and blocked the shots—all three bolts struck. He fell forward, but pushed Jack into Rondee's arms.

"Dad!" the boy cried.

"Jack, go! I love you son," he called in a strained voice before his head slowly sagged against the stone floor.

"No! Dad! Dad!" the boy wailed.

Manasseh's body suddenly began to convulse on the floor, limbs contorting, and he sat straight up. He acted differently; his body moved stiffly, but it was his eyes that said it all. They were pearly black, with no pupils.

Bridazak felt a familiar chill tingle the back of his neck. He was certain of what his senses were alerting. "Get out of there!" he shouted. "It's not Manasseh!"

Rondee quickly brought the struggling teenager to the dragon. Zeffeera began to lift away. The Wild Dwarf, still in his giant size, grabbed onto her leg.

More troops were coming up the stairway to the Tower. Abawken summoned an air elemental to keep them occupied and then flew after the others. He grabbed hold of the dragon's other leg. They looked back to see King Manasseh, or what appeared to be him, on the balcony watching them fly away.

"This is far from over," the evil being said in each of their minds—the voice smooth and sinister.

"That was not Manasseh. Who was that?" El'Korr asked.

Bridazak paused, "Xan knows who it was, he told us about it."

"I do?" the Elf was surprised. He paused for a moment, but turned white as he realized the only tale Bridazak could be referencing. He turned to the others, "That was the dark ruler of Kerrith Ravine."

El'Korr snapped, "How do you know this, Xandahar?"

"That level of power—it had to be him. It is the only thing that makes sense. He was controlling the Tree and Manasseh, all along."

The heroes sat dumbfounded as they soared over the scattered undead army remnants and soon caught up to their own men. Only four hundred of them had survived. The pursuing horde had fallen after the power of the Tree was severed and destroyed. The dwarves were now deep into the Desert of Guilt, a layer of ash and dust clung to their bloody armor and matted hair.

Zeffeera landed and everyone was reunited. There was a solemn exchange of good tidings; no cheers, just appreciation for survival. Their loss was heavy.

"You did well, Geetock, all of you did," King El'Korr announced.

"Without Raina's power and your successful mission of defeating the Tree, we wouldn't have made it," he responded.

"The Orb was destroyed before we could get it to the Tree. We are uncertain as to what happened."

Bridazak stepped forward, "The Orb. It changed color."

"I am not following you, what do you mean?"

"It changed from gold to red. I think it," he turned his head away to compose himself. "It knew it was going to be destroyed."

"But why? I don't understand."

"Neither do I, but—"

Xan cut Bridazak off, "We have a problem."

"What is it?"

"Dulgin is not responding to any of my healing spells."

"No," Bridazak quickly rushed to his fallen friend.

The others gathered around with concerned looks. Dulgin had lost a lot of blood through multiple wounds.

"Is there nothing we can do?" El'Korr questioned Xan.

"I am at a loss. Perhaps being in close proximity to Kerrith Ravine has blocked any healing, but I can't be sure."

Bridazak no longer held back his tears and buried his face into Dulgin's armored chest. "Don't leave me Dulgin," his voice cracked.

"I just got my brother back. Find a way, Xan!" El'Korr demanded.

"I have given him my most powerful healing spell, but still he is dying. I am sorry."

Suddenly the Ordakian lurched in surprise and looked around at each of them.

"What is it, Bridazak?" Spilf asked.

"You didn't hear him?"

Their puzzled looks answered him.

"The voice of God said 'the Holy City'. That's it! We need to get him there."

"Bridazak, are you sure? I saw the Orb destroyed in a vision; I promise you it is no more."

"I know his voice, and so do you El'Korr. You told me you recognized it when you heard it before. You have to trust me!"

El'Korr was hesitant, "The city has not been heard of for centuries, and Kerrith Ravine stands in our way."

"I don't care. I'm taking him there!" He turned toward the dragon, "Zeffeera, will you take us?"

"No one is able to fly over the Ravine, and the other side is blocked by a sheet of darkness. Some say it is a void. I can take you to the edge of the Ravine, but no further."

"That's good enough. Someone help me with Dulgin."

Abawken and Spilf immediately responded to his request. Xan and El'Korr assisted in getting the Dwarf situated on top of the bronze creature. They finalized Dulgin's position with Bridazak straddling the ridged spine, when Geetock suddenly shouted, pointing back toward the castle in the distance, "El'Korr, look!"

Everyone turned to see a huge, swirling funnel touch the ground. It whipped along, lifting the fallen bodies into the air. The twister was massive, and it appeared to be heading their way.

"There's another one!" someone shouted to the right of them.

"Over here too!" came from their left.

These black twisters were each coming in to trap them, and the only direction they could travel was now toward Kerrith Ravine.

"Let's move out!" El'Korr commanded.

Spilf and Abawken climbed aboard the dragon to join Bridazak and Dulgin.

"I'm staying with my army. May God help us all. Tell my brother that I am sorry," El'Korr prepared to part. Xan approached him, but the dwarven king ushered him to leave, "You need to be with them. Save my brother. Now go!"

"C'mon Jack! You too!" Bridazak called down to the saddened and lost boy. He climbed and settled in behind the Ordakian.

Zeffeera jumped into the air; her powerful wings pushing them further and further away. El'Korr watched them depart. He was about to take his remaining army into their original goal, from centuries before. It was his destiny and it awaited him.

21

Kerrith Ravine

The vile god of darkness returned home to Kerrith Ravine. Manasseh had failed him, but there was no shortage of power-hungry humans willing to take his place. The problem was the Tree. Centuries he'd spent perverting the sacred relic, gone. The trophy he flaunted before his enemy in the heavens was now destroyed, and access to its darkness lost forever. He seethed in anger.

"Sigil, send my followers to rise up and crush the insignificant beings above."

"As you command."

A low hum throughout the halls increased in volume until it was recognizable—monotone horns sounded the order. Out of the pitch-dark came the stirrings of the evil within Kerrith Ravine—a hidden dimension, nestled inside the realms; a shadowy harbor reserved for the eternally hideous. Those dwelling within its confines began to awaken with fury. There were sounds of claws scratching at stone, and growls oozing out of grinding teeth. Indescribably contorted faces weaved in and out of the rock wall as they climbed to the surface where the dwarven army stood. They thirsted for their souls to be devoured, and longed to pull them into their world of torment. The twilight sky above grew closer as the thousands of shadow creatures raced to the top.

"El'Korr, why are the wind funnels not approaching?" Geetock asked.

"I'm not sure. It's like they are waiting."

"Waiting for what? We are at the edge of the ravine. We have no place left to go."

"We also don't know what happened to Zeffeera and the others. They have not been seen."

"Maybe they made it?"

Just then, several of his men shouted alarms of distress. "They're coming!"

"This is it, boys! Prepare your spells of light and fight like there is no tomorrow."

The warriors could now hear the sounds of the reegs. They backed away from the ledge to give some distance. A deathly chill ran through them all. El'Korr began to bash his shield with his weapon. The others followed suit until the cacophony of clanging sounds was deafening. They would combat fear with courage.

"Look!" Someone yelled.

They watched the black whirling wind tunnels slowly dissipate. The blackness fell like water and it was quickly understood that the very essence of the tornadoes were the shadow creatures themselves. They were surrounded and there was no escape.

"There! Do you see it?" Bridazak pointed.

"*Yes, you were right,*" Zeffeera was surprised.

"What is it, though?" Xan asked.

"*It is an opening. A tear in the curtain that is Kerrith Ravine,*" Zeffeera announced into everyone's mind, amazed to see it for what it truly was after all this time.

Approaching fast, the bronze dragon soared toward the brilliant rays shooting out of the blackness. They each raised their hands to shield themselves from the blinding light. Zeffeera closed her eyes and ducked her head, preparing to ram whatever may be on the other side, and shot through. The sounds of their world, the cold whipping wind, became muffled, and were replaced with a soft, melodic, warm breeze that soothed them all with an overwhelming sense of peace. All their fears, anxiety, and troubles faded within the surreal environment. They knew those feelings existed, but they could no longer be found in this place. There was light everywhere, and soon a glorious city emerged into view.

"It's the Holy City!" Xan announced in unbelief.

White marble, crystal cathedrals, and streets and pathways that glistened like gold; it sparkled and took their breath away.

"What is this place?" Dulgin asked, now awake.

"You're alive!" Bridazak embraced his friend.

"Yeah, I'm alive, now get off me. What's going on?"

"This is the Lost City! It was never destroyed after all; it was hidden! We made it, Dulgin!"

Zeffeera landed at the foot of the steps leading up to the Great Temple—the grandest and most beautiful place in the entire city. No legend ever spoken of it had done justice to what they saw as they looked up in awe. It was situated on the highest spot while the rest of the glorious structures cascaded down all around it. There stood two beings at the top of the marble stairs; they had wings and held swords that gleamed so brightly, they appeared to be fashioned from light itself. Their faces weren't quite visible, as they were bathed in a brilliant glow. Each of them started the trek up the stairs, and the huge double door entrance was pulled open by the winged creatures. The golden portal revealed the purest white luminescence they had ever seen, and small sparkling spheres danced about inside of it.

"Our clothes?" Bridazak noticed, alerting the others.

"They are white and clean. How can that be?" Spilf questioned.

"Your hair!" Bridazak pointed.

Spilf reached up and felt his hair, and even looked down to see new growth of brown fur on top of his pads. He was healed of all the damage he had taken from the hand of the evil king. The Ordakian smiled brightly.

The heroes now wore white clothing of a material they had never felt before—so soft and soothing to the touch. Their weapons and gear had vanished, but they did not long for them, as there was no feeling of fear. Bridazak stepped through first, followed by Dulgin and Spilf, then Abawken and Xan, with Jack between them.

Brilliant colors of the entire spectrum and new colors they had never seen before fanned out like kaleidoscopes from the throne of white light before them. Wild smells of wonderful fragrances beyond their scope of understanding filled every breath. The high walls faded away from their sight, endless and indescribable. The sound of rushing water came to their ears in the form of a powerful voice.

"Well done, good and faithful."

The sense of love was so overpowering that they fell to their knees in a place that had no floor or ceiling. Tears flowed down their cheeks as their heads bowed. There was no question in anyone's mind; they were with God.

"Rise, my child."

Abawken obeyed, and stood to find himself alone before God. Abawken peered into God's eyes, bluer than oceans, vibrant, and full of vitality. His skin glowed in perfection and his brown, silky hair cascaded to rest upon his broad shoulders. The human God was drenched in majestic robes that flowed off of him like water that never ended.

He spoke, "I'm so proud of who you have become, Abawken. Your faith is beyond measure."

"I am at a loss for words my God, my King," Abawken tried to respond.

"Come and share your heart with me. Let us speak for as long as you like. I will fill you with great and wonderful knowledge."

"What about my friends?"

"You never cease to amaze me. Always caring for others, but this time it is all for you, Abawken Shellahk. Your friends are with me even as we speak."

"I have so many questions," Abawken said, unsure of where to begin.

"And I have all the answers you need, but first, let me share a story."

God began to stroll with Abawken by his side, and not too long after, two marble thrones rose from the iridescent floor. They were slightly angled toward each other; God motioned for him to sit. Abawken nodded and took his seat. He was pleasantly surprised to find the stone to be comfortable, like a pillow of air.

His deity began to weave his tale, "There once was a desert. Sagebrush and honey thimbles splayed across rolling orange dunes as far as the eye could see."

"Sounds like home," Abawken whispered.

"In this arid desert, people wandered aimlessly in search of..."

"Water," Abawken answered.

"Yes, water, but none could be found. Though water was scarce and precious, a community nevertheless was formed. Water had to be brought into this desert gathering, and the value of it overcame gold. The wealthy flourished while many mothers and children barely survived; always longing for the prized water." God ended his tale and waited for Abawken's response.

The human paused and then slowly shook his head, "I don't understand the meaning of your story. This is the way of the desert."

"You are using your mind. I ask for you to search your heart, Abawken."

The human suddenly blurted out, "In a desert, water is life."

"Exactly," he nodded as Abawken was starting to understand his leading. "You asked me many nights why I brought you there when you were a child. Do you remember?"

"But I was just a boy, and thought selfishly."

"No, you thought with your heart."

"I questioned my life many days and nights. I thought I was cursed, to have been brought into such a desolate land."

"Yes, you were *brought* to that desert, my son."

A sudden flash of realization hit the fighter, "I'm the water," he whispered.

"And a stream comes from a source which can sustain life forever. No one is where they are by accident. Each has his purpose. I have set destiny in the hearts of everyone, but knowledge, though it has its place, can prevent the heart from seeing the truth."

"Why did you call me away from this land, then?"

God lightly laughed, "How does a fighter become a master swordsman?"

"Training and practice," he answered.

"Abawken, you were always destined for greater things, but you needed to be prepared in the desert first."

The warrior was perplexed, "But why use anyone at all; why allow the evil to continue in the world? You are God, Creator of All, why not put an end to the suffering?"

"What kind of God could I be to a people if I broke my promises to them? I gave you free will to make your decisions, to make your mistakes, to live according to your own methods. One act stripped the good of the world and so it was, one act, to restore righteousness."

"You speak of the Orb of Truth, but it was destroyed."

"My voice can never be silenced. I have placed eternity in the hearts of all, and many hear their calling while others resist. I will not, I cannot, force anyone to love, but the choice is there for all to make. As their Father, I await to hold them in my arms and restore their full inheritance as my sons and daughters. A time is coming and for some has already come when the scales covering their eyes will fall away, and they will behold the Truth."

Abawken leaned in, "I want to hear more."

"Russo, di cende."

Spilf slowly lifted his gaze to see a beautiful Ordakian wearing flowing topaz robes. It was God, smiling so full of joy at the sight of him.

"Where are we?" Spilf looked around, but saw only endless light.

"Where would you like to be, Spilfer? Perhaps on top of a calm lake?" God spoke, and they were there, standing on glassy water surrounded by an assortment of colorful trees in the distance. Spilf recalled the sensation he'd felt when he travelled through the portal out of the Oculus chamber, but this was different. It wasn't magic; they hadn't really even travelled. They were simply there. He felt no fear, only wonder. He grabbed hold of his God's hand, and they walked together. Each step the King of Kings took produced a bed of lilies; colors sparkling off of their uniquely shaped petals. Spilf watched in awe as clusters of vines raced up from the depths of the crystal clear water to meet his next step.

"This place seems familiar to me," he looked in amazement.

"It should. It was your home, when you were a boy."

Spilf had forgotten his childhood, remembering only life on the streets up until he met Bridazak, but God's words seemed to unlock something hidden, and he knew it to be true.

"Where is my family?"

"They are still of the world, Ruauck-El."

"They are alive?"

"Yes."

"Why did they leave me?"

"I will give you eyes to see for yourself, Spilfer Teehle. Behold."

The Ordakian watched as a scene from the past unfolded before him. He could feel the cool breeze coming off of the lake shore and hear the water lapping up against the smooth pebbles. He turned, trying to discern the origin of the smell of fresh baked bread, and spotted a simply-clothed male Ordakian with his young boy, breaking a loaf in half to share. *"That's me,"* Spilf thought. Then a female Dak stepped out from the open door of the cottage, and kissed her husband.

Suddenly, screams erupted from the other side of the small village. The simply-clothed Ordakian man grabbed the child and ran to the lake. He placed the boy inside a small canoe and ushered for his mother to join him.

"Son, you must go to the far side and wait with your momah. I will meet you there. I promise,"

"Bapah! No! Come with us."

"Honey, he will be okay. C'mon let's go," the mother said.

"But what is happening?"

"Your bapah will explain everything once he gets back."

An arrow suddenly slammed into his mother's shoulder as she reached for an oar. She fell out of the small boat.

"Momah!"

She bobbed back up to the surface and stood in the shallow water. Her hands reached to the canoe and she pushed it with all her strength, screaming through the pain. "I love you, son. Don't come back. Don't look for us. Hide!"

The vision ended and he was suddenly back with God. Tears streamed down his face and he embraced God with sadness and understanding.

"They saved me."

"Gundi, te chiva."

Dulgin stood, but stubbornly refused to raise his head.

"What troubles you?" the deep voice of God spoke. His hand reached out and lifted his chin.

Tears tumbled from Dulgin's eyes. God wiped them away and continued to wipe each new tear that fell. Dulgin was now looking at the most powerful Dwarf he had ever seen; such pride and love came from him. A flowing cape of gold fluttered behind his broad frame, and a well-groomed white beard adorned his face. It was the only thing he could recognize, as the rest of his features were blurred by his overwhelming beauty.

"I am torn," Dulgin said.

"But why?"

"I have a sense of loss that I can't explain."

"Perhaps a gift will change that." The mighty Dwarf God produced a grand battle axe. Brilliant orange and red gems littered the shaft. A gleaming, perfectly shaped, axe head fanned out on top with magnificent etchings beyond all imagination.

Dulgin was overwhelmed by the beauty of the weapon and the gesture, but hesitated to take it.

"It doesn't feel right, my Lord. I don't know how to explain my feelings right now."

"Why would you want that old beat up axe you lost?"

"How did you know? Well, I guess you would since you are God and all. It was given to me by my father when I was a boy and for some reason I have never wanted anything else. It's like I have a piece of him with me."

"I understand Dulgin, more than you can comprehend," he smiled and continued, "You hold the inheritance of generations before you. It is something that cannot be seen, only experienced."

A flash of light erupted from behind Dulgin. He turned and there stood his father, holding his old axe.

"This belongs to you, Son."

Spirit images of past generations stood behind his dad, beginning with his grandfather and extending out five generations beyond. Dulgin stood in humbled astonishment.

"Take it with my blessing. My pride for you has moved the fathers who came before me to stand with you."

Dulgin reached out and grasped the battered battle axe. He felt restored, and tears tumbled out once again.

"I love you, Dah."

"I have never questioned your love, son. Let us embrace and cherish this moment together."

Dulgin held his father like never before. They separated. "Dah, you left us. Why?"

"Chiva, I can only say that I am sorry for not being there when you both needed me most. After the loss of your mother, I fell into despair and lost sight of you both."

"Where is Mah?" Dulgin looked at his father and then back to God in excitement.

The dwarven deity responded, "She is waiting, let us go and see her."

"Russo, di cende."

Bridazak recognized the voice; the Orb of Truth. His head lifted, excited to finally see the face which matched the sound he had come to love more than anything. He found an Ordakian, and he marvelled at the perfection of the glorious being. A soft glow encapsulated him. Bridazak noticed his robes flowing endlessly behind him. The material rolled like forming waves and revealed two colors on either side: gold and a deep red; the same colors of the Orb had borne. Bridazak's elation dwindled and he slowly looked down, away from his deity, reminded of his failure.

"What is it?" God asked.

"Why did you choose me?"

"Why not choose you?"

"Because I failed, and I am a nobody."

"You did not fail. I orchestrated every step so that every promise and prophecy made would be fulfilled. I created the Orb and only I could destroy it. You, Bridazak, faithfully carried me through my plan, so again I say, well done. Well done. I knew you before you were born, before the world was ever created. You are special and you matter so much that I would sacrifice everything to have you with me."

"But you are God, and I am just a thief."

God laughed, "And a good thief you are."

"I don't understand."

God placed both of his hands on Bridazak's shoulders, "You are a good thief because you stole my heart."

Bridazak's face began to brighten with a smile. "I wouldn't have thought of it that way. So, you are not mad at me?"

"Of course not! I'm proud of you. I knew that I chose the right Ordakian for the task. You fought through the darkest hour, and risked everything for me and your friends."

"I know you sent Abawken to help, but did you set all those things in motion for us? Bringing me to the Seeker bow and arrows, and meeting Billwick... and learning my Bapah's name?"

"Your steps were ordered and never without my hand's guiding," he paused, "Matter of fact, I have another gift for you."

Bridazak protested, "You have already given me more than I could possibly imagine. What else could I want?"

God smiled and extended a closed fist, turned it upright, and then opened his hand to reveal two clear gems in the form of teardrops.

"What are they?"

"Your gift."

Bridazak held out his hand and God dropped them into his open palm. The gems splashed onto his skin like water. He looked at God with a puzzled face, not understanding.

"Those are prayers offered up to me that I have reserved, and will now honor."

"We didn't abandon you, Son," a female voice echoed forth from behind him. Bridazak turned around, and there she was. Her long brown hair had beautiful flowers laced within the ornate braid-work. She wore a white dress that elegantly draped to the ground. He recognized her, though he had never seen her before, he knew it was his momah. Then his bapah, Hills Baiulus, stepped out from behind her, greeting him with a warming smile of admiration. He couldn't believe what he was seeing.

"We are so proud of you. To have you here is the greatest gift for us."

"Momah? Bapah? Is it really you?"

"Yes, Son."

"I don't know what to say."

"We were always meant to be together, and finally, it is time." There it was, like the dawn of a new day breaking free from the bondage of night—the connection, the final link, from the beginning when he first received the Orb of Truth inside the box, now came full circle. *"It is time."* It was his parents who had delivered the box, the message, and the mission.

"The One that was, that is, and will always be, allowed this."

They embraced and cried together. Bridazak glanced up and looked into the eyes of Truth and silently mouthed, "Thoss vule." God smiled, his face like that of a proud father.

22

Darkness and Light

The celebration feast was in full swing. All the heroes sat together with their families at the massive table set before them with God at the head. Vibrant, colorful food covered the dining table-top from end to end. Jovial conversations abounded, erupting into laughter at different intervals. They ate to their hearts' content; the tastes of each morsel elicited moans of enjoyment. Golden goblets filled with wine clinked and sloshed over at each toast.

Their God laughed and enjoyed each of them at his festival. Each of the heroes looked at their King of all Kings and saw him in the form that represented their kind. Sitting before them was love in a tangible form; no longer just a word or feeling, but instead something they could physically touch, see with their own eyes, and hear with their ears.

Bridazak was seated with his family and surrounded by his friends. He took notice of Xandahar, with his wife next to him and his son on his lap, the pure joy of their reunion displayed across their faces. Dulgin caught his attention next, when his Mah slapped the back of his head, scolding him about something. She, like her son, had red hair bursting like a volcano from her scalp. Bridazak smiled as he realized where Dulgin had inherited his attitude. Next to them sat Jack and his father, Ghent, pointing to the magnificent array of cookies and pastries, deciding which to try first. Then his eyes caught a familiar Ordakian; directly across from him, Billwick Softfoot raised his drink, and smiled as if he had known all along that it would end like this; maybe he had. There was no place Bridazak would rather be. He pulled more grapes off the table—beautiful, deep red, plump beauties draped over a silver stand near the center. As he pulled a portion of the vine laden with fruit away, he saw his reflection in the polished silver. As if caught in a trance, the clank of utensils and chalices around the table jolted him back to memories of the former realm he had come from, and resounded like a distant clash of battle.

God was suddenly standing behind him. "What is it my child? What do you see?"

Others at the table hushed to hear what was going on.

"It's nothing," Bridazak responded, not able to explain his feeling.

"Then let me make this announcement. I will be making a new realm. One that will never be corrupted. One where there will be no pain or suffering, only joy and love."

Goblets rose up into the air in gleeful acceptance—all except for one.

"Bridazak, is there something wrong?"

"What will happen to the old realm?"

"It will cease to exist."

"But what about the people that are still there?"

"My judgement will fall on those who have turned from me."

"But what about El'Korr and his army?"

Others at the table mirrored his question with mumbles of concern.

"They will be invited guests, of course. They have fought valiantly for me and will be rewarded."

Everyone loved his answer, and returned back to drinking and eating. Bridazak asked another question.

"What about other people—who don't know you?" A hush returned.

God countered, his peaceful demeanor never wavering, "What about them, Bridazak?"

"Don't they get a chance to know you? You created them."

"Yes, I did, and do you think that I have not given them a chance? Do you think that I have not spoken to them in their dreams? Do you think that I have abandoned them or that I do not feel the loss of every soul that chose to ignore my calling?"

"But what if there were one?"

The question lingered in the room. Everyone waited in anticipation of the answer.

"Who will reach that one? Who is willing to speak to them in a world filled with evil and darkness?" God asked.

There was silence and then a lonely voice answered.

"I will," Spilf chimed.

Everyone turned to him.

"My momah and bapah are still alive, and I want to go back for them."

Bridazak glanced at his parents, who exchanged knowing looks, and smiled at their son. "I will join you, Spilf," Bridazak said.

"You can't go anywhere without me, ya blundering fools."

One by one, Bridazak, Dulgin, Abawken, and Xan, volunteered to go back, including young Jack, who tightly embraced his father, then stepped out to join his heroes.

God's face beamed with pride as he looked upon each of them, "Know this, heroes of Ruauck-El: you will feel the pain and suffering of the world and will be vulnerable in your mortal bodies once again. You will not be able to see me, but know that I will never leave you nor forsake you. I am your God and you are my people. Go out and gather those who have been lost. Spread the good news that I wait for them at the city gate. Do all in the name of love. You will be my hands and feet, treading through darkness, and you will bear my light."

They were now alone with God who sat on his throne. The heroes stood before him. There was a sense of duty calling them back, and love was at the core. It was time to leave and help the suffering, and fight the evil works of the enemy of their king.

"My sons and daughter, I send you with the blessing of a Father."

Bridazak looked down the line of them and was confused.

"You meant to say sons, right?"

God smiled and did not answer. A female voice behind them startled the group.

"Clearly, I am not a male."

They turned to see Raina, glorious in her white robes.

All of them rushed to hug and embrace her, except for Xandahar. Smiling, she greeted each of them, until her eyes met her fellow Sheldeen Elf.

"Xandahar, please forgive me. Here and now, in this place, all that was behind us feels meaningless. Let us set our differences aside and join together once again."

He stared at her for a long moment, searching his emotions as her words penetrated his heart. He felt the wound of the centuries-old ill-exchange now healing. He had blamed Raina for steering El'Korr and his army to Kerrith Ravine, instead of to the Tree. She'd commanded him away for his open dissent to her orders, and he had always been ashamed of obeying her, instead of insisting to stay by her side; moments later, he heard the explosion, and she and the troops were ensnared into the ever-burning flames.

"I have missed you, and I accept your apology." He rushed over and lifted her off her feet, his arms wrapped around her tightly.

Bridazak had sensed the separation between them ever since the curse of the Burning Forest was broken. "Dulgin, do you know what is happening?"

The Dwarf shrugged, "Maybe a lover's quarrel."

Xan released his grasp of Raina, his countenance towards her completely transformed from a hardened tone to one full of joy. He smiled as he announced, "Rejoice with me, for my sister was lost, but she has now returned!"

Bridazak let out a deep sigh as all of his former misconceptions now formed into an understanding of their tension—a longtime sibling disagreement.

"Zeffeera awaits for you outside. It is time," declared God.

Bridazak tilted his head slightly, pondering God's choice words once again. *My parents sent me this message, but did God give it to them to begin with? Did he know we would go back?* He looked to God, who winked back at him. Bridazak smiled and whispered, "Will it ever *not* be the time?"

Golden doors appeared and then broke open to reveal the outside. The bronze dragon was perched at the bottom of the stairs.

"Ah, there you are," her booming voice rang inside each of their minds. *"Climb aboard, this dragon is leaving. Next stop, Ruauck-El."*

Just then, she spotted the Elf mystic, *"Raina! You live!"*

"Yes, I am alive, and eager to get back. It is good to see you, old friend. Ruauck-El has not seen the last of the Sheldeen Mystic. I told you that you would not be rid of me."

They all smiled and walked down the stairs to reunite with Zeffeera.

"El'Korr, we are not going to make it!" Geetock yelled.

"We will be taking out as many as we can, then!"

Geetock growled, "These Reegs will see what happens when you back a Dwarf against a wall. It has been an honor, my Malehk."

Screams of horror filled their ears as the first of his army were hit by the life-sucking beasts. The surge of dark shadow creatures came over the lip of the ravine while more evil gathered around them from the other three sides. Flashes of light sprang up throughout the hundreds of remaining dwarves, humans, and elves to combat the sentient dark-souls. The clerics of old fought valiantly as gurgled bursts of pain amongst both Dwarves and Reegs resounded like a cacophony of screeching sheps being slaughtered in scores. The burly, bearded clan bolstered each other with yells of triumph. None would admit defeat and each motivated swing of vengeance encouraged them to fight on. El'Korr was surrounded by his elite Wild Dwarves. His fearless brigade of protectors were a lone vessel amongst the endless sea of dark Reegs. The Dwarven King relentlessly hurled his magical hammer, thunderous impacts of light bursting forth at each connected hit. Horrific screeches of torment flared and then faded away as their souls were blasted back to the pits they had come from. Their heroic stand, mighty as they were, would never be enough, as the seemingly countless numbers of Reegs continued to flood deeper into their ranks. Their end was in sight; the inevitable was upon them.

Suddenly, a brilliant flash, like that of the glorious sun emerging over the horizon, ignited the darkened sky and caused many of them to look to the distance, including the reegs.

"Dear God Almighty," El'Korr stared in awe.

"There they are, Zeffeera!" Bridazak pointed to the cluster of battling dwarves below.

"I see them."

"It seems like time stopped while we were at the Holy City," Spilf noted.

"How are we going to save El'Korr and the others?" Abawken asked.

"Look, the Reegs are scattering!" Dulgin pointed out.

"But why?" Bridazak asked.

"They must be scared of old Zeffeera," Spilf chimed, patting her scales.

"Impossible," Raina said.

The heroes were now back in their normal attire, though still clean and pristine, their armor and weapons shining like new.

They watched the violent enemy flee back into the darkness like cockroaches caught in light.

Jack was riding in the back and tapped Xan on the shoulder, "Um, you should see this."

Xan peered backward and his mouth dropped open. "Everyone, look!"

They turned simultaneously to see hundreds of thousands of God's army. Winged creatures of light soared in from the tear in the veil that hid the ancient city. Cheers erupted from the remainder of El'Korr's men.

The voice of God sounded through the open portal as the angels continued to pour out, "I never said you would be going back alone. You will hear me in new ways, no longer are my words contained inside an orb. I have many rooms and even now prepare for your return with the ones you find scattered throughout the lands. Always remember, my love for you is greater than anything."

Zeffeera landed and everyone aboard climbed down to properly embrace El'Korr and the others who survived.

Geetock commented, "You are all glowing."

The returned group noticed it for the first time, and then Bridazak announced, "We made it. The Holy City has returned."

El'Korr charged ahead of the others, to greet his kin. "Dulgin, you're alive!"

"Good to see you, Brother!" During their embrace, El'Korr spotted his fallen mystic.

"How is this possible?" El'Korr asked as he looked upon her with his own eyes.

Raina bowed her head, "By the grace of God."

Bridazak sat atop a large moonstone rock, overlooking the rag-tag military encampment El'Korr had established. This was a spot he frequented daily, his special location to get away and think, to pray and to process. He focused in on the multitude of sounds around him, closing his eyes, longing to pinpoint and hear the voice of God once again, hoping he would speak to him. Life felt strange now; he had grown so accustomed to calling on the voice at any time, but now there was a gaping hole without his presence. When he closed his eyes, sometimes he thought he could hear God whispering in the wind that rustled through the treetops. It brought him peace during the moments of uncertainty and a new hope filled his emptiness.

His hairy feet dangled over the ledge as he chewed on a sugar stick and watched his surroundings. He smiled slightly when he spotted Abawken, his faithful warrior friend, purposely intercept Raina. The human was infatuated with the Elf, but unfortunately the Sheldeen Mystic didn't seem to notice; she was preoccupied with her studies of recent history in Xan's library—catching up on the centuries she had missed while held captive in the curse. Bridazak gave Abawken credit though, he was persistent—there was not a day he didn't try. On this particular day, he watched the tanned human's clutched hand spring from behind his back, wielding a freshly picked bouquet of wild flowers. Raina was stunned at first, as she slowly took the gift into her hands. Abawken didn't wait for her response; he bowed his head and quickly retreated. Bridazak finally saw a reaction from Raina; she smiled and brought the scented petals to her nose. The mighty warrior had indeed delivered his message, and it was finally received.

So much had changed since they had marched back to the Moonstone Mountains to regroup. It was a good location for El'Korr's battered army, for the time being. Scouts had been sent out to invite those of their races still scattered across the realm to join forces with them. Rumors abounded throughout Ruauck-El of the fall of King Manasseh. The cracks from the pressure of a new era began to show; each week that passed brought new Dwarves, Elves, and even some Humans to the newly formed encampment at the Moonstone Mountains.

Bridazak shifted his gaze to his right when he heard a sudden yelp. "Ow! That hurt!" It was little Jack, the decade and a half year old human boy. Xandahar had been training him daily in the art of sword fighting. It was also a daily event for the young lad to get his butt swatted by the elven cleric-fighter. "It won't hurt if you protect yourself," Xan countered.

Then, his long-time dwarven friend lumbered into view. Bridazak chuckled when he saw the beat-up armor he still adorned. It was dented, scratched, and seemed more of a liability than a protective barrier, but Dulgin had been adamant with God, so he said, to leave it be, mystic-hole marked, Varouche-slashed, and all. He made his rounds, addressing the squads of training dwarves. Bridazak chuckled again as he mouthed his friends exact words on cue, "Not like that, ya blundering fools!"

"Am I interrupting something?"

Bridazak turned to see Spilf and smiled, "No, come sit with me."

They both watched the coming and going of the dwarves, elves, and humans for a few minutes when finally Spilf spoke, "Do you ever wish you hadn't left the Holy City?"

"I do miss it, but I know it waits for our return. I miss the presence of God the most. I imagine it will be difficult for us all to adjust, but it gives me motivation to see others come to the revelation of a God who loves them more than anything."

Clanks of metal clashing and pounding of shields accepting the impact of a blade, filled the background of their conversation. Spilf changed the subject, "It is strange, but I have no desire to steal. Before, I was always looking for the next score, the chest of gold, or that diamond ring."

"Yeah, the same with me. I'm sure our skills will be used on our way to Baron Hall and beyond, but it feels different. It's difficult to describe, but I feel like I can see things more clearly now, and I can choose to use those skills for the good of others and not for the good of my pockets. At the very least, they might come in handy to help you find your family."

"I know we are searching for Misty Lake, but I'm not sure if that was the actual name, or a nickname we called it when I was a child," Spilf mused to himself.

"Either way, going back to the Western Horn lands, back to the beginning where Dulgin and I first found you, to see what we can find, is our best shot."

"Mmm, I'm sure the old Baron will love to see us again," Spilf contemplated the location.

"It's been so long. Perhaps he forgot about us."

A new voice interjected, "Doubtful, that wretched son of an Orc is one stubborn bastard." Dulgin and Abawken now joined them at Bridazak's formerly quiet spot. Abawken produced a map.

"This should help us navigate."

"Great. Did you get the other supplies?"

"Yes, Master Bridazak, and I was even able to get us a horse and ponies."

Dulgin glared at the human and said through gritted teeth, "I don't ride ponies, nor horses, damn it! Bridazak, if this is some kind of joke I'm gonna beat the Dak crap out of you!" he stormed away in disgust.

"Did I say something wrong?" Abawken asked innocently.

Spilf and Bridazak laughed heartily, "No my friend. It's just good to be readying for another interesting journey. Looks like we will be walking, though."

"Walking? Really?" Abawken questioned.

Spilf smiled and responded, "Tell me about it. I still don't know what happened and I'm not sure they will ever tell us."

"Please excuse me, I need to mend or apologize or... I'm not sure, actually," Abawken back-peddled and took off to catch Dulgin.

Bridazak and Spilf laughed and then silently waited for the scene below to unfold, until Spilf broke the silence, "I do have a question that remains to be answered, though."

"What is that?"

"Where did you get this?" Spilf reached into his tunic and withdrew the bright yellow plume with beige spots, the famous Varouche feather.

Bridazak smiled, "You found it! I thought it was lost."

"Can't wait to hear this story."

"Well, you're going to have to wait a little longer," Bridazak pointed toward Abawken who just intercepted the perturbed Dwarf. "We should get down there. When we get out on the road, we can fill our time with our tales. Besides, you still have to tell me about Ross' giant rat."

Spilf chuckled when he thought about it, "Oh yeah. Well, this is it, I guess. We leave tomorrow."

"Yep."

"Do you think we will find them? My parents?"

"Of course. They are out there, and," he paused, smiled, and finished, "it is time."

Coming Soon

The Dragon God

Book 2 of the Four Horn Series

Raina, the Sheldeen Elf mystic, focused her attention on the power-ful magic she weaved in the secluded Moonstone Mountains. After the fall of King Manasseh, she took it upon herself to investigate the realms of Ruauck-El. She had been held captive for centuries by the curse of The Burning Forest and she knew knowledge was power.

In the weeks following, she had been strategizing with King El'Korr and others planning their next objective. The first phase was to gather all remaining races of dwarves, elves, Ordakians, and anyone else, into one location in order to oppose any Horn King military action. Moonstone Mountains was a good place to do battle, but it would not be able to con-tain the masses or allow for a strategic defensible position.

El'Korr had suggested a place called The Shield, which centuries ago had housed the largest gathering of dwarves ever known and they remained separated from the outside world. It is uncertain if they still reside there or if it has fallen. Raina was going to find out, but first wanted to check in on the three remaining Horn Kings.

The information flooding into the encampment spoke of tyrant leaders from former King Manasseh's troops, taking over regions and establishing their own power hold on the surrounding communities. Some of the evil leaders had fallen while others to this day still fight to keep their reign alive. The borders are crumbling but the West and East Horn Kings are holding back until they have more information. It's likely they don't want the Southern Horn King to come up behind them if they try to take more of the land in the North.

Raina stood before a pedestal with a basin on top filled with water; formed from the Moonstone itself. She was thankful to the have the privacy of her brother's home nestled into the rock cave away from the hustle of El'Korr's troops building barricades and exercising their military skills.

She leaned low, with her face almost touching the calm water, and staring at her reflection, whispered, "Show me what I need to see."

The water rippled and images began to replace her reflected face; revealing to her four colored stones, no bigger than the size of a man's fist; black, white, red, and green. The ripples churned and flashed to another scene; a mystic in dark robes, gold stitched with the emblem of the West Horn King. He was standing before a monstrous black dragon. Raina recognized the beast. It was the same one who had captured Bradazak and delivered him to King Manasseh on top of his tower.

"What are you up too?" she asked herself.

She gasped when two green scaled humanoid Dragoons dragged in King Manasseh's lifeless body and laid him before the black monster. The vision then ended.

A library of ancient tomes surrounded her. Her thoughts churned like the water in the basin as she held tightly to the rim.

"Very interesting," she contemplated. "Four stones and a fallen king. What do they mean?"

For the next several hours she scoured through the books, bound parchment wrapped in leather, strewn about the room. Xan had kept a grand collection over the centuries and there was much information to be gathered.

"Here we go," she said aloud to herself. She read the passage in the book entitled Tales of Power, "The ancient dragons of the dark-side searched for ways to prolong their spirits and worked with a human wizard of unknown origin. The wizard promised the old wyrms of the five colors that their spirits could be harnessed into younger bodies and they could live for eternity. However, he betrayed them and harnessed each of their powers into his own spirit. The wizard was known as The Dragon God, but was destroyed by the elements created to counter the effects." Raina suddenly stopped as the next sentence spoke volumes. "The evil power of the wizard and the dragons were separated and scattered throughout Ruauck-El in the form of five colored stones."

"Five colored stones," she whispered. "They have four. They are looking for the fifth stone, but what does Manasseh have to do with this?" A flash of realization hit her.

Xan suddenly entered the room. The door was partially blocked with stacks of books and a couple rows fell over with his sudden intrusion.

"What did you do to my library?" he exclaimed.

"You won't care once I tell you what I have found brother. Come, we need to talk with King El'Korr."

She whisked past him as he stood in the entryway looking around the disheveled room; his cherished collection of manuscripts tossed without a care. Shaking his head, he closed the door and said under his breath, "Damn you Raina. This better be good."

ABOUT THE AUTHOR

Brae Wyckoff was born and raised in San Diego, CA. He has been married to his beautiful wife, Jill, for 19 years, and they have three children; Tommy, Michelle, and Brittany. He has a beautiful grandson, Avery. He is an active leader within his church body at The Awakening in Carlsbad, CA. He and his wife are the founders of The Greater News Facebook page which reports on miracles, signs, and wonders from around the world. Brae has been an avid gamer since 1985. His passion for mysterious realms and the supernatural inspired him to write The Orb of Truth, the first in a series of fantasy action adventures. He is also working towards a Psychology degree and is currently officiating weddings on the weekends.

http://www.theorboftruth.com/
http://orboftruth.blogspot.com/
https://www.facebook.com/theorboftruth
https://twitter.com/BraeWyckoff

15749234R00140